For
Helen Maserati –
with best regards!
Kurt Feldbärker
Vancouver ²²/₁₀ – ₉₄

TWILIGHT COUNTRY

KNUT FALDBAKKEN

Twilight Country

Translated from the Norwegian by
JOAN TATE

Quarry Press

© Gyldendal Norsk Forlag A/S 1974
© Knut Faldbakken 1974
English translation © Joan Tate 1993

UNESCO Collection of Representative Works
European Series

Originally published in Norwegian as *Uar: Aftenlandet* by Gyldendal Norsk Forlag A/S
and in English translation by Peter Owen Limited London
First published in Canada by Quarry Press Inc.
PO Box 1061 Kingston Ontario K7L 4Y5

The publishers gratefully acknowledge the assistance of the Arts Council
of Great Britain, NORLA and Gyldendal Norsk Forlag in the publication
of this book

ISBN 1–55082–077–X

Canadian Cataloguing in Publication Data is available

PART ONE

Allan Ung and Lisa moved out to the Dump one afternoon at the beginning of March. It was late in the day and the great iron gate was locked, but some boys, probably, had smashed the padlock and it was easy to push the gate open. Allan had planned it this way, so that they would not be seen by anyone. Although it was not prohibited to go to the Dump, their suitcases and the big seaman's bag would have aroused any guard's suspicions. Were there any still around out there, even in working hours? Unlikely. He couldn't believe anyone would go to the expense of employing a guard to look after a refuse tip, whether public or not, anyhow not under present circumstances. The city had expanded, the economy stagnated and all public services had been curtailed. As he humped along the case and heavy bag, Allan thought that although the crisis was obvious, in a strange illogical way life had become easier. All the pessimism and hopelessness, the restrictive measures and cuts in various public services had given him a sense of freedom, of being able, or rather being *forced* to play a decisive part in his own life. That was new and stimulating to him.

He looked at the gate with its smashed padlock, at the high rusty wire-netting fence threatening to collapse in several places, and he thought how only a few years earlier, what he was now going to do would have been much more difficult to carry out, if not impossible, even inconceivable. What would his architect colleagues at the office have thought? 'A place of employment in a free and stimulating environment', but nonetheless with clear directives, sharp edges, competition, rush and stress, like everywhere else. It was good he had got away from that.

Janson at the petrol station knew of his plan and supported him to the extent that Janson could now concentrate on other things apart from his own worries, his insomnia, his ruined digestion and premature ageing.

Allan pushed open the heavy gate and heaved the case inside. Lisa stood in silence, their four-year-old in her arms, and looked thoughtfully along a track which was no more than two deep ruts over uneven ground. It was mild, very mild for the time of year, and there was no wind.

Lisa was carrying the boy and the lighter of the cases, Allan the other case and the seaman's bag, as well as a carrier full of minor items, food and supplies they had bought on the way, some vacuum-packed bread, a carton of margarine, a jar of jam, some 'meat' paste, her favourite spread, some mineral water (water would be a considerable problem and he had already speculated on several ways of acquiring some), two bottles of orange juice (the boy didn't like milk and drank only soft drinks, an expense now he was too old for the infant food ration), some tins of pre-cooked food, two packets of biscuits, some cocoa, matches and candles.

A reddish sun was shining over Paradise Bay, making the oily water gleam. He had closed the gate behind them, then looked round. No one in sight. No guard to chase them off, telling them they couldn't stay there and the gate should be locked. He had reckoned on that, but the relief was still great, for the actual gate and the wire fencing extending rusty and man-high, apparently into infinity in both directions, had taken him aback. Only a few years ago there had been guards with dogs keeping watch over public property, protecting law and order. The city had been progressing and expanding, a model of economic growth, social welfare and political stability. Much had changed since.

'Over there.' He pointed.

Lisa and the boy had gone on ahead along the track and she was now looking back uncertainly, awkward in uncomfortable, high-heeled shoes, her spindly legs helpless-looking in thin nylons. ('I haven't anything else!' she had cried, angrily, when he had reproached her as she was packing.) The sun was so low Allan felt as if his lungs were filling with sulphur whenever he breathed in. It had been unusually warm recently. That also suited his plans — the first nights would not be so cold as he had feared and he would soon be able to rig up a stove.

Boy, the child, was restless, whining and waving his arms about, wanting to get down. Lisa let him run. He soon fell, got up again, then fell again and started crying, unused to the slippery, uneven ground after floors and pavements. She helped him up and scolded him. Allan came up behind them and smiled. Apart from them, there was no one in sight, no one to stop them, to bother about them or ask questions. He had hoped and imagined it would be just like this, peaceful, a place to themselves, not at once invaded by other people – by the city.

It was easy for him to find the camping van. He had towed it out there only a week ago. It was not all that badly damaged, either, but enough to satisfy the insurance people so the owner got his claim. The owner, a busy man annoyed by all the fuss over the accident, had offered Allan money to tow the 'trash' away for him. Allan had been handed a folded banknote, given an indifferent nod, an impersonal smile – and a gust of expensive aftershave: 'Fix it for me, then, will you?' The accident had happened out on Abbott Hill Road, not far from the petrol station, so it had been a simple matter to leave the van on the station parking lot for the time being. But Janson clearly did not like it taking up the space, so Allan had had to get it out of the way. That was when the idea had occurred to him.

He caught up with Lisa and heard her gasping for breath. He was also struggling, their luggage heavy although they possessed so little. The boy was shuffling along behind them, refusing to be carried.

Lisa turned to Allan, a pale oval face under a profusion of reddish blond hair, even paler and redder in this strange light – his child bride, his teenage wife, Lisa.

'Is it far?'

'No, just down there. Behind those mounds.'

'Can we have a rest?'

'All right.'

They put down the cases. A gust of wind cooled them and brought with it the smell of smoke and decay. She stared around, wide-eyed.

'Can you hear?' she suddenly exclaimed.

'What?'

'Our breathing! And heartbeats. I can hear my own heart beating. Can you?'

He listened. Neither said anything.

'Yes.'

7

'How quiet it is. How fantastically quiet it must be, to be able to hear your own heart beating,' she said with an amazed, childlike smile of wonder.

'Mm.'

'I don't think I've ever been anywhere so quiet before,' she whispered.

A wind blew in from the bay. Not a sound came from the city, the city that was just visible as a dark grey mass, vast in extent and shape, an eruption of urban geography far inside the narrow bay, sprawling out over the land and hills around it, an area neither Lisa nor Allan could remember any longer. Nor could they even recall hills, land – countryside. The wind whisked away even the distant, unceasing roar from the elevated Motorway as they stood listening to that strange quiet.

'How lovely!' She was enthusiastic now. 'How nice. So quiet. I'm glad we came after all. Aren't you?'

A gust threw up a piece of old brown paper.

'Yes,' he replied, breathing in the sulphurous air. They were standing on a small rise of garbage and loose clay soil packed down by the weight of the countless tons of waste carted along this track every day to be tipped further out. He wanted to say more, to express his great relief, the satisfaction he felt, but he had always found it difficult to express himself in words.

She had sat down on the corner of the big suitcase and was staring in the same direction as he was, across Paradise Bay, the incoming wind softening their memories of the city behind them – Sweetwater.

2

The Dump was the name given to the long, narrow strip of land which lay to the east along the bay. The area had previously been intended to be an extension of the harbour in Sweetwater City, and a plan had existed to construct new docks, more warehouses and shipyards. But the project had never got off the ground and the thousands of tons of garbage carted out there over the years now lay like dunes in a desert, or lava, crumbling mountains of soil and gravel and stones sloping down towards the dead brackish water. It was easy to see remnants of the start of the new installations – a row of huts and a derelict warehouse, its roof fallen in and window frames empty; a railway line starting nowhere and ending in a crater of mud, overgrown and rusty; tipping wagons sunk in the mire after years of wet weather; pieces of machinery; a few discarded trucks and a caterpillar tractor from which everything of use had long since been removed — all abandoned, as if someone had brought them there with a heroic effort, then lost heart, many years ago. Rust was flaking off from the once solid constructions, falling in drifts and great flakes, gathering into indeterminate patches of colour in the clay ground — fleeting enterprises, a dream of progress, prosperity and comfort the years had devalued, all now turning into soil, slowly dissolving into basic elements, dust to dust, metal to liver-coloured soil, all traces of activity eliminated.

Little by little, the Dump had become the city's garbage tip, private as well as public. Fleets of the cleansing department's heavy vehicles drove across the tip, relieved themselves of their stinking loads, then turned back for new loads of what the inhabitants of the city no longer needed or wanted to know about, the cinders of city life which had to be removed if people were not to be suffocated and destroyed by waste they themselves created, by their own excrement and odours, in the great, stagnant harbour city with the proud name of Sweetwater.

Everyone used the Dump — ridding themselves of surpluses accumulating in their attics, back gardens and basements, defective and useless objects, worn-out things, things too old, dangerous or out of date, or simply no longer as practical or suitable as they had once been. The Dump was the dark side of Sweetwater, of people's lives in a city stripped of glamour and eye-catching elegance. On the Dump was everything that surrounded and decided all human life, except human beings themselves. Anyone who cared to search could find all he needed to stay alive, creating a crude caricature of a life which in its essence would be identical with the good life of Sweetwater.

Sweetwater's refuse covered only about half of this area — a wedge of land between Paradise Bay and the Motorway — for it was very large, and although the mounds of waste towered far above eye level, most of the neglected area was still flat, barren land. Some distance farther east, the mounds of refuse became slightly less overwhelming, a more intimate, compact and unnatural landscape of slopes, hills, low ridges, all formed by possessions left behind by human beings, in a communal attempt to dispose of it all. But to no avail, for more and more kept appearing, to rust away and sink deeper and deeper into the soft ground after every autumn down-pour — a labyrinth of paths, alleys, narrow passages and tunnels running between the mounds of refuse. Two old buses with a 'roof' between them made from a door frame and some corrugated iron formed an 'arcade'. A cupboard with no doors, or an upturned van with its interior burnt out became secret caves. It was easy to get lost, although the mounds were seldom higher than a man.

Then finally the area began to open up, distances growing longer between car wrecks, piles of mouldering furniture, discarded gas stoves, sludge of old magazines, until at last the sea became just visible, revealing the closeness of the shore and the sour odour of polluted seawater. The stony ground there was strewn with cans, paper and scrap, but no longer covered with refuse. Stiff dry grass grew between the stones and a bush or two had managed to survive in the polluted yellow soil. Even farther out was a deserted stony shore, once the glory of Sweetwater, where there had been dis-creetly secluded villas with private beaches and moles for pleasure craft. At low water the remains of wooden jetties became visible, pillars side by side on parade, overgrown and rotting. At one time happy people in colourful beach clothes with parasols, radios and soft drinks had frolicked in the clear waters of this shore. But that was long ago. The villas had gone now, most of them demolished when the Motorway was being planned. Old and slightly decayed, most of them had belonged to a vanished era even then. The sites were compulsorily purchased for huge sums, for the road network had to be extended — progress was necessary. The two or three houses left had soon been abandoned, for no one wished to live with the Motorway rising threateningly in the background — a mountain, a majestic mass on its raised foundations. The roar of traffic was incessant, loud and destructive, spheric vibration assailing the ears, like a song, pulverizing all thought, shattering the sense of well-being. So those houses had also long ago decayed. Here and there, their ruins could just be seen in the undergrowth and thickets, all that was left of idyllic gardens — a bare gable, a heap of stones overgrown by the years, a subtropical garden enjoying its wild state, shaping itself and flourishing, occasionally forming a strip of im-penetrable, jungle-like forest with tough creepers, their lush green leaves soon becoming colourless under the layers of dust falling in a fine powder from the Motorway.

Out there, on that side of the Dump, protected and hidden by the mounds of refuse and with easy access to the shore, was where Allan had planned to settle. He had towed the buckled, scratched but largely undamaged camper quite far out to the east. The petrol station's sturdy recovery-vehicle had been relatively easy to drive between the mounds. He had uncoupled it at a suitable place between a pile of old tyres and a stack of packing cases (fine for wood should it turn cold), then manoeuvred the van in. A plan was already forming in his head. The camper had been a stroke of luck, a pointer helping him make the decision he had long been brooding over. And he had even been paid for his trouble. When Janson, the manager of the PAC station, had seen the banknote the owner of the van had thrust into Allan's hand, he had spat and mumbled something about times not being such bad times after all. Not for everyone, obviously.

Janson was always jealous when Allan was given a tip.

3

Times were bad.

Lisa was still resting on the suitcase. She had crossed her legs, taken off one of her shoes and was rubbing her ankle. Cheap shoes, poor shoes, difficult to walk in, they had been a bargain at the shoe store. That had been over a year ago. Since then there had not been a sale, either there or anywhere else. Shoes had become more and more difficult to get hold of, and nor had they the money to buy any. They seldom had money, so whatever they bought was cheap trash, but all that was to stop now.

The sun was low, seething in chemical colours over the flat strip of land on the other side of the bay – Saragossa, the delta plateau where Sweetwater's industry had originally been built on marshland: factories on piles, on vast rafts of reinforced concrete, the workshops of prosperity with all their filth and noise kept to the wilderness west of the city, on the other side of the river. Rows of chimneys shimmered and trembled in the evening mist, hissing bluish flames as they burnt off the dangerous gases (window dressing – gases escaped anyhow, the polluted air of Sweetwater causing sickness and deaths) crackling out of some of them, others cold, as they already had been for months, perhaps years. Restructuring, cuts and failing investments. Conditions in commercial life had become more and more restricted. No one had escaped. Times were bad.

As they rested, Allan thought about the bad times people kept talking about and which he read about in all the popular papers. 'Bad times – will our standard of living go down?' But he couldn't understand – people lacked for nothing, at least nothing essential as far as he could see. Some cuts had certainly been made in the flood of goods, but there was no direct shortage, at least not yet. According to their own statements, the government wished to ensure no one would suffer want. And yet people complained and talked about how times were bad.

To Allan, the times were good, even promising. He had suddenly seen the opportunity of *doing* something, felt a sense of freedom to do something with his life. Perhaps just what they kept calling 'bad times' was what had enabled him to see possibilities apparently not there before. People appeared to have had enough and were less concerned with what other people did, the rules and regulations of the almighty State, 'law and order', as one of the slogans had been. 'The struggle for existence', as the illegal pamphlets had so challengingly called it, had perhaps become harder. People had perhaps become more activated at work to ensure their own welfare; anyhow, they seemed to accept that they were trying to solve their various problems in different ways. Some taboos and conventions were losing their content and rigid forms were dissolving. People were actually beginning to help each other.

And, too, cuts in public funding meant the loopholes in the regulations the state was based on were becoming clearly visible. Laws, orders and decrees had become so complicated, involving everyone's daily lives, that compliance with them simply could not be enforced without a massive extension of the whole apparatus of surveillance – inconceivable in the present situation. The extent of the judicial system was limited, so priorities had to be decided on. Naturally the most important were concentrated on – organized crime, fraud on a grand scale, financial manipulations and open speculation – all of which flourished in times such as these, threatening the welfare state. But that almost exhausted resources and the authorities were more or less forced to turn a blind eye to the many who solved their private problems, small or large, in their own way, far beyond the periphery of legality.

It was a time of opportunity for Allan. Slowly the decision had grown in him to get out of the city, away from noisy April Avenue, the cramped, uncomfortable, almost uninhabitable apartment in

12

the old four-storey block, the neighbours. . . . Rumour had it that the block was to be demolished and the whole street razed to make way for a modern office block. But rumours of that kind often went round and nothing was certain, except that that kind of building was the most common in the city at the time. But they were told leases would not be renewed when they ran out, and they had been pleased because no one liked April Avenue, the apartments or the life there. The trouble was that in all likelihood that also meant they would end up in an even worse place if they were put out on the street – probably one of the tower blocks in the North West Zone. The public-housing department spent its time moving people out of areas to be cleared, which were much sought after because rents were low and fixed. Cramped, inconvenient and decayed as it was, they were nevertheless fortunate to have found the apartment in April Avenue at the time. No one wanted to live in tower blocks, at least no one who had any choice. So the idea of moving, getting away, had grown in him out of sheer necessity. Life was unbearable in Sweetwater and would soon be impossible. Then on a Friday afternoon in the middle of the weekend exodus (which according to Janson's pessimistic calculations was steadily increasing but brought in less money: 'They watch their pennies and drive till they stop before filling up. . . .'), the accident had happened with the camping van. A car carelessly overtook him and Allan suddenly had both the means and, after a little thought, an aim in mind. Suddenly the opportunity was there, and real.

'Is it far?'

They were both still sitting on the cases, her childish face pale, the setting sun bringing light freckles across the bridge of her nose. She would soon get a better colour, he thought, and would be brown and healthy after a few weeks out here in the sun and fresh air. He noticed faintly the acrid smell coming from the brackish water of the bay, but on this side they were far enough away from the stench of the huge tipping places.

'No, not much farther,' he said, pointing. 'We'll be able to see it when we get up on that mound there.'

'My shoe's rubbing. . . .' She had slipped off her shoe again and was rubbing her ankle.

'We're sure to find a better pair tomorrow. Come on, now. We must get there before dark.'

'Where's Boy?' she said.

They both looked round in the unfamiliar stillness, then saw him a little way away, down on the ground between the wheel tracks, investigating some shiny metal, and digging in the soil.

'Oh, Boy, look how filthy you're getting. Come here!' She sounded lost, unrecognizable in this situation. Boy stayed where he was, pretending not to have heard. She called again, anger in her voice.

'Come here, I tell you, at once!'

Her voice sounded hollow and meaningless in all the desolation. Perhaps that was what made her uncertain, sharp and scared. She still had the open wonder of a child on her expression, even when she frowned. Orders and duties were still strange to her.

Allan had got up, a medium-tall, sturdy figure in denim overalls, solid boots and leather jacket.

'Look, he's coming now. It's all so new to him, so much to look at. It doesn't matter. . . .'

'How am I going to get him clean?'

She was not usually particular about cleanliness. The unfamiliar situation made her fasten on that, and she could now see Boy staggering towards them, mud all over his knees and elbows. He had never got dirty like that in the city.

'It'll work out.'

He was suddenly certain things would go well for them, that every problem had a solution easier to find there than in the confusion of the city. Madness living in the city, he thought, although both of them had been born in Sweetwater, grown up there and had never really been anywhere else.

'Come on.'

He grasped the biggest case. She had reluctantly put her shoe back on and was stamping on the ground to test it.

'It's not far. Just over that slope there. I can take Boy if you like.'

Boy had come right up to them, his arms held out, and he was staring upwards.

'Look, Dad. A plane!'

He was a thin pale child, anaemic like his mother, and he looked much younger than his four, soon five years.

'Plane!'

'Yes, yes,' said Allan, lifting him up. The jumbo jet was leaving two thick red streaks of condensation across the fading sky. He could still just see the gate. They had not walked all that far, yet it seemed a long way. Perhaps it seemed longer over these great mounds of packed garbage, refuse, loose soil and gravel. Anyhow he felt as if they had already covered a long, dangerous and important stretch, and had left major obstacles behind them. The traffic was building up on the motorway; the evening rush hour became a roar they could hear from where they were standing. He was already finding it easier to breathe, easier to live.

'Come on,' he said. 'It's not far.'

4

'How pretty the lights are,' she said.

He had pulled out an old car seat and manoeuvred it up on to the heap of tyres just behind the camping van. They sat close together in the soft evening air, looking across a strip of the dark shore to the bay, and the long gracious bridge bearing the Motorway across Paradise Bay through the industrial area on the other side, then on inland to the west. The night activities of the industrial area of Saragossa, the basis of the city's prosperity, were reflected in innumerable points of light glittering and dancing over the metallic surface of the water, lending a ghostly light to the mist always lying over that part of the city.

But she was watching the cars coming in their hundreds and thousands in long lines, close together, gliding across the bridge.

'Look at the lights. Look how they wriggle away. And they never come to an end. How many do you think they are? Hundreds? Thousands?'

He said nothing. She was still young and seldom carried away by anything, rarely showed enthusiasm, or indeed had any need to.

'If I screw up my eyes, they become stars, white stars driving to Sweetwater, red stars driving away. How lovely it looks at a distance like this. Don't you think it's pretty?'

'Yes.'

He had turned his head so that he also had a view over the city. He had never seen it like this before, enveloping the end of the narrow bay behind them in a cloud of glittering lights. The high-rises round the centre were just visible as amazing blocks of living and dead windows, shopping malls, commercial properties and office complexes. In the background and in both directions was a shimmer of vivid patches of light, clusters of stars lost in the night.

As they sat there together outside it all, allowing impressions to flood over them, Allan had to admit it really was beautiful, this strange landscape, the only landscape he knew – it had a synthetic beauty of its own. The same strangely repelling beauty had always drawn him to roads, cars and petrol stations ever since he was small. Out here, away from the noise, the filth and dangers involved in every moment of city life, he was able to say, Yes, from here it does look beautiful. Sweetwater City: dreamily beautiful, unreal, a glimmer in the mist, the tail of a comet from infinity to infinity – and slow lines of earthbound headlights gliding to and fro.

'Boy should have seen this,' she said.

'He can see it another time. He must sleep now. He was flat out, poor little devil,' said Allan.

Boy was asleep in the van, chocolate all round his mouth. He had wanted nothing to eat and had been restless and difficult and in the end Allan had become angry and slapped him, leaving him sobbing on the floor, until they had calmed him with chocolate. They themselves had been as hungry as hunters and had greedily eaten cold spaghetti in tomato sauce straight out of the tin, washing it down with artificial fruit squash, suddenly starving after the un-familiar exercise, the tensions and changes. The bus they had taken to the Dump had bumped along for an eternity along a winding route criss-crossing the eastern outskirts of Sweetwater, and the other few passengers had stared suspiciously at them and their suitcases.

He had promised he would make a stove the next day so they could have some hot food. The camper was well equipped but the gas cylinder was empty, and carrying gas cylinders to and from the Dump was unthinkable. One window was broken and he had temporarily covered it with cardboard. He would have to find some plastic and repair it. What a lot he had to do the next day. He was pleased.

As darkness fell, Lisa at last got Boy to sleep. He curled up in a corner of the bed Allan had made for all three of them on a foam mattress he had bought cheaply and which covered most of the floor. Boy lay on the mattress, hectic red patches on his cheeks, exhausted by all the unfamiliar impressions, his hair plastered over his hot grimy forehead.

'He'll probably like it here,' she said into the darkness. 'Did you see how absorbed he was in all kinds of things? What a lot of things he'll be able to play with here. How much freer he'll be!'

He had thought so, too. Their cramped apartment with access only to the street and an unhealthy backyard had been prison for the boy. So it had been not least for him. . . .

Allan belched and the taste of his undigested meal, the acid tomato sauce, came into his mouth. There hadn't been much to eat, but things would get better. Lisa rummaged in the carrier and lit a candle. He looked at their remaining stores. They had been greedy – they had eaten and drunk too much. They would have to bring more supplies from the city. He hoped they would be able to find most things out there, but they would have to be careful. They were not particularly well equipped for this undertaking. They were both city dwellers, and neither of them had ever had to cope without the services of the city – supermarkets open round the corner day and night, and although they had been poor, it had always been possible to get *something*. They had never really lacked for anything – not poor in *that* way. The city had seen to that. But things were different here. They would have to plan, to economize, be content – and their very first evening, they had already eaten too much of their food.

But it had been good! Allan could hardly remember the last time food had tasted so good. Tomorrow he would make the stove.

She yawned and shifted position. The car seat creaked.

'It must be late. What's the time?'

'I don't know. My watch must have stopped.'

He could feel the fatigue in his body after the past two hectic days. Departure. Much had had to be arranged, although packing their few possessions had not taken long. Allan had never acquired things just to have them. To him, owning things implied permanence, a desire he had never felt, to have something at once. Hitherto he had seen his life as a slow gliding from one phase to the next, from age to age, and now that he had reached an important new stage of development, with or without his active participation, he found it unnecessary, even painful to be reminded of his past. Acquiring possessions was like being held responsible for something he had done in an earlier life, and Allan was not proud of anything he had done, nor did he feel any particular pleasure in anything, except perhaps a loathing of what had gone before.

He was pleased with and almost proud of one decision he had taken, and that was that he had found the courage to resign from his job at the office. After qualifying as an architect, he had wasted four years of his life designing refrigeration units for large warehouses, multi-storey car parks and ventilation systems for commercial premises. None of them ever got further than the drawing board. Routine work. He had been the youngest. The more experienced architects with 'names', took on all the major assignments. His chance would no doubt have come one day, but he had resigned when he saw that he would never in the long run be able to stand planning airy architectural dreams on white paper while life contracted round him. So he had resigned and drifted until almost all his money had gone. Then he had got himself a job at the PAC Station out on Abbott Hill Road – earning less, of course. They had had to give up the apartment, move to April Avenue and apply for welfare to manage, the child making the high cost of living truly felt. But Lisa had not complained and he had enjoyed the job, inasmuch as that kind of work can be enjoyed. At least it was real – morning shift, evening shift, ten hours a day, five days a week – strictly speaking one working day more than the new labour laws allowed. But that was one of the things to which a blind eye was turned. It was difficult to get people take such jobs despite high unemployment ('Lazy pigs,' growled Janson. 'They'd rather lie about and draw benefits.').

It was a fine night, unusually still and mild for March. He looked at the slight, pale contour of Lisa as his side. She was so young, just eighteen, and he had wondered whether she would cope with this, whether she was strong enough. But she had never complained or raised any objections. Perhaps she didn't grasp the extent of what they had set out to do? As if to ease his conscience, he had tried to calm her, although she had shown no sign whatsoever of being upset.

'Do you think we can find some kitchen utensils out there?' was all she had said. 'A frying pan, for instance? If so, I'll throw this one out. It's so awful.'

'Yes, for heaven's sake. . . .'

He had told her about how people got rid of perfectly good things just because they wanted something new. He had heard of several people, at the office, for instance, going out to the Dump to look for things they needed, spare parts for cars, furniture (the fashion was for restored old furniture). She had believed him, and he had almost been touched by her trust in him, but at the same time irritated by how helpless and impractical she was. He had impatiently watched her packing on the afternoon they were to be off. He gave her orders, criticized her, told her to hurry. She fumbled, dropped clothes on the floor, near to tears, and he had realized he couldn't blame her for being so incompetent. No one had ever taught her anything. But it irritated him. She made sure of including two or three things she was childishly attached to — two small lacquered boxes, one inside the other (she said they were old and rare and from a country in Asia), and a ring with blue stones in it she had once found in the street (he had asked her to pawn it once when they were very short of money, but she had refused — a rare occurrence when he asked her to do something). These were the small 'treasures' she was not going to part with, or perhaps toys she was attached to in some mysterious way. Otherwise she seemed indifferent to possessions and took all the changes, all shifts in their relationship for granted, as if she scarcely noticed them, or they were simply something she should accept as stops along a course of events which she perhaps did not care to understand.

This childish defencelessness and her fatalism were what had attracted him to her the first time he had met her. Just the sight of her on that plastic-covered bench at a table, on her own at the back of the juke-box place called the Café, had affected him. He had spoken to her almost for fun as she sat there, pale and shy, with that crown of reddish blond curly hair. He had taken his tray over and asked if he could sit at her table, and she had nodded, then started talking quite unguardedly about herself, telling him she had left home and didn't know many people in this part of the city. She talked in a loud, childish voice and she gazed round as if astonished at all the impressions she was taking in. But she had not seemed scared. only excited and curious. He soon realized what she was really after was somewhere to live, and without really thinking, he had offered her house-room in his own apartment.

Her directness and trust had disarmed him and nullified all his objections the moment he had spoken. He was not even sure he wanted anyone else in his apartment, and anyhow, why choose a girl scarcely adult? But she agreed at once and took his hand as they went out on to the relative quiet of the pavement, where at least the noise from the juke-boxes didn't reach them. He was determined not to exploit her situation, but that very evening, he was again surprised, this time by her experience, the warm eagerness inside that spindly body. She had suggested it straight out, assuming quite naturally that it would end like this. He was as careful as he could be, though he felt brutal and crude, so much bigger and heavier as they lay in his narrow bachelor bed. But she was unafraid, and unrestrained (she told him later that the girls at school had played a game in breaks. They had sneaked across the street to a day-and-night discothèque); she had made him forget himself and seduce her. . . . The next morning she had told him she was not yet fourteen and had run away from home after quarrelling with her parents.

They had married a month before she was to give birth. Dispensation was not necessary once she was fourteen and pregnant. She had almost fainted in the cramped, hot waiting room at the city registrar. Cigarette ash, crumpled forms and other rubbish lay strewn all over the floor, and the seats were occupied by couples all dressed up waiting for their turn. Her slim, veined hand was clasped convulsively round a bunch of violets as she leant against him, breathing heavily. The trip on the underground to the City Hall from April Avenue had affected her and she was swaying in her seat. Allan had tried to open the window behind them, but it was nailed shut. She was looking even paler than usual, with dark circles under her eyes as she turned them on him, trying to calm him as he struggled with the window. Her cheeks and chin were plumper and now there was a fine down on her upper lip. He had observed her over these months, fascinated and frightened as she expanded, and the unmistakable shape of woman broke through the girlish slenderness, making her mature and different. Her condition demanded a consideration on his part he often found frustrating. Things were not as they had been before. She was no longer a spirited girl he could play with. Pregnancy had made her more 'his', but had restrained him, made him fearful, afraid of the responsibility. But he had been part of the decision to have the child. They had talked about it and agreed it would be best, as well as right. She wanted a child, a baby (a doll), and he, deep down beneath his reluctance and confusion, he sensed that a child must be a plus in life, something he instinctively felt he would find joy and profit in, not just effort and duties.

But it had been largely effort while they were living in April Avenue. Pregnancy and the time after Boy's birth with its necessary consideration and caution had ruined much of the joy in their married life. Boy was often sickly, and living at such close quarters was suffocating. After a sleepless night, he had occasionally regretted the whole affair, both that he had been so incautious as to bring a child into the world, and that he had become involved with this girl who, after two days on Central Station, where she had sat on a bench scarcely daring to move from the spot for fear of thieves and rapists, watching the trains silently gliding back and forth above her head, had been so exhausted, she was prepared to go with anyone who would offer her house-room.

She yawned again in the darkness.

'We must go to bed,' she said. 'I'm falling asleep.'

'Of course.'

He had been sunk in his memories. He seldom thought about the past and now it came back to him, perhaps because of the quiet, or the panorama of lights from Sweetwater, the feeling of at last being free, at a safe distance, left to his own devices and ingenuity, his own ability to survive.

'Yes, let's get to bed.'

He put his arm around her shoulders. She sighed. He felt closer to her than he had for a long time, and grew warm with desire for her.

They undressed as quietly as they could so as not to wake Boy, now sound asleep with his thumb in his mouth and chocolate on his cheeks. They shivered a little. As he crept under the covers beside her and felt her body as close as that first night together, he was again overcome with desire, a sudden uncontrollable appetite for her, her broad angular pelvis and pointed breasts (even after the birth her figure had remained unchanged, younger, more innocent than she herself was), the child-wife whose needs he had neglected so often recently. Now he wanted her.

She had known since he had put his arm round her up there on the mound and fingered her breast through the thin material of her sweater.

'We must be quiet, Allan,' she whispered. 'And careful. Think about Boy. . . .'

He grunted his assent, his arm round her − nothing could stop him now. She sleepily gave herself to him, wavering, almost reluctantly fired by his crude wooing.

'Just be still there. . . .'

One of his feet touched Boy, who moved in his sleep. Allan felt a small hand with sticky fingers fumbling over his bare leg. A wholly new feeling, a sense of *closeness* suddenly came over him − here he was, coupling with his wife at the same time as he could feel his son's little movements. He drew a deep breath. Now were they a real family for the first time. They said nothing, not even a whisper as they lay there, both striving for satisfaction, to still their hunger. But all the time he felt Boy's presence down by his foot, warm and soothing. This is nature's way. Human beings had coupled like this since the dawn of time. He could no longer hold back and emptied himself, groaning, grunting, struggling, fighting with this wild happiness the changes had brought with them, and at the same time weeping into her thick hair as she lay beneath him.

5

The first morning.

The flies woke them. Boy was restless and thirsty. Yesterday's lemonade was flat and tepid and inside the camper it was hot and stuffy, so after struggling to get Boy dressed, Allan opened the door and let him out. Then he rolled up the mattress and pushed it under one of the seats to give them more space to move while getting breakfast. He could see the yellow sphere of the sun trembling in the mist above Abbott Hill, an uninhabited hill rising behind the grey concrete of the motorway between them and the lower-lying eastern zones of the city. Allan yawned, feeling rather stiff, but rested. It must be late.

'You promised to fix a stove today.'

'Mm.'

He couldn't consider all the practical things at that moment, he was so full of his amazing dreams of the night and his great delight at being able to dream them to the end and wake to this quiet. The sun's rays, all sulphur and phosphorus, slowly came through the window, warming the cramped space. Peace and quiet. This was just what he had hoped for in the mornings of their new life. The flies were something they would have to put up with.

Lisa was dressed and rummaging round in the bag of food.

'If you don't do it now, I can't make coffee.'

'All right,' he said, suddenly in a good mood. 'We'll make coffee over a fire and I'll fix up a stove afterwards.'

Outside, the air was moist, the chill of morning hours, a faint smell of smoke and the stench of ebb-tide wafting over towards him on the breeze. Boy was nowhere to be seen. A vehicle in low gear whined far away in the distance. The cleansing department. They

22

had started already, but were tipping far away on the other side of the Dump, so there was no danger.

He scouted round and found some bricks and a metal plate, collected some wood, sticks and newspaper, then crouched down to get a fire going on his primitive hearth. The wood was damp from the dew, but eventually caught.

Lisa came out and poured mineral water into a small saucepan. 'Great. We'll eat out here.'

The water soon boiled on the hot metal plate.

'Have you seen Boy?'

'No,' he said. 'But let him play. It'll do him good. He'll come as soon as he's hungry.'

'Supposing he gets lost?'

'He can shout. You can hear for miles out here. He has to learn to help himself.'

She made powdered substitute coffee in two cups and they sat on two car seats from the wreck Allan had plundered the evening before. Dim sunlight began to come through the mist. She raised her face and brushed the hair away from her forehead and cheeks.

'You can sun yourself . . . it's almost like the country. But much better. The country's so lonely . . . so sort of deserted.'

They had once talked about moving out to the country. 'The country' – the words alone sounded so strange, so tempting to them. Neither had ever set foot outside Sweetwater's ever-growing urban sprawl. Tempting, but also frightening. A park with no limits, forests with no paths, plains, hills, woods, mountains . . . no dividing lines, no firm definitions. There were people in Sweetwater who loved 'the country' and went there (where?) every weekend and every holiday although it was expensive and an effort. Sweetwater kept growing, enclosing its inhabitants in a constricting net of urban obstacles; the roads from the city centre out to the periphery were long, incredibly long measured by distance; measured in traffic lights, queues, traffic jams and orientation difficulties, they were more or less insuperable. But people came back sunburnt, full of loud praises for 'the country' and their stay there, for just the things Allan found so strange, almost frightening and difficult to reconcile himself with: the wilderness, natural beauty, uninhabited stretches, and qualities such as 'natural', 'genuine' and 'untouched'. That made him dissatisfied with the 'countryside' he knew best, parks and avenues, flower beds and municipal gardens, lawns always needing cutting, pathways, small bridges over artificial streams, ponds full of ice-cream papers and half-tame ducks and other water fowl chasing after the bits of bread thrown to them by children in particular. All round the 'countryside' he knew were benches to sit on to observe others who had made their way out to this 'countryside' with their prams, dogs, friends and lovers. . . . He preferred it that way, 'countryside' in small, disciplined doses.

Largely out of curiosity, they had once gone to find out what it was like 'in the country'. That was their first concrete action to show that there might be something more than day-dreams in the talk about getting out of the city – a ridiculous, innocent expedition out into the unknown. They had gone by bus – when they had finally found one, as not that many went from the city – to Pleasure Cove, a small village by a shallow lake where a purification plant had been installed – now proudly advertised as infection-free bathing. Pleasure Cove was popular in the high season and had golf courses, go-cart tracks, riding paths and signposted walks in the low hilly area where there were occasional rows of cypresses or pines, perhaps even the odd deciduous tree. Allan knew all this from what he had seen in travel brochures.

It had been late when they had arrived. Lisa had thrown up on the bus. Boy was only two and had slept all the way. They had taken a room at the first motel they saw, calling itself a 'guest house', decorated inside and outside with wheels and old ploughs, pans, buckets and antique agricultural implements, but nevertheless unmistakably a motel. They had taken a room and gone at once to bed, exhausted by the journey.

Breakfast was served from eight to ten in the morning, boiled eggs, toast and butter (*real* butter, it said on the folder on all the tables in the dining room), marmalade of indefinite origin and colour, coffee or tea. Lisa had felt sick again at the sight of dirt on the eggshell and could eat nothing.

'Fresh eggs from our own chickens', their hostess had said beaming, a large sturdy woman with a red face and bright friendly eyes behind misty round glasses. She wore a chef's hat and her forehead glistened with sweat. She told them their guest house (motel) was one of the oldest there. They kept to tradition and regular customers had come over many years. She was disappointed so many people preferred the new, more resplendent lakeside motels. She had an accent Allan had difficulty in understanding at first. That had irritated him and he avoided her, although she was very friendly and let Boy pick fruit out of her garden.

24

The weather was fine and in the morning they had gone for a walk – they had come to the 'country' to enjoy 'the countryside' and the fresh air, hadn't they? But they hadn't gone far before Lisa said she was tired and wanted to go back as soon as the cluster of houses round the bus stop was out of sight. She had suddenly felt deserted and ill at ease in open country – no houses or proper road to walk on. She had to take Allan's hand and he had led her on along the pathway, remembering he had thought it might be great to make love to her in such a place, in the grass, in a meadow with nothing but plants, trees, insects and birds and blue sky all round them. That was what he had thought before they had come. But the pathway kept going unpredictably up and downhill, and there were hills beyond the hills, mountains far out on the horizon, farther away than any human being could imagine.

So they felt like strangers, and she squeezed his hand, and he hers, as if to be sure of not losing each other. They felt small in that great expanse of 'countryside' (where indeed there were trees, just like in the colour pictures of the brochures), and light as they walked in all that openness. A gust of wind could have seized them and blown them away from each other under that great wide sky.

They had an early lunch and while Lisa rested, Allan had strolled around on his own. He went down to the edge of the lake and walked past all the men fishing with rod and line, casting and hauling in, casting and hauling in, totally absorbed in what they were doing. It had bored him to watch them.

He had tried taking a nap in the hammock behind the motel, but had been disturbed by the ginger cats playing in the long grass under the trees. As he lay watching them, lulled by tiredness into a semi-slumber in the hot afternoon sun – the cats' quick supple movements as they chased through the grass, their wildness expressed in rough games as they rolled round each other and scratched and hissed, their animal instincts at work – he found it all frightening, even terrifying. Like when the wind turned and sent a shudder through the poplars, bringing with it the heady scents of the overgrown garden. Was this 'countryside'? It was wildness. He thought he would disintegrate in this quietness, all this emptiness, the lake, the meadows, woods and the hills behind him, all saturated with smells, strange sounds and movements. His breath came quickly, his hands shook and the sun winked from a cloudless blue sky.

On their way home, Boy had a stomach-ache from too much

fruit, and late in the evening, when they were at last walking down the litter-strewn pavement in April Avenue, they had both felt profound relief to be back.

That had been their trip to 'the country'.

'How lovely,' she sighed, putting her head back and closing her eyes. They were enjoying the hot coffee and the gentle sunlight through the mist, which nothing, neither wind nor seasons, ever changed – a chemical addition to the atmosphere.

'We can sunbathe all day here.'

With one swift movement, she pulled her short-sleeved sweater over her head and sat there topless, her naked torso white and unfamiliar in the daylight.

'No one can see us,' she said, when she saw him looking at her.

'No,' he said. 'There's no one else here.'

The sight of her sitting there, half-dressed, out of doors in the middle of the day, excited him, but also made him uneasy, as if she had gone too far, as if she had taken their new-found freedom further than was proper. Is it all right? he thought. By nature he was reliable and sensible, with a sense of proportion, and he disliked exaggeration. Wasn't this just that? Exaggeration?

No. She was sitting there on the shabby car seat, giving herself to the sun, slender and pale, her stomach flat, her breasts modest, her cheek resting on one hand, a picture of innocence. He regretted he was not impulsive like her, that he could never do what he felt like, what he *felt* was right. He was aware of her talents, and knew the strength in his own arms and hands, the weight of his body and thought, half reluctantly – it's all right, of course it is. Out here. Who would see us? Who would come? But his thoughts also worried him. He could feel himself sliding. He had never had any difficulty controlling his desire for her, had never been particularly impulsive when it came to approaches, nor did he have mechanical Saturday-night-Sunday-morning habits. But that had perhaps been because there seldom seemed to be any reason, because of the child, work, where they lived, the whole of their 'regular' existence. But now it was all right! He was sliding. He could feel it.

'Why don't you take everything off?'

His voice was actually shaking. He was being bashful about immodesty – this was neither the time nor the place – he had a lot to do, make a stove, get things they needed, scout out their surroundings, evaluate the possibilities – it seemed unnatural to do it out here, just because of its naturalness, primitive – yes, just that, *primitive*.

She had caught what lay behind his words and smiled a little shyly. She was surprised, for he normally never showed much interest in her body, indeed appeared bothered when she stripped naked, as if her slender shoulders, slim back, her thighs and knees reminded him of something less pleasing – perhaps that he was almost twice her age and had seduced her, made her pregnant and married her, and now felt obliged to make the most of a difficult situation.

'Supposing Boy comes. . . .'

'He's right over there,' he said impatiently. 'Anyhow, he's seen you naked before. Come on.'

She giggled as she stepped out of the short skirt and pulled off the scarlet tights, knowing his eyes were on her, restless, uneasy and twitching. His desire for her was an uncomplicated, indisputable fact, with not the slightest consideration for her. He went over to the van, opened the door and grabbed a rug from inside, then spread the blanket out on a flat patch on the ground a few steps away. All with the sureness of a sleep-walker. Then he got up and unbuttoned his shirt.

'Come on.'

But she hesitated.

'Come over here!'

She saw that he was going through some violent upheaval and went straight over to him, carefully, to avoid cutting herself on the metal and glass lying around.

Afterwards, he lay whispering to her, holding her close to him, like an affectionate great animal, and she tried to find expression for all this strange contradiction between what she was used to and what was beginning to happen.

'How lovely,' she said. 'Lovely to do it out of doors . . . lovely.'

Satisfied, but uneasy deep down, he thought they had been like cats in the sun, wild and supple, rolling round each other, like 'savages', like those cats in the grass.

Then they slept again.

A rustling sound woke him. He looked over to where they had been eating, at the few bits of bread and a piece of cheese they had left. A large brown rat was gnawing at something, ignoring their presence only a short distance away. He lay still, watching it as it sniffed and snuffled, as if testing the food before setting about eating it. Then he saw another rat nosing its way out of a rotting shutter leaning against the pile of tyres. The first rat crawled in its direction, then sat up and bared its teeth. But the other rat came right out and cautiously crept round in a circle, approaching the food from a safer angle, its thick hairless tail rustling over the paper and cheese had been in. Lisa was asleep. Allan fumbled round, grabbed his shoe and threw it with all his strength. In a flash, both rats had vanished.

'Damned vermin!'

Lisa woke and asked what the matter was.

'Rats. Two huge rats eating our food.'

'Ugh!' she said, sitting up.

Allan was used to rats. That wasn't it. The back of April Avenue had crawled with them. He didn't really have anything against the filthy creatures, but suddenly having them so close seemed provoking. Suddenly it was a battle for food, for the place. They were vulnerable now. Their situation out here was exposed.

'Bloody horrible creatures.'

6

Boy came running back.

Lisa had got up and put her tights and skirt back on again. She was half-heartedly clearing the space in front of the camper, but with little apparent effect. Allan was still sitting naked on the rug.

'Food! I've found some food!'

He was dirty and excited, his clothes in disorder, eyes bright in his not very attractive face. His mane of untidy hair was thick like his father's, but fairer, softer. Then he stopped suddenly and stared at his father's unexpected nakedness.

'I want to take mine off, too. Take mine off, too,' he began.

Allan got up quickly and pulled on his trousers.

'No, we'll all get dressed now,' he said, a touch of embarrassment in his voice. The boy's wondering look had again made him think he must be on his guard, not let their 'freedom' make him lose grip on himself. A great deal was going to be demanded of him, he was sure.

'But I *want* to,' sniffed Boy.

'What have you got there?' said Allan, pointing at the boy's hand.

'Cake. I found it.'

'Cake?'

'Yes. Good!' He held out a lump of dough.

'Have you eaten some of it?'

'Yes.'

'But you mustn't eat things you find.'

'It's *good*,' the boy insisted. He would soon be five, but could easily be taken for three, though a stubborn intelligence occasionally flickered over his face.

'Yes, yes,' said Allan, trying to be patient. 'But it might be bad for you.'

'Where did you find it, Boy?' said Lisa.

'There. . . .' The boy pointed vaguely.

'Can you show us where?'

'Ye – es. . . .'

'It's not necessarily dangerous,' she said to Allan. 'Loads of bread and cakes are thrown out every day.'

She had worked behind the bread-counter in a supermarket before she had become pregnant, so she knew. New health regulations prohibited the sale of bakery products over a day old. Some of what was left over at the end of the day went into employees' own bags or under the counter for friends – the management turned a blind eye – and the rest was carted away.

'We're sure to be able to find bread,' she said. 'It's worth trying, anyhow. Come on, let's go and see if we can find some more, Boy. You can show me the way.'

'Put something on first,' said Allan. She seemed to have forgotten she was semi-naked. It didn't really offend him, but he had regained control now, the control he had been so afraid of losing, over his *life* as he wished it to be. The thought of how easy it was to lose control frightened him.

Later on, they took a walk along the shore.

Boy was tired now, trudging along behind them, throwing stones into the water and whining occasionally. Allan had four or five packs of bread on his back. They had found the place Boy had discovered on the other side of the Dump, closer to the tip. He couldn't understand how Boy had got that far and found his way back. Piles of trays of stale cream cakes were scattered about, the name of a large bakery in Sweetwater on the cartons. Bread, too –

rats had already made a feast of most of it, but they managed to rescue some that was relatively untouched. Carrying bread on his back, food they had found themselves, gave Allan a feeling of self-sufficiency. There was sure to be a lot more discarded food. All they had to do was to look. They would have to *learn* how to stay alive. As things were at the moment, no one knew how long they would be able to fetch essentials from Sweetwater. They would have to cope on their own.

'We must go back there again on Saturday,' said Lisa. 'That's when most is thrown away. It's all too stale by Monday.'

She was strutting along beside him in a pair of long leather boots he had found under a heap of mouldering clothes. They were worn and stiff, but fitted well. He had said he would find something to grease them with to make them softer. She was delighted and was about to throw away the high-heeled patent-leather shoes that caused her so much trouble. But he stopped her. 'We mustn't throw away anything usable,' he said. 'There may be a use for everything.' So she was dangling the useless shoes from their straps.

He was pleased about her enthusiasm. Her spells of passivity, almost apathy, has worried him. Sometimes when he had come back from work, he had found her in their small bedroom sitting on the same chair as when he had left that morning, staring into space, Boy filthy and uncared for, a whimpering bundle on the floor or in bed. Or she turned night into day, wandering restlessly about, smoking (which she never normally did), drinking glass after glass of soft drinks, or looking at the pictures in the stacks of weekly magazines she bought or stole. Or she would spend hours in the shower. He had talked to her, asking her to pull herself together, at least for the sake of the boy. She had promised she would, weeping, saying she didn't know what had come over her, but she refused to talk to the doctor at the Health Centre. The only explanation she gave was that every now and again everything became overwhelmingly 'heavy' – life in the apartment, looking after Boy – as long as he had been a baby she had been almost over-devoted to him, but when he was older, she seemed to lose interest, as if the first small signs of an independent will in him confirmed his independence of her, and that meant 'opposition', a will in him to break away. It made her retreat from him, although he was only two. The task of keeping everything in some kind of order, the shopping – three flights of stairs carrying the boy, six blocks to buy bare necessities, the crowded shops and pavements, the noise of the through traffic in April Avenue, block after block of decayed old apartment houses, the dust, the polluted air that made it hard, even harmful to breathe, dust filling the pores of her skin and fastening everywhere, on people, buildings and objects, like a membrane of grey corrosive decay – all descended on her now and again, plunging her into a despondency which paralysed her will to go on living like this, to live at all. And yet she knew they were *fortunate* to have found the apartment and that things were worse for other people.

'Some of those clothes looked quite wearable. . . .' She admired her boots as she walked beside him making cautious plans.

'I'm sure we can find lots that can be used. If they don't quite fit, they can be altered. And if some have come apart, they can probably be sewn together again, can't they?' She had never sewn anything before, but now it seemed to be possible.

Allan was thinking about supplies. The first thing he had to concentrate on was their water. Not that they would at once be without after they had used up the mineral water they had brought with them, for they could easily get more. It was on sale in all the kiosks, supermarkets and food stores and many people preferred it to the public supply with its added 'purifying' chemicals. But that was no long-term solution. Mineral water cost money, and supplies might dry up, as they had with so many other goods. He would have to arrange some other method. He thought about how damp it was everywhere in the morning, the dew dripping off the van. Later, when summer came and it was really hot, there would be rain in the afternoons, and in the winter it sometimes rained all day. He had to find some means of collecting it – that was the answer. He had had little experience of practical work, but he had learnt *something* at the school of architecture, if only in theory, and he could be fairly handy if necessary.

'They're good for walking,' said Lisa, looking at her boots again. 'But they're an odd shape. The legs are so stiff. I've never seen anything like them before.'

'Riding boots, I expect,' he said absently.

'Riding boots?'

'Yes, boots people wore when riding horses.'

'Riding horses? Ordinary people? When did they do that?'

'It was a kind of sport. I don't think anyone does it any longer. There aren't any horses, anyhow not around here, apart from at Camp Avenida.'

Camp Avenida was a large military base north of Sweetwater.

Rumour had it that the mobile forces had started breeding horses to use for minor disturbances in the inner city and political unrest – there had been quite a lot in recent years. And trouble over supplies of fuel for cars.

'Oh, you mean soldiers on horses? I saw that in a film once.'

'Mm,' he said with a sigh. Her naïvety, her total ignorance even of elementary things, occasionally both saddened and annoyed him. He himself had stopped reading the newspapers as they had grown thinner (shortage of paper), the articles and news always similar and empty, reflecting publishers' interests and readers' prejudices. But some of what was going on had trickled through to him and could be put into context.

'Riding boots,' she mumbled. 'Fancy. . . .' They were walking along the shore, Boy falling farther and farther behind as he kept finding things and calling out to them that he was tired and wanted to go 'home'. The camper was already home to him. It was a fine calm day, the small waves leaving green and reddish strips of scum behind as they broke on the stony shore.

Allan went down to the water's edge, squatted and lifted a handful of the brackish water to his mouth, sniffed at it and tasted it cautiously. It smelt of nothing and tasted only slightly acid, cloying, hardly salty at all. The poisonous effluents from Saragossa had largely been responsible for ruining the water in Paradise Bay, while the drains from Sweetwater ran through purification plants. But like the laws limiting dangerous emissions from industrial plants, they had been started too late to save life in the sea, and the stench and danger of infection had by then already reached unacceptable levels. Over the years things had improved, but the bay was 'dead' and would continue to be so. No laws could reverse the fatal processes tons of poisonous industrial effluent had begun in the shallow bay.

'You could do the washing here,' he said.

She screwed up her nose. 'In that sewage?'

'It's not sewage, only chemicals.'

'What would I wash in?'

'We'll find a tub or some kind of container,' he said, looking round. A low, half-eroded concrete construction protruded out into the water, a mole or perhaps the foundations of a quay, quite wide and flat on top. Here and there chunks had broken off and were lying like flat, smooth rocks out in the water.

'You could *thump* the clothes clean on that,' he said, pointing.

'What?'

'Like they do in the South Sea Islands. They put their clothes on flat stones in rivers and thump them with sticks until they're clean.'

'South Sea Islands? Where are they?'

'Miles away somewhere. I once saw them doing it on the television. We can do that, too. Back to nature.'

'But what about detergents?'

He shrugged. It was true he had once seen an old documentary about the South Sea Islands. Palm trees along the shores and calm lagoons. Little villages with animals running round between strange little houses. No streets. Dark, smiling people in flowery clothes. Perpetual summer, the commentator had said. It had made an impression on him. He had dreamt it would be like that away from the city, out in the country. Or something like it, idyllic and peaceful, happy and harmonious. No desolation or worries, no hostile surroundings such as he had come across: a landlady speaking an incomprehensible language, car parks and hoardings everywhere. Or cats, sneaking cats playing their games in the long grass, an image that had taken hold in his mind as a symbol of wildness and unpredictability in the 'countryside', a wildness he had thought dangerously near to taking over his mind that morning on the rug in the sun with Lisa. Out there on the Dump he felt a concrete presence, a 'countryside' they knew, a 'countryside' based on the same basic materials as their own existence – it was *their* 'countryside'. Though a wildness lay in wait and they would have to be on their guard.

'Won't that be terribly hard work?' Lisa frowned at the remains of the concrete jetty and the dark algae slopping about down both sides of it.

'Well, no worse than lugging the washing five streets to the laundrette, waiting for half an hour in the steam and stink, waiting for the machine to finish, then putting the wash in the dryer . . . and back again.'

'But will it be clean?'

'I expect so. We can try.'

He liked the idea of seeing her standing out there in the water thumping the washing clean. It fitted his vague idea of how things should be. That was the nearest he could get to describing an idyll.

A shout of delight from Boy made him look up. The boy came running up with some object he had found and they had to stop to see what it was – a doll's head with long yellow hair, its eyes flapping at them from the flat ruins of the face.

'Pretty!' cried Boy with delight. 'Pretty! Pretty!' He held the head by its gleaming yellow hair and swung it to and fro.

Allan was startled. There had been so many impressions since they had come the day before – and now all those images, his images were coming back to him. He had almost forgotten. He had lived without them for years, but now they flooded back one after another. The yellow synthetic hair. His mother's wigs on knobs beside the gilt-framed mirror in the bedroom of their crowded three-roomed apartment. 'Youthfulness' preserved in her thirty-ninth year, eleven years younger than his father. Vanity, discontent, accusations: 'Here I am trying to keep myself pretty and slim for you . . .', her hands on the round hips in a skirt too short and narrow, her hair in flaring colours. 'Throwing my best years away here. . . .' Part-time work in the drapery department of a store: 'To escape perishing here at home!' Cigarettes, low-cut dresses, cosmetics and massage oils, slimming cures. She had given Allan sex manuals ('So that you don't become like your father . . .'). Painted eyes, painted lips and always a mop of stiff shiny hair in improbable colours.

Then the same face smashed, the same shiny metallic hair sullied with blood. His parents had been killed in a road accident when he was eighteen, in a multi-pile-up on the Motorway during the great Sunday rush. The irony of fate – they had often taken him with them to see the huge multi-crashes which occurred nearly every weekend, particularly in the autumn when thick fog swept in from the bay. When he was told, he had seen them quite clearly in front of him, sitting jammed in, crushed in the remains of the big car, a heap of smoking, blackened metal, just as he had occasionally glimpsed other victims of accidents. His father used to lift him on to his shoulders above the heads of the crowd which always collected whenever there was an accident. Some people took photographs. Some ate snacks they had brought with them. He had loved the drama of these hectic, improvised outings. He had loved being held back by policemen in leather uniforms, helmets and goggles. Then in the evening they had watched the news and seen pictures on television of what they had already seen in real life.

He had also watched the news the evening his parents had been killed, but the accident had been a minor one, so was barely mentioned. But the image of his mother's gleaming hair plastered with blood, the scorched remains of their car squashed between other wrecks had remained with him, as clear and bright as the wigs she left behind.

'Oh, no, Boy, you'll get *wet!*'

The child had suddenly kicked off his shoes and was happily wading in the calm water.

'Come here at once.'

Lisa's voice was sharp again; her maternal role usually returned in any conflict. She would have liked to ignore the small boy who was around and was her responsibility, making demands on her at all hours of the day. She was too young and had quite enough to do protecting herself and her childish reality from everything around her. She had not yet grown out of being self-centred, with the right to be so – *had* to be in order to survive. But she also had a child and reproached herself for her egoism. Her sense of inadequacy made her exaggerate and she was over-protective whenever she felt strong enough to adopt the role of mother. She had even insisted on breast-feeding him, although that had not been easy, since she clearly had insufficient milk for him. The result was that Boy was thin and weak and always crying, causing even more irritation and self-reproaches.

'Come on out of the water at once, do you hear!'

'Leave him alone,' said Allan.

'But he'll get so *wet.*'

She was again anxious over what was a new situation. They had never taken him to a shore before and he had never waded in water.

'A little water won't do him any harm. Don't you see how pleased he is? He likes it here.'

The doll's head with the squashed face and gleaming yellow hair lay abandoned on the shore.

Allan spent the afternoon looking for pieces of corrugated iron. He also found an old-fashioned iron tank and hauled it back with him together with plastic sacks, large sheets of plastic and bits of tarpaulin he found everywhere. He took them down to the shore to clean them, then set about covering the heap of tyres with plastic and canvas, a tricky job when the slightest gust of wind was enough to lift whole pieces and blow them away. He collected them again and weighted them down with stones, making sure they overlapped properly so that the patchwork cover formed reasonably level surfaces leading into the corrugated iron chutes. He was building this edifice to accumulate water and collect the dew; the chutes led into the tank. The area covered was not large, but he had to see if it worked first. If it did, there were enough mounds and slopes round about to use the same method. Should a shower come now . . .?

He was sweating with the effort. He was used to manual work, but this was tough going. He had taken off his shirt and looked down at his powerful chest and the bulge of his stomach. He was getting fat, so work of this kind would no doubt do him good, he thought, panting but pleased.

He watched a flock of crows flying in on a sea breeze and settling behind the farthest mounds over by the tips, croaking hoarsely, black and inelegant, flapping through the misty air on their ragged wings. Crows and rats – the only living creatures he had seen all day. There had once been gulls in profusion out there. He could remember clouds of them following the boats in and out of the approaches. But like all the other sea birds, the gulls had gone. A great fuss had been made at the time, but that was long ago. No one gave them a thought these days. The innumerable crows had taken their place, ineradicable, flapping low over the rolling landscape of the Dump in search of carrion.

Dusk was setting in. He had improved on the stove, and now could see saw Lisa crouching over it, opening a tin of stew. She tipped it into a saucepan with a little mineral water, then put it on to the metal sheet, the fire crackling underneath. Boy was exhausted after the exertions and impressions of the day and was lolling on a car seat. Allan relished the sight of them. It gave him a feeling of having done right. He was satisfied with his first day's work on the Dump.

After their meal, he went over to the place he had selected as a latrine and squatted down over the shallow ditch half-filled with rusty brown sludge. He relieved himself and sighed with pleasure, a breeze cooling his skin. His own smell did not seem unappetizing to him. Even that was better out there. As he sat there, he could see the endless headlights winding their way to and from Sweetwater. The newspaper on his lap told him of the threat of industrial stagnation and difficulties with the distribution of wealth – an old newspaper. The bad times had already come to Sweetwater. He finished, but stayed there for a moment longer, relaxing in this rare feeling of satisfaction, almost happiness, his hands automatically tearing the newspaper up into suitable sized pieces. Only a rustle somewhere on his left (a rat?) and the silent headlights on the bridge disturbed the total stillness.

Allan had decided to go on working part-time at the PAC station, at least until he knew how self-sufficient they could be on the Dump. He had agreed with Janson to do the long Sunday shift and the Saturday afternoon. That meant sleeping on the old mattress in the store-room overnight, as the pumps did not shut down until eleven on Saturday night and they opened again at seven-thirty on Sunday morning. That made getting back on Saturday impossible, considering the distance and unreliability of the bus service. Overnighting on the hard mattress did not worry him, for he had often done that before after a late shift. It was all part of the job. Nor did he mind this connection with his old life, although the trip back and forth, the waiting and changing buses were both boring and tiring.

Taking the job at the petrol station had been his first step out of Sweetwater, his first break with views, attitudes and ambitions imprinted on him without his knowing it. Such as being an architect, perhaps with his own office, his name on the door, modern furniture and intercoms. Allan had never been much of a scholar and nothing had come easily to him. He had docilely struggled through his higher education, choosing architecture as he had a certain bent for practical work and had ideas about the need for houses, social housing, people-friendly buildings, a future revolution in city planning. But that had never come. Unemployment among graduates had come instead, and he knew he was lucky to have found work with a good firm immediately after qualifying. He had to compete with several applicants with better qualifications than his, but it was well known that established firms did not take on the best qualified applicants. They wanted reliable employees, not people with intelligence, vision and unconventional ideas.

Allan's father had always said: 'Get yourself an education, then you're safe, and things won't be the same for you as they've been for me.' His father was a typographer. He had been retired early owing to (among other things) the shortage of paper which resulted in cuts in the printing industry. He stuck to his view, ignoring the thousands of unemployed graduates living on welfare benefits. 'Be an architect,' he said. 'An architect or a doctor. People always want houses and are always falling ill. Architect is best. A clean job. Then you don't have to rummage about in people's innards. I don't suppose you're clever enough to be a doctor, anyhow. . . .'

His father had been a dreamer. Small, balding early, he used to sit on the narrow concrete ledge called a 'balcony' outside the living room window of their seventeenth-floor apartment, just wide enough to take a stool jammed between the railing and the wall, and talk about things Allan did not understand. Every summer afternoon he had sat there in his blue and white striped undershirt, his legs stretched out, a can of beer in the hand resting on the rusting railing as he stared up into the misty city sky and talked about something he called 'swallows'. 'The swallows!' he had declaimed with a gesture. 'Where have the swallows gone? The incarnation of free thought, the messengers of beautiful desires, the lightning writing of wild yearning across the sky. . . .' He had talked like that, and about other things of which Allan had then understood little, on the balcony in the heat of summer as ash floated down over the city, leaving a sticky grey layer of decay on everything and everyone. His father's hand clenched round the can of tepid beer so that the muscles stood out like ropes on his forearm, thin but not disabled, trained in his craft, one of the last, and now redundant. 'No, my boy, be an architect or a doctor. Our whole civilization is based on new bousing and sick people. But try for an architect. You're probably not bright enough for medicine.' His allotted measure of leisure out there on the stool. His allotted measure of beer, and *her* in front of the mirror in the cramped bedroom, trying out new bras, new wigs, new nail varnish, all to satisfy her frustrated dreams of eroticism, of sex with a pot-belly and flabby thighs.

Allan had had his own dreams. Since boyhood he had had a secret desire to work at a petrol station. Not because he thought the work in itself particularly gainful or interesting, but because something about the atmosphere attracted him. He thought petrol stations were beautiful. He liked their simple, practical layout, the pumps with their meters and the bright lights advertising the brands, the black tubes with shiny snouts on moveable arms, the cars gliding in and out, being served with routine and purposeful operations, then disappearing into the darkness again (it was always dark). Allan thought it a thrilling and beautiful spectacle, even the smell of petrol and rubber. Speed, strength, efficiency. . . . The corner petrol station, with its multi-coloured lights and rotating advertisements, was the only thing to brighten the dismal street he had lived on as a boy. It was his dream and he carried it within him long after he realized how destructively boring it must be to work in such a place; and no less important, had discovered that petrol stations were a part of the system which had probably been the greatest single factor in the destruction of the pleasures of city life. The dream was still there, or its shadow, as in a popular tune of long ago called 'Apple Blossom Time', about the flowering of fruit and love, though for him it always completed the vision of cars gliding in and out of brightly lit petrol stations, being served with quick, practised movements and rolling on into the darkness. Apple Blossom Time.

His father had also talked about his annuity. It clearly gave him great satisfaction to discuss this sum of money, which had a double objective. One was to ensure his old age if he lived to sixty-five, the other to make sure he left 'something behind him' should he suddenly die. Allan had quietly considered the latter possibility and what he would do with all that money. But at his parents' death, the sum had inexplicably shrunk when he had finally wrung the money out of the insurance company with the help of a lawyer. When as a young man his father had signed the contract with dreams of an old age of untroubled luxury, it had certainly seemed a handsome sum. But time had reduced it to a very unimpressive amount: some expenses were involved, minor debts had to be paid. Allan had had to find somewhere else to live, for at the death of his parents the apartment reverted to the local housing authority and their offer of an apartment for a single person had not tempted him. He had decided to look around on the open market, an expensive diversion when practically all housing and most city properties had been nationalized. He found an apartment, larger than he had intended and certainly larger than he needed, but all that space had temporarily given him a sense of freedom. He had started furnishing it but that had been a costly and exhausting affair, so he lost interest. That was when the money ran out. He had not earned enough in the last two years at the architects' firm to maintain such an expensive flat and a reasonable standard of living, so he had had to make inroads into his 'fortune', particularly after Lisa had joined him. The year between his resignation and the decision to take on the job at the PAC station had put an end to what remained. Almost. He had not let things go that far, and had kept back a little for emergencies. He had drawn that out the day before leaving April Avenue and he now kept the ridiculously small remains of his father's trouble-free old age in a pouch on a leather thong round his neck.

The PAC station was on Abbott Hill Road on the north-east out-skirts of the city. Houses were spread out there, with a few stores and offices along both sides of the road, rather like the centre of a small town. Otherwise there were older buildings with gardens, some shabby, some deserted or razed. There was a park and a large leisure area which had previously been a recreation ground, but had gradually become plots for public housing during one of the many attempts to solve the housing shortage in Sweetwater. But priorities had changed, building projects had been postponed or abandoned, and the area known as the Park was now useless. No one went for walks there, or sunbathed, or took part in sports, or used it as had originally been intended. Most people had no time to spend on such things.

Abbott Hill Road had been one of the major traffic arteries in and out of Sweetwater before the Motorway had been built. But now the surface of this once busy route was poor from lack of mainten-ance, traffic had declined drastically and two or three other petrol stations, a couple of shops and a drive-in cinema in the district had had to close.

Allan was sorry about the cinema. He used to put a chair up on the flat roof of the office building on warm summer evenings and watch the films on the gigantic screen about a kilometre away. The colourful sequence of pictures silently flickering across the wide screen created a garish, two-dimensional world in which he had to guess the dialogue and action. Owing to the lack of sound, the colours, shapes and absurd incidents could be seen as an expression of something beautiful, as the PAC station below was 'beautiful', with its six cylindrical pumps glowing in the garish yet 'beautiful' neon lights, the advertisements, the pennants on the flagpoles and down the stays . . . 'Apple Blossom Time'. As he sat with his back to the still-warm ventilators, and heard the cars driving past on the road, fewer and fewer (that gave him more time on the roof), he imagined the painted women and tanned men on the screen 'beauti-fully' linked with the pump-eyes of the PAC station, the smell of rubber and humming of meters counting litre after litre as it poured into tanks, then the cars starting up with a cough, whispering away into the darkness again. Then he knew that a dream had been fulfilled despite the long wait, the bad pay and the dirty, boring work.

Allan was largely preoccupied with the things they needed and he would have to get, as he purposefully made his way over the mounds of garbage back to the big gate that first Saturday on the Dump.

It was about midday. He was not sure what the time was as his watch had stopped, but he tried to calculate roughly from the sun. The afternoon guards came at half past three, and he had to be sure to catch one of the few buses that swung down the road. He also reckoned he would have to wait for a connection at the East Terminal.

He had to admit it worried him slightly having to walk along the road to the bus stop, then stand there waiting – for other people might be there – then sit in the bus till it reached the terminal, wait again with another lot of people, change buses and perhaps even have to stand pressed up against other passengers on the Saturday-full bus out of the city. They had been living on the Dump for four days without seeing anyone, and he already felt uneasy at the thought of mingling in the crowd, perhaps being stared at and pointed out, although there was nothing to distinguish him from anyone else. Nothing about him would say he had turned his back on the hostile city. He was wearing the same clothes he had had on the day they had left. But there was one important detail which already distinguished him from city dwellers as clearly as if he had come from another planet: he had shaved in two inches of water in a cracked cup. He knew the value of water. Which of those other clean-shaven gentlemen on the bus had ever thought about the possibility of one day being without water? That perhaps one day he would have to collect cupfuls to have enough to survive? That shaving, washing and even going to the toilet would be an impossibility? He had lived on the Dump for only four days, but already felt the distance. He felt wiser, knew things they did not, *could* not know because they lived as they did, a life he had left behind him.

They had used those four days on the Dump to explore the area round the camping van. They had taken things back they thought might come in useful, and they had made some headway in the practical reorganization of their life. In the evenings they had sat together, warding off the sense of loneliness, trying to enjoy the unusual, unreal stillness. The excitement of the first evening had gone and they felt not a little forlorn when darkness fell. But they fought off the loneliness and he reckoned they had conquered it. That was another experience – knowing he was alone in a rather different way from being alone in the city. . . . Nor could he get away from the 'wildness' – his sudden need to make love to Lisa could obsess him, overwhelm him – both of them – without warning, often at inconvenient moments, whether owing to the warmth of the sun, the fact that they were undisturbed or the dawning certainty that *they were on their own*, free to do whatever they wanted. That was tempting, so charged with possibilities of 'wildness' it was easy to lose one's grip and slide . . . all this seemed to have already created a stillness in him, a distance from others, everyone outside the Dump. It gave him a kind of peace, a security that would distinguish him from others as surely as if he had given off a smell. But this certainty he had felt beginning to build up inside him over the four days was a security which concerned him alone. He sensed it would be just as vulnerable, as easily disturbed as an animal's. It gave him no chance to overcome the uneasiness he felt about other people. On the contrary, it gave him an *instinct* for the increased attention required if they were to survive, a knowledge of what was essential and what was not, a sharpened awareness of the many dangers there would be . . . after only four days he could feel his senses had sharpened. Even the asphalt pavement under his thick soles felt alien and he moved along it with increased care, as if on hostile ground, towards the bus stop, a desolate concrete cube often used as a urinal. He could see two or three people already assembled there, so a bus must be expected soon.

They needed more tinned food, margarine, biscuits, chocolate, coffee substitute, vegetable 'bacon', candles and matches. He could buy them at Sweetness's grocery kiosk by the petrol station, the only one along that stretch not closed down. They had found more bread. They ate it in the ordinary way until it was too hard, then Allan had ground it up into crumbs and soaked them in water to form a dough. He then shaped the dough into small cakes and fried them on the metal plate. The result was a kind of biscuit which tasted good. He had also found some bags of vegetables on one of his trips: cabbages, onions and potatoes lying about, probably thrown out as spoiled, though some of them were edible.

As he approached the bus stop, he grew more and more nervous about the long bus trip together with so many people, but he told himself he had to pull himself together and concentrate on what he had to bring back, the food they needed. After four days they had run out of almost everything. The next supplies must last a week. That was what mattered most now.

Once at the petrol station, he found Janson in an agitated mood. Janson had sacked Roy Indiana. He had forced the boot of the boy's huge old Ford and found it full of things stolen from the stores: plugs, windscreen wipers, seat covers, splash guards, reflectors to fix to the car body. . . . Janson could hardly get the words out, he was so angry. He had at once gone to the youth and told him to leave. He had long suspected something was going on behind his back, things were missing from the stores (true, soon *everything* was missing from the store as it became impossible to replace supplies of goods), and he had never liked the sight of that pup, anyhow: it was good that he at last had an excuse to get rid him.

But what was worst of all, what had really made Janson's blood boil had happened afterwards, when he had pulled himself together and phoned the police to report the thefts, grinding his teeth with fury at not having locked the scoundrel up himself so that they could have come and fetched him and put him away as he deserved. For the police had not taken Janson's report seriously. At first they had insinuated that Janson himself had rigged the theft for the insurance, so that on the quiet he would be able sell the 'stolen' goods on the black market — they had even threatened him in-directly with the possibility of investigating *him*.

When Janson told them he had caught the thief red-handed but had thoughtlessly let him go, they dismissed the whole matter as unimportant and gave him a dressing down for wasting their precious time. Didn't he know the Force was undermanned? What did he mean by overloading them with such an unimportant mat-ter? But Janson had not given up. He was tough, and insisted that the value of what had gone came to a large sum of money. He had a right to demand that they investigate the matter.

Then the voice at the other end of the crackling, at times scarcely audible wire, curtly requested that he draw up a list of what had been stolen, a detailed specification with descriptions and values of every single article in question, which of course poor Janson had not been able to do. He had not kept an inventory of his stores for years, and he had no idea what existed, or should exist. So they had hung up on him with a threat that if he wasted their time again he could expect some unpleasantness.

'Christ, I only just escaped being taken in for questioning myself,' said the old man bitterly. 'The Peacekeeping Force — Christ!

They're too busy making sure of their share of the black market and dealing with street trading, and that's a fact! When honest folk try to get help, they get threatened with being locked up. When a crime's committed, they lock up the first person they get hold of and say the case is solved, then fix the evidence afterwards. Bastards! I know them, all right! And that rogue . . . if I had him here I'd damned well. . . .'

Roy Indiana was a youth Allan used to share the weekend shifts with when there had been more to do. But he had not seen much of him recently. Roy usually took over Janson's stint whenever Janson complained of being ill with his various internal pains. Roy was an introverted youth, thin and sickly, with cropped hair and grubby skin, completely absorbed in his great hobby and only passion – old cars. He and Allan had got on together all right, but Allan had disliked the way Roy evaded the heaviest jobs. Roy and Janson had always been bickering over something or other. Roy could take liberties because he knew Janson needed him at work and it was almost impossible to get help nowadays. Janson had grumbled and fretted.

Only a few years earlier, Janson used to go around whistling out of the corner of his mouth as he chain-smoked cigarettes. Now he was old, his skin yellow, his jaw long, and life kept playing one trick after another on him. His profits shrank as the traffic declined. A few years earlier he could have looked forward to an old age free of money troubles, but now he had to take his turn at the pumps to ensure his livelihood. The petrol station itself had long since started to show signs of decay: the paintwork was flaking; two pot-holes, one at the entrance, the other at the exit where the pavement ran into the roadway, had become great gaping holes, the toilet door swung on one hinge, the mirror inside was broken, and light bulbs kept going and were not replaced . . . and the traffic steadily declined. If fuel rationing grew any tighter, he kept saying to Allan and to himself, there was nothing he could do but close.

They were out by the pumps, the spring warmth making the smell of petrol rise. Thin and grey, Janson stood there grumbling while Allan gazed round, taking in the decay, but finding some consolation in that. All the way in, he had been afraid of feeling alien when he got there, just as he had felt at the bus stop and inside the bus, crammed among strangers whose smell he did not recognize.

Now that he could see the rubbish, old newspapers and scrap

lying about, the plasterwork flaking, the buildings crumbling and grass coming up through cracks in the asphalt, he felt better and realized neither he nor his new life was threatened. On the contrary, the Dump was threatening Sweetwater. The anarchy of the Dump was creeping in, showing itself in the cracks, consuming the city, slowly dissolving it into individual basic elements. Allan suddenly realized that these two opposites, the metropolis and the rubbish tip, would one day be identical.

After Janson had gone, Allan went into the store and started looking for some plastic containers he once remembered seeing there. He needed a small one which would hold about twenty litres. He had to take water back with him, in case of an emergency. They were not right out of water, and his experiment had produced a few cupfuls each morning, less than he had hoped, but enough for them not to suffer as long as they rationed it and used water from the bay for everything they were not going to eat or drink. But that would not last and they had to have some reserves until he hit on something better. He found stacks of the containers under a tarpaulin and had no scruples about 'removing' one of them for his own use despite Janson's indignant tirades that afternoon. He felt this was his right. He needed water. How else was he going to carry it back? The containers were just lying there gathering dust on the shelves. He annexed the container as naturally as he would have grabbed a lifebuoy had he fallen into the sea. He needed it. It was important to them out on the Dump. That was enough.

The idea of carrying twenty litres of water in a plastic container half way across the city did not worry him. The city water supplies often broke down, and that meant people having to fetch their drinking water from the tankers the city health authorities sent out, announcing the routes through deafening loudspeakers. One man lugging a container of water was a perfectly ordinary sight in Sweetwater.

8

After Allan had gone, Lisa sat for a moment outside the van wondering what to do, overwhelmed by a profound sense of loneliness. Loneliness was nothing new to her. All her life she had felt more or less excluded from contact with other people. It had been worst in April Avenue, where her isolation, her protest against the life she had to live there had occasionally left her in a state of mental and physical immobility as profound and depressing as she had felt before she had run away from home. Even Allan's persuasiveness and well-meaning caresses had had a negative effect on her, as nerve-racking as the fussiness of her parents – her well-meaning but uncomprehending parents, about whom she thought so seldom it was almost as if they didn't exist; they read books on child psychology and always blamed each other for what went wrong. What she had wanted more than anything else at home had been peace and quiet, to be left alone. All she could do was to pretend her parents didn't exist. As she had sat on the Central Station watching the trains gliding silently above her on their elevated tracks, hour after hour, registering the bustle round her, and she had realized no one would ever notice her as long as she stayed on that bench, then it had almost seemed to her that she herself had ceased to exist – she was a nothing, a speck, nix – and then she really *was* as lonely as she thought she was, without the irritating care of home that had always depressed her to such an extent that only pills had helped. She had stayed on that bench all that first night, scared to death, the difference between day and night marked only by the hands of the clock on the wall. She had sat there, clasping a small leather bag containing a few banknotes stolen from her father and her make-up, not daring to close her eyes for a moment – but that had been better, more 'right', more herself, more like her life. . . .

But out on the Dump, solitude was different. For four days she had seen no one except Boy and Allan. The quiet rang in her ears when no one spoke, when the wind did not blow or the crows shriek. Here, at a safe distance from the crazy *closeness* in the city, perhaps for the first time, she was able to think about people and occasionally even miss having someone around.

Not that she had much time left over to feel lonely. There was plenty to do and they were by no means idle, although the passage of the sun and other natural rhythms decided their activities. They got up when woken by the daylight, ate when they were hungry, slept when they were tired, lay with each other when desire overcame them. In between, they had more than enough to do with daily tasks they had scarcely given a thought to before, but were now tests of their sagacity and ability to adapt, demanding all their energy and ingenuity. She had spent all morning down on the shore on the ruined concrete ramp trying to wash clothes in the way Allan had told her, thumping them with a club. She had thumped and thumped, rinsed and thumped again until her arms and back ached and the sun coming through the sulphurous mist flushed her skin and brought freckles out of her forehead, across her nose and the backs of her hands. But it didn't seem to be much good, so she gave up with the remainder and just dipped them in and rubbed them against the rough concrete. That had the same effect, the worst of the dirt rinsing away while what remained spread itself evenly over the clothes – they at least *looked* a little cleaner. When she had spread the clothes out over stones to dry, she saw her rough treatment had made holes here and there. But what did that matter here? As she was working, she had suddenly made a discovery – she could take her own time. That gave her a great feeling of satisfaction, although it was heavy and unfamiliar work. For the first time for as long as she could remember, she stopped hurrying to get things done in time. Other things decided the pace, the rhythm of the work, the pace of her thumping and rinsing, the scrubbing against the wet concrete ledge, the work itself – everything had to take the time it took. That was a consolation, for it was heavy work and she wished Allan would come and help. But he was busy improving the stove, his job for that morning. As he struggled on, she thought, he is near enough so that I can call him if I really need help. That was also a consolation, for she was neither strong nor persevering, her attention easily diverted.

Saturday afternoon and so quiet! The stillness was like an endless distance between her and the life she had left, and she suddenly knew she missed people. It made her uneasy. A thought which had scarcely occurred to her before now came into her mind and stayed there. Were they to live like this *always*, so alone, just the three of them? There had been so much to do just to get away from April Avenue once they had the chance, the question had never really come up, at least not aloud. But now it worried her. What was he really thinking? Could he mean it that they would live like this, as if in the wilderness, with no contact with anyone? That would be all right for him. He had a job and bus trips into the city to look forward to each week. But what about her and Boy?

Boy lay in the camper, sleeping the laborious sleep of a four-year-old, cheeks flushed and forehead clammy with sweat. He seemed to have a temperature, though she was not quite sure what the matter was. Perhaps it was just reaction to all the changes of the last few days? To the sun and the fresh air, the freedom of movement. He was never still for a moment, not until the sun went down, by which time he was usually totally exhausted and fell into an uneasy sleep without even having anything to eat. But they had not tried to curb him – on the contrary, they were pleased to see him spreading his wings after the restricted life of April Avenue. Small for his age, he had always been slow to learn and was backward and underdeveloped in various ways, but now he seemed to want to catch up. After every expedition, he came back with cuts and scratches, so excited and eager he couldn't get the words out to tell them what he had seen and done.

Boy was asleep, and Lisa was watching the flapping crows above the rubbish heaps over by the new mountains of refuse on the tipping places. She was feeling depressed and lost, wishing she had a pill now, a 'pinkie'. But they could officially be had only on prescription now, though they could be got hold of anywhere and even her mother had taken them.

Should she take a walk down to the shore? She got up and started off slowly, aimlessly walking along the tortuous route they usually took between the mounds when heading in that direction. She noticed they had already made the beginnings of a track, a path, on the many trips they had taken there and back. She could see the glint of water only a short distance away, but before she reached the more open ground where the rubbish heaps ended and the shore began, she suddenly stopped, crouched down and froze like an animal on the alert. She had heard something, a sound, not the usual rustle of rats or the wind in dry paper, but the sharp clang of metal against metal. She sat quite still, waiting to hear if it would be repeated and trying to guess where it came from. Then she heard it again, a rhythmical banging as if someone were hitting iron with a hammer. She stayed where she was, but the terror which had struck her and made her seek cover was gradually replaced by an almost uncontrollable curiosity. She had to find out who or what it was. She had nothing to fear from strangers, for as far as she knew, they were not doing anything directly illegal and they possessed nothing of value to anyone else. So she crept on, bent low, in the direction of the sound, as if obeying some instinct. She could see nothing for a vast heap of rotting mattresses blocking her view. Cautiously, she started climbing it, then lay face down at the top and peered carefully over the edge.

Directly below her a man was leaning over the engine casing of a wrecked car, a small leather case of tools beside him. The tools glinted in the sunlight like precious objects, strange against all the rust everywhere. He was struggling with something right down in the rusty engine. She stared, noting every detail of that back. Never had she observed a human being so carefully before. He interested her. So did what he was doing, because he was *there*, out on the Dump, and for a moment he filled the vacuum inside her. Absorbed, she watched his efforts, finding comfort in the sight of this stranger, so occupied and apparently with no hostile intentions.

When he seemed to have completed what he was doing, he straightened up and inspected the heavy cylindrical object in his hands. He was an elderly man with snow-white hair down to his shoulders. He wore small round spectacles and his face was deeply lined, though with regular, pleasing features. He was not tall, his stocky figure in patched old dungarees, the braces replaced with a piece of rope over one shoulder. His shirt was also worn and faded, but the hands examining the lump of metal he had rescued from the car were strong and shapely. Despite his age, the long white hair and old man's fumbling movements, Lisa knew she liked him. In fact she liked him so much, she almost called out to him to let him know she was there. He looked kind, almost distinguished despite his long hair and dilapidated clothing. She was no longer the slightest bit afraid. It would be nice to talk to him. But she couldn't bring herself to call out and found she could not make a sound, as if she had to respect what he was doing, as if the calm, competent way he had been working on the wrecked car had created an atmosphere she simply could not break into. Without really understanding why, she was suddenly aware that relations with other people were bound to be different out there on the Dump. In this quiet, everything said must be significant, and everything done, revealing, providing others with a pointer to what you were *yourself*. She could see from the man's tools, his slow and measured movements and his almost careful treatment of this clearly precious piece of scrap metal that he was kind, a human being who considered others. Allan's self-confident and resolute way of treating things around him rose in her mind. To her his thoughtless skill with his hands now seemed unfeeling, almost brutal.

49

The old man bent down and put his booty into a sack containing other objects. She thought for the first time that he probably came from 'outside' and was plundering the wreck to make a bit of extra money. She had imagined he somehow 'belonged' out there, in the same way that she did. That was a disappointment. She looked at his clothes, at the whole man, the way he moved, and simply couldn't believe he lived in the city. He *looked* as if he also belonged on the Dump. He got out a rope and tied it round the top of the sack, slung one end of the rope over his shoulder and started walking away, dragging the sack behind him.

She had half expected him to swing to the left and head over towards the gate, but he went straight on along the strip of sand, stones and barren land which had once been Sweetwater's best bathing beach, dragging the heavy sack along behind him. It made an uneven furrow, like a street in the soft ground, wiping out his footprints.

She lay staring after him until she became aware of a slight movement by her legs. Boy. He had found her as surely as if he had been able to follow her scent or her tracks. He really was amazingly good already at making his way about.

'I woke up.'

He was whispering, although he couldn't have known she was spying on a stranger.

'What are you looking at?'

'Oh, nothing,' she said in her normal voice. The old man was too far away now to be able to hear anything. She slithered down to Boy. She had no desire to share her discovery with him.

'Just looking across the shore.'

'I want to go to the shore,' said Boy. His eyes were shining, his cheeks red and he was breathing quickly. He had little resistance and had been very ill when small, with an almost permanent cold in the winter.

'Want to go to the shore!'

'No, not now,' said Lisa. She climbed up again and casually looked across. The old man had vanished, and there was nothing but the furrow from his sack left on the shore.

'No, let's go and see if we can find some bread. Then we can make supper afterwards.'

'All right,' said Boy.

A little later, he said, 'When's Dad coming?'

'Tomorrow,' said Lisa. 'Late tomorrow evening.'

She wondered what Allan would say when she told him about the old man. Although she would have liked to have kept it to herself, to have saved it in some way, she knew she would have to tell him.

She told him as soon as he came back on Sunday afternoon and was surprised by his reaction, although she hadn't really known what to expect. He mostly seemed troubled, as if preferring not to hear about what the old man he had been up to and dismissing the whole incident as most likely a pensioner topping up his meagre income by selling scrap metal. But he did not sound sure. Nor was he. He knew it was not easy, particularly for an old man, to get out there from the city. Communications were poor, the way long, and also, if that had not been so, hordes of people from the city would have been out there looking for things. As it was, only the best equipped could make it. His colleagues at the office had told him that, and they did not go out there often. Perhaps the man Lisa had seen was an exception.

As soon as Boy was asleep, however, she persuaded Allan to go with her to the place where she had seen the old man.

'There,' she said, pointing. 'By the car. Then he went straight across there and he disappeared.'

'I expect you can get up to the road that end, too,' said Allan, reluctant to abandon his theory that the man was just an ordinary old man, perhaps even a vagrant.

'Couldn't we follow the track and see?' she said.

'Tomorrow,' he said.

Darkness was falling and the smells from the mattresses, the decay all round them wafted over in the twilight, just as the scents of grass and trees and flowers in a meadow are stronger just after sunset.

'No, let's go *now*.'

She insisted, perhaps the first time *she* had experienced something she could show *him*. She was so persistent, he gave in, goaded by her enthusiasm.

The track left by the sack was still quite clear in spite of the poor light; the shore glowed white between the dark strip of old garden and the water, the narrow strip of sand washed clean. The rough ground above was covered with stones and refuse and overgrown with coarse grass and occasional stunted shrubs with low, muddy oval leaves. In daylight the yellow and rusty brown colours reflected the mild summer's day in the misty clouds over the bay, but now they were only grey with deep shadows. On the other side of the bay, Saragossa was already a jumble of glittering industrial lights.

They walked in silence along the furrow made by the sack, perhaps rather more quickly than would appear natural, as if a restlessness had come over them now they had at last decided to follow the stranger. The track gradually swung almost imperceptibly to the left in towards the thickets that had once been a row of well-tended gardens, and farther on it swung away abruptly and disappeared into an undergrowth of nettles and bracken between two cypress trees.

'Whatever would he want in there?' muttered Allan.

The gardens had become a veritable forest, thicker than would have seemed possible if seen from a distance, and in the failing light, every bush and gnarled tree cast a dark shadow, making this amazing, indeed unnatural forest (*forest*, out here?) mysterious. . . .

'Just weeds,' Allan said to himself, but they stopped and stared at the incredible lush growth, so unfamiliar, so large and dim after the clearly defined shapes they were used to, outlines of mounds on the Dump, the line of the shore, the bay.

Allan took a few steps in through the bracken.

'There's a path here.'

The path was hidden by the thick bracken. They cautiously made their way through this forest, up towards a thicket that had once been a hedge, now covered with ivy and a tangle of other ramblers. The path grew firmer and wider, then they were walking on flagstones, garden flagstones. Allan spotted a half-open rusty gate leading into a narrow gap in the hedge. He pushed his way through, alert as if there were enemies everywhere in the semi-darkness around him. Lisa followed close behind, peering over his shoulder.

'Look!' she whispered. 'Ruins.'

To her, this last stretch had been a journey through an enchanted landscape. As a child she had watched programmes on fairy-tale journeys to unknown places where cave-dwellers lived, or sea creatures, or woodland spirits. . . . They had both delighted and frightened her.

'A house,' he whispered back.

A little way ahead of them a gabled wall topped by a chimney rose out of the undergrowth and beneath the foliage and thick mat

Duthie Books

■

MAIN STORE
919 Robson Street · 684-4496

■

4255 Arbutus Street · 738-1833

■

4444 West 10th Avenue · 224-7012

■

2239 West 4th Avenue · 732-5344

■

LIBRARY SQUARE
345 Robson Street · 602-0610

■

MANHATTAN BOOKS & MAGAZINES
1089 Robson Street · 681-9074

■

TECHNICAL & PROFESSIONAL BOOKS
1701 West 3rd Avenue · 732-1448

■

MAIL ORDER
1701 West 3rd Avenue
Vancouver, BC V6J 1K7
toll-free: 1-800-663-1174
toll-free fax: 1-800/730-3765

■

VIRTUAL BOOKSTORE
http://www.literascape.com/

■

E-MAIL
infodesk@duthiebooks.com

■

The image on the reverse was reproduced
from a series of bookmarks designed in 1959
by Takao Tanabe.

■

BOOKSELLERS SINCE 1957

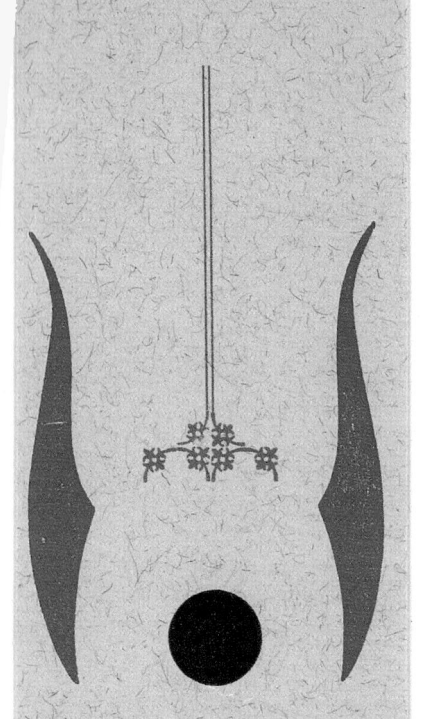

DUTHIE BOOKS

901 Robson Street

Vancouver, Mu 4-2718

of climbers, leaves and branches, they could see where the steps leading up to the front door had been, now nothing but an overgrown heap of stones.

'A luxury villa, too. Hacienda style.'

He was familiar with this type of building from his architecture days and it had been popular among the upper classes many years ago.

Then Lisa suddenly spotted something else and pointed.

'Look!'

A roof, an intact wall, clearly visible, a wing of the house still standing. And a light! A light coming from the dark outline of this building. As they stood there staring, they saw a shadow momentarily gliding past, then the light went out and the shadow glided away. There was someone there.

'So this is where he lives,' Lisa whispered. She was slightly scared, but at the same time excited, just as she had been watching those television programmes. Other worlds. . . .

'Come on, let's go.'

Allan turned abruptly and grasped her arm. They cautiously made their way down the path back to the shore.

They said little as they sat on either side of the warm stove over their evening coffee, biscuits and chocolate, both thoughtful, wondering what this discovery would mean to them.

'So we're not alone on the Dump,' Allan said.

'No . . . but he looked awfully nice,' she said quickly. 'I'm sure he's nice. Maybe we should go and see him? Tomorrow, perhaps?'

'We'll see.'

He had to think it over. The unlimited freedom they had enjoyed would now be restricted. But there might be situations when it would be good to have other people around. Everything depended on who the man was and what he was like. They would have to see.

9

The water Allan had brought with him from the PAC station tasted foul the next day, so he raised no objections when Lisa wanted to wash her hair. They also seemed to have plenty for the moment, with the container plus what a late evening shower had produced in his tank. They had soon learnt how to reduce their use of water to the bare minimum.

Lisa was kneeling with her head over a buckled tin bowl she had found a few days earlier, using the last of their precious soap. She wanted to look presentable that day. Although he had said nothing about it, they were going visiting. She knew that from his restlessness and the glances he kept making in the direction of the bay. They would *have* to go back and find out what the man was doing there, what kind of person he was, a friend or an enemy.

Friend or enemy? Ever since the day she had watched him and his kind face and good hands, she had had no doubts at all that he was a friend. She even felt more secure at the thought that he was also living there, no further away than that she could see if she climbed up the pile of tyres.

Allan was repairing the window in the camper. He had found some transparent plastic and glue at the petrol station, where things in the stores had been lying about as if no one was responsible for what was there. It never occurred to him he was stealing. Concepts such as 'theft' were used by the authorities and meant something else when one possessed nothing and simply needed things. Allan was working quickly and efficiently but absently, his thoughts elsewhere. Yes, they had to go and find out more about the old man, cross boundaries that had to be crossed, exchange experiences – as long as the man was not just a miserable, incoherent vagrant – as was most likely. But even so, they would have to come to some kind of understanding. They could not afford to ignore anyone.

He glanced at Lisa's slim back bent over the bowl. She was just tipping the last handfuls of water over her head in an attempt to rinse the remains of the soap out of her curls. He was thinking about her optimism and expectations. She had never shown the slightest interest in other people when they had lived in Sweetwater.

Boy's temperature had gone down, but he was still so weak, he made no protest when they put him to bed and said he was to stay there until they came back. He seemed uninterested in where they were going, and soon dozed off to wherever his dreams took him.

Boy was dreaming about a man – the Man. His head was full of the Man. The Man was his great secret, perhaps his very first secret. Something had told him he must keep quiet about the Man. The Man was something so extraordinary, no one was to spoil it for him. Boy was dreaming about a figure lying asleep under flattened cardboard boxes, one arm protruding and apparently waving to him. That was how he had found him. The big chubby hand had a dull ring deeply embedded in one finger. Boy was dreaming he was taking gold buttons off the Man's clothes. The man had one arm over his face as if asleep. He was large – very fat. And might wake at any moment. But the buttons fell off his clothes, and they were gold. Boy dreamt he was picking gold buttons, and the Man who was his, his find, his secret, simply lay still and let him do it, allowing him to take the buttons. No stern expressions or reprimands.

The wild garden looked less mysterious in daylight. The gnarled shrubs were choked with weeds, roses had gone wild, and there were three or four fallen trees, their roots exposed. The narrow path was a shadow under the bracken and the rusty gate creaked. The chimney, the first visible part of the ruin, was covered with moss, disintegrating and not nearly so majestic as it had looked the evening before.

They found a track which ran round the back of what had once been a luxury house, then over towards the still relatively intact wing – at least compared with the rest of the building. There were climbing plants everywhere – the roof was a carpet of tangled ivy, its shoots weaving in and out of the cracks in the wall. A knot of roots had shifted a corner of the wall – the whole old house appeared to be under pressure from the plant world. Three or four poplars and a cypress tree towered above the undergrowth and they could see more trees in the background. Above and behind those, they could just glimpse the lines of the Motorway and its solid columns. They could also see a thin layer of powdery dust on the broad lily leaves round a hollow which must once have been a swimming pool.

Although he no longer feared this meeting, Allan walked along the path very quietly and stopped as they approached the far corner of the house. The place looked so deserted, he had to pull himself together to remember they had seen a light there the night before. Where had it come from? If from the windows facing them, they were covered with foliage. It again occurred to him that perhaps they had stumbled on a nest of vagrants and last night's inhabitants had already moved on. But the well-trodden path contradicted that explanation.

'Come on . . . .' He felt Lisa's impatient touch on his shoulder.

As soon as they rounded the corner, he at once saw the half-open door, inside it the end of a carpet on polished red brickwork. On a clearing outside the door was a rocking chair with a worn, folded rug on the seat, and beyond that, by the end of the wall, a ramshackle shed with three walls and a roof of rusty corrugated iron. Inside it, they could just see rickety shelves and a number of bags and boxes arranged in piles and rows. Tools hung on the walls in neat rows, coils of rope, fan belts, large cog-wheels, various machine parts and outside a heap of rusty scrap-iron. A man was kneeling in front of the shed with his back to them, concentrating on what he was doing. Lisa at once recognized him and put her hand on Allan's arm.

They stood staring for a moment – a cleared space, a tool shed, a rocking chair and an old man busy in the sunlight. Then an unfamiliar twittering sound broke into this peaceful scene – some kind of birdsong, four long flute notes followed by a crackle, like nothing they had ever heard before. The old man had also heard it, straightened and looked up. Allan saw his chance, took a step forward and cleared his throat. The man turned round and stared at them. His round glasses were held in place by an elastic band round his head. His shirt was so faded with wear, washing and sun, its original colour was impossible to see. He laboriously got to his feet and came towards them.

'Hullo,' said Allan. His voice failed him and to his annoyance he found he was quite nervous.

'Good-day.' The old man smiled. 'So you've found your way here at last?'

So he knew about them. It sounded almost as if he had been expecting them.

'You must be the people in the camper over on the Dump. Is that right?'

They nodded.

He had come over to them, his voice friendly, but he spoke slowly and rather hoarsely, as if not used to using his voice.

'I saw your water system,' he said to Allan. 'It'll probably work at this time of year. But when it gets hot, it all evaporates before you've got up in the morning.'

'I had to try. . . .' Allan started. 'Until I hit on something better.'

'You must have a well,' the man said. 'That's what you need. But it's not easy to find the right place to start digging. . . .'

He seemed to be about to add something, but changed his mind.

'I'll probably manage,' said Allan. The way the man was talking made him optimistic. He seemed to be experienced at living out there, and he also seemed to have simply accepted them.

'Yes, you probably will, if you've the time.'

'We've time.'

'Good.'

Allan dared ask the question, although he considered it the old man's right to ask it first.

'How long have you lived here?'

The man thought.

'Getting on for eleven years, I think . . . since I stopped working.'

He paused again.

'I was a doctor in Sweetwater. I had a small practice. . . .' He mused again. 'Yes, well, I suppose I should introduce myself. Fischer. Dr Anton Fischer. Call me Doc. You must excuse me. . . .' He smiled slightly. 'I forget formalities of that kind. One so seldom sees people out here.'

'Allan Ung,' said Allan, holding out his hand. 'This is Lisa. We're married.'

They shook hands, and it was something more than an ordinary greeting.

For the first time, the old man looked directly at Lisa, smiled and nodded. She smiled back and looked down, her newly washed hair a reddish-gold cloud round her head.

'How old are you?' he asked mildly. 'You look so young.'

'Eighteen,' whispered Lisa.

'And you have a child. I've seen a little boy with you. I've seen you now and again on my rounds.'

'Yes, he's asleep. He hasn't been very well.'

'You need a strong constitution on the Dump, especially in hot weather. Be careful about sores and grazes, too. Lots of infections around. Some inflammations aren't to be played around with. Lice?'

'N-no, I don't think so. But we do have rats.'

'Oh, you'll have to learn live with them. They're reckoned as neighbours. Incredibly intelligent animals. But the fleas will come, just you wait. . . .'

He kept looking at Lisa. She averted her eyes, for now she was close enough to touch him, she realized he really *was* old, that 'old' was not just a word used for people older than herself (she considered Allan 'old'), not just long white hair and slow movements, but also being able to look at a person with a calm steady gaze of friendliness and warmth, having lines in your face, wrinkles round your eyes and mouth which showed whether you were bad or good, happy or disappointed. She thought Doc Fischer must be a happy person and a good man. She had not met many old people, in fact could scarcely remember one. Not many old people were to be seen on the streets of Sweetwater (what had happened to them?). She had never learnt to read anything in the features of other people. But she thought Doc Fischer must be a good man and that could be seen in the wrinkles round his eyes and mouth and in his gaze, which was so steady, so calm and full of warmth and admiration, she couldn't bring herself to meet it.

'So young,' he mumbled to himself. 'So young and yet mother to such a big boy . . . but I'm forgetting my duties as host,' he suddenly went on in a louder voice. 'You must come in and meet Marta. Perhaps you'd like a cup of tea?'

They were taken aback. Lisa giggled uncertainly. It was all so unreal. Invitations to tea were only found in school-books. Tea. How old-fashioned it sounded. So impossible there. It reminded them of their expedition to Pleasure Cove and everything that had been so strange there.

Doc Fischer was already over by the door. Despite his massive torso, he moved relatively lightly on his broad feet in their down-at-heel shoes.

'Marta!' he called. 'Come on out. We have guests.'

He turned around.

'My wife doesn't often go out,' he said, slightly apologetically. 'She's not very well.'

They wondered why he should be apologetic on that score.

Then they suddenly heard the bird again. Three long flute-like notes and a crackle, clear and unexpected from the back of the ramshackle shed.

'Greenfinch,' Fischer cried, his face brightening. 'That's the greenfinch. Everyone thought it was extinct. Chemical sprays and poisoned grain. Hedges cut down, marshes and undergrowth cleared. There are hardly any small birds left – officially. But here in my garden . . .' He flung out an arm, taking in the wild undergrowth, ' . . . they've come back. Everything here has grown wild for twenty years. We've almost got back to the original vegetation. They can live here, some of them, anyhow. We have squirrels and moles. I've also seen rabbits, and the birds are coming back little by little. Everything round us is growing, growing all over the ruins of the old. . . .'

An elderly woman had come into view in the doorway, walking with difficulty and leaning on a stick. Her face was sharp, deeply furrowed, her eyes dark, her greying hair brushed back and fastened at the nape of her neck, apparently unkempt, but it was thick and strong, clearly once an adornment. She was thin, her shapeless full-length dress hanging like a dark sack.

'We have guests, Marta!' cried Fischer. 'Come and meet Allan and Lisa. They live in the camping van over on the Dump.'

The woman screwed up her eyes against the light.

'Well, if you think the Dump is the place for young people to settle, you're welcome,' she said as she looked them up and down. 'I know what *I* would do in your place.'

'Now, Marta,' said Fischer.

'I'm just saying how it is,' she went on. 'No one should think I live here because I like it.' She stared at him until he looked down with a faint helpless movement of his hand.

'Well, come on in then,' she said. 'I'll make some tea – if there is any.'

She turned and went back inside the house.

'She's plagued with arthritis,' said Doc, as they hesitated, not knowing whether to follow her in. 'It makes her unpredictable and moody. But she's better now. Sometimes she's bedridden for weeks, even months at a time.'

They sat in Doc Fischer's room and drank weak, tasteless tea with sugar and ate sweet biscuits, the conversation slowly expanding, largely on practical matters. How did anyone subsist on the Dump? *Off* the Dump? Doc told them he sold scrap metal, machine parts and 'antiques'. Every month, a man came in a van along the service road behind the overgrown gardens, once used when the Motorway was being built, and the man took whatever they had. The demand for metals, for instance, had become great since the authorities has started rewarding production based on recycling, a result of the threatened shortage of raw materials. Other things such as knives, forks, household goods, screws, nuts, steel wire, taps, tubing, cable, gaskets and various tools were sold on the market stalls in Dock Road. There was an increasing demand for second-hand goods now that it was becoming impossible to buy new, and more and more people were earning extra money from mending defective articles. Poverty had long been invisible, but had now become visible, despite state welfare and increased social benefits. Welfare and benefits never reached those who really needed them, Fischer said. Poverty was not something that could be captured on forms. These days even people with middling incomes were poor, perhaps worse off with their status and duties to preserve.

Allan knew what the old man meant. He had seen ladies, married women, well dressed with hats and gloves, taking bottles they could get money back on out of rubbish bins and concealing them in handbags which had once cost a lot of money. That had had nothing to do with *him*, but was part of the picture in which decay could be seen, one of the danger signals telling him the time had come to get out of the city.

Doc Fisher talked about governments and politics and social theories as he sat there in his ramshackle rocking chair, now brought back inside, the afternoon sun glinting on his glasses. The contents of the room had the unmistakable imprint of the Dump, found and repaired with whatever was to hand – crate timber, wire, twine, even tough root fibres. Everything was tidy, clean and well kept, but the Dump was unmistakable. The thick foliage covered all the windows except one, producing a dim green light – an atmosphere of the underworld – and the network of plants along the beams in the ceiling and in and out of the cracks between slates formed natural binding material holding the ruined house together.

'The ivy keeps the roof on,' Doc said cheerfully. 'If I started cutting it down, the whole house would collapse.'

A fireplace was bricked up in one wall and a paraffin lamp hung on a hook above the table.

'We had electricity as long as the service road was in use. A cable ran along there, so I brought a cable in here. But then the current was cut off. The construction camp moved on I suppose . . . God knows. We get paraffin from Dos Manos, the man with the van – he's an old friend, by the way – in exchange for scrap. Gas, too, and some other things we need. But we find most things for our ourselves.'

They could see into the little kitchen through a half-open door: a glimpse of saucepans, buckets and glass jars containing various kinds of grain and seeds. Doc had told them about his kitchen garden where he sowed and planted things they could eat, and about the maize field running from the end of the garden jungle right up the slope towards the Motorway, the remains of an abandoned farm that had flourished before the city had sprawled out there many years ago. Allan looked all round, inquisitively, hungrily, as if it were important to take in every single detail, as if by absorbing everything in that crowded narrow room, he could learn the art of survival, as the old man opposite had learnt it – in fact seemed to be an incarnation of it.

Doc sat with the warm afternoon light on his face, looking at Lisa, almost unable to take his eyes from her as she sat with her wild mop of hair dancing round her slender face. What a delightful child! He was amazed she was married and had a child. He had seen her with her son, but it was still hard to take it in. He had seen them all together by the camper four days ago as he was passing on his rounds. She had been on her knees getting breakfast in front of the stove, so fragile and clumsy with those crude vessels. Then *he* had come out of the camper and stood looking at her for a moment, the morning sun warming him. He had gone over to her, put his hands on her shoulders and stroked her back, then suddenly lifted her up and carried her half-smiling, half-protesting back into the camper. The little boy had clutched at his father's legs and cried. He had stood watching this whole incident, but his sight was poor, and at that distance he had not seen how young she was, how amazingly innocent, how *beautiful*.

Lisa could feel his gaze on her and she felt safe, safer than she had felt since they had moved out to the Dump. Safer than she had ever felt since she was small and had had a father – another father, a larger, calmer, kinder, *older* father – who had left them and betrayed them, as her mother said, but whom the new, handsomer, younger and loud-voiced father, so interested in psychology, had never been able to replace.

They sat in Doc Fischer's room with its shabby but practical and comfortable furniture, talking about what mattered most: how to survive on the Dump, how to collect things and sell or exchange them for things they needed. Their fellowship became a warm protective bond – not because they had suddenly come closer personally – but because they had important things in common. They were all in the same boat and the same conditions prevailed for them all.

Doc put a pinch of crumbled tobacco on to a little paper, rolled it up, licked it and made a cigarette. He offered it to Allan, but he declined it. He had given up smoking several years ago. Synthetic tobacco blackened the teeth and was no real stimulant, though it was cheap, and like artificial chocolate, it was proffered as if such things would make people forget the shortages of other, rather more important items.

Doc told them it was real tobacco. He had stored some away when it had still been available and now mixed it with what he grew himself. To Allan, smoking was unnecessary and old-fashioned. He maintained people could no longer tell the difference between real and artificial tobacco. So Doc smoked his thin cigarette on his own. The two men belonged in their own eras, swearing by their own small pleasures. But what were Allan's small pleasures, when it came down to it? What pleased him? Did he know any other pleasure apart from sitting on a car seat on a heap of rubber tyres, staring at the lights of Sweetwater – just as he had once stood in the window of his boyhood room, staring at the lights of the petrol station going on and off and lighting up the street with their marvellously clear colours? Doc's pleasures were relics of another era, a ceremony he wished to maintain. Today, to Allan's genera- tion, pleasures were fabricated, products, as synthetic as consumer goods. So pleasure was really an an unknown concept to Allan, while for Doc it was an almost vanished concept he could remember if stimulated in the right way.

That did not disturb the sense of fellowship warming them as they sat, closer now, so close not one of them could be entirely unmoved by their very existence, despite the distances and differ- ences between them.

'I have a well,' said Doc, as they were about to leave. 'I didn't mention it at first, but I have a well. You can fetch water from it when you need it. I'll show you where it is.'

They went out and Doc showed them a track winding between thorny bushes round at the back of the ramshackle shed. There, in a hollow, was an iron cover surrounded by slabs of stone.

'Look. . . .'

Doc struggled with the heavy cover.

'There's plenty at this time of year.'

The well was a dark hole in the black soil, the surface of the water glinting like an eye some way down. Doc got down on his hands and knees, a scoop in one hand. His hand and arm vanished into the hole and they could hear a splash as he pulled his arm out again with the scoop half full of brownish water. What he had done was an amazing ritual to Allan and Lisa. They had never seen water brought up from the earth before.

'There. . . .' Doc lifted the scoop and took a sip, then offered it to them.

'Can you really drink it?' said Lisa.

'Of course. I guarantee it tastes better than that mix of chemicals out of taps in Sweetwater. That'll come to end, too, anyhow. Did you know every inhabitant of the city uses a hundred and fifty litres of drinking water a day? And that's just for direct use. Manufacturing processes use incredible quantities. We're quite simply running out of water. Actual ground water levels are sinking. I notice it in the summer when the water in the well is low. The water tastes brackish. That means they're overusing it to such an extent, sea water is seeping into the subsoil water.'

Doc had raised his voice and was gesticulating towards the city. 'There's enough water for people to survive. There always will be, but not enough to maintain technological civilization. It'll all collapse one day. Sweetwater's eight million inhabitants will have no drinking water. That'll be the Day of Judgement.'

Allan took the scoop and cautiously tasted the water. It was cool and fresh, compared with the tepid liquid he had in the plastic container.

'What do you want for the water?'

'What?'

'What do you want in payment?'

Until a week ago, water had been the most obvious thing in life and he had never given it a thought, apart from the moments when it had been cut off as a result of some failure in the supply. Now it was just as obvious that Doc Fischer's offer could not be accepted without offering something in return. Water was more important than anything else. To be offered it ensured their survival. It was more than a service.

'Payment, no. . . .' Doc looked at them, two young people, and found himself unable to make demands, soft-hearted as he was even after his years of toil out there.

'But you *must* have something in exchange for water!'

'We-ell. . . .'

They stood there irresolutely until Marta settled the matter. She had come out with them, although the pain in her joints grew worse toward evening, but she did not want to lose sight of these two, this sudden element from the world outside, the world she thought of with longing, a world she had missed every single day over all these years. For it had not been with goodwill that. . . .

'No,' she said, 'Doc Fischer has never taken payment for his services. It's always been like that. It was the same with his abortion practice in Sweetwater. He – the idealist – couldn't even bring himself to ask for fees for the vile work he did.'

Then it all poured out, the bitterness that had been hidden behind those half-closed eyes as they had sat in the room drinking tea, the bitterness that made her life into a long slow struggle against 'the unfortunate circumstances' forcing her into such a life, against *him*, although she knew the battle was lost and that she would die out there.

'Ask him why he had to leave a good practice in the city, why he was thrown out of the Medical Association and had to find somewhere to live on a garbage tip because he was too *proud* to admit he had been wrong.'

'Marta, dear, what are you saying?'

Doc attempted a protest against her vilification, but faced with her intensity, he seemed resigned and powerless.

'I am against the abortion laws,' he said. 'What I did was consciously breaking a law I found both stupid and inhuman. I knew the risks I was taking. Taking to sackcloth and ashes would be to deny everything I believed in. And still do believe in.'

'Huh!' she said. 'What kind of view of life is it, doing illegal ops on flighty girls, free, too. . . . Listen to me,' she went on, turning to Allan. 'You have to know what this is all about. We can't just give our water away. Let's say a bucket for five kilos of iron, five buckets for a kilo of copper and a kilo of lead. If you find anything else, we can agree on that later. Is that reasonable?'

Allan glanced at Doc, who just nodded.

'O.K.,' he said. He thought it a reasonable agreement. He was thinking of all the wrecked cars, the defective machines of various kinds he had seen all over the Dump, and here, too, along the road. It wouldn't be difficult to accumulate enough metal to ensure their water supply for a long time.

They walked back along the shore.

'Why was she so horried to him?' said Lisa.

He shrugged. The old people's private quarrel had not affected him as it had her.

'I expect they've lived there for so many years they've begun to get on each other's nerves.'

'But if she's so angry with him, why doesn't she leave him? If she's so dissatisfied with living here, why didn't she move out long ago? No one has to live with anyone he or she doesn't like.'

'No, but once upon a time there was something called fidelity and loyalty in marriage, "until death do us part", you know. Maybe they believe in that. I think that was an old-fashioned happy marriage we saw and heard. I think it's often like that with older couples.'

She thought for a while.

'What do you think he meant by "sackcloth and ashes?"'

'Something to do with "honour". A man is not supposed to go back on his word. Then he loses his self-respect. Something like that.'

'How odd,' she said. 'You can't think and mean the same things all your life, when things change so quickly.'

'No, you can't.'

He had never really known what the word 'honour' meant, either.

'How *old* they are,' Lisa went on. 'Did you see their wrinkles? And his hand was like leather to hold. But it felt right – quite natural, I mean, though I've never touched such an old man before. I don't think I've even *seen* anyone so old, with such white hair . . . and her, bent double and so wrinkled. Have you ever seen anyone so old before?'

'Mm, maybe. Not often. It used to be quite common to see old people, but not any longer. I don't know what happens to them. In old people's collectives, perhaps?'

The old were invisible in Sweetwater. The statistics said people were living longer, but they aged more quickly and disappeared. Children didn't know about them. They looked on their scarcely middle-aged parents as 'the old' in a society that had no use for knowing what approaching old age did to a human being, either good or bad.

But different, more practical thoughts were occupying Allan as they walked side by side along the narrow strip of shore. Doc Fischer had managed for eleven years. So it was possible. Then it should be possible if times got worse. Allan had kept his eyes open. He had seen his ideas put into practice. He had noted every detail inside and outside that room. He had to look and learn. He had noted Doc Fischer's possessions, his store of metals, tools, screws, nuts and bolts, machine parts of all kinds, all of them scrap, but still valuable, barter in a society where most things were in short supply. Not yet obvious, but undeniable. He had seen the transistor radio, a pair of binoculars, a gas refrigerator, a row of sharpened knives in the kitchen, and he had wondered what Doc Fischer possessed that he *hadn't* seen. Not because he envied Doc Fischer his possessions and was thinking of stealing them, but out here, possessions in themselves took on a quite different light because they were immediately bound up with *needs*. Just as the lives of their fellow human beings could no longer be a matter of indifference, possessions – regardless of who owned them – had become something of importance to them all, concerned them all. Like water.

'That look in his eyes. . . .' Lisa was basking in the old man's obvious admiration. 'I don't think anyone has ever looked at me like that before. But it wasn't unpleasant, just safe, in a strange way.'

Whether they liked it or not, they were already involved in a new and indeterminate fellowship with the other inhabitants of the Dump.

When they got back to the camper, it was late afternoon. Boy was asleep on the mattress who they came in, at first glance just as they had left him, but then they found various objects lying beside him which had not been there before.

'He's been out,' whispered Lisa. 'Look, he's got his shoes on. Poor thing, perhaps he's been out looking for us. We shouldn't have stayed away for so long.'

Allan bent down and picked up something from beside the boy's bed. Half a dozen shiny buttons were strewn all over the mattress. He examined them. They had a coat of arms on them.

'They're official buttons. I've seen them on postmen and social workers,' said Lisa. 'Where do you think he got hold of them?'

'Oh, everything can be found on the Dump,' said Allan. But he was thoughtful. Among the stones and bits of glass on the mattress was a wrist-watch, the rotting strap half off. Without another word, he collected up all the objects and put them on the shelf above the folding table.

It was warm inside the camper. The boy's forehead was hot, but he was breathing evenly. His fever seemed to have gone.

Allan went out to collect firewood for their coffee. Lisa came out with food, bread, a bowl of fat from the pieces of bacon they had fried for dinner — the last of their old provisions — a tube of fruit paste tasting of blackcurrants and a piece of vegetable cheese wrapped in plastic, which Allan had bought at Sweetness' kiosk. Their movements as they prepared their simple meal were calm and sure. They had acclimatized. They had time to spare. They knew they were safe — to the extent that anyone could be sure of anything — from disturbances from the world outside. They had adapted to the surroundings they had chosen for themselves. They did not talk. Allan squatted by the fire and let his eyes run over the camper and what was around it — the heap of tyres, two more mounds and the open space where they ate. He knew every detail now and had summed up all possibilities. He had paced every square metre innumerable times in the course of the ten days they had lived there and it had become *his* territory.

10

Weeks went by. Months went by, and their life acquired a pattern of its own.

The heat on the Dump began to plague them as early as late May. The whole area was suffering a heat wave that simply went on and on. Experts speculated on whether the cause was chemical effluents and fumes from industry, heating and traffic, creating disturbances in the atmosphere which in their turn created meteorological ir- regularities — local at first, but with inevitable knock-on effects. Doc told them the reports indicated that half the continent was affected by drought. He listened to the radio and also read newspapers Dos Manos brought out to him.

'Carbon dioxide in the air increases the intensity of the rays of the sun. That was already known in my time,' he said despondently. He was on his knees measuring the water level in the well.

'Looks as if we've managed to change the composition of the whole atmosphere of the Earth. First we get this heat, then comes drought, crop failure, shortage of water, shortage of food . . . just wait and see.'

He did not go on. Even talking was too much of an effort in that heat. Doc carefully hauled the plastic bucket up out of the well. The supply was not great. The buckets were precious. No one knew when rain would come.

Allan was patiently waiting beside him.

'Have you noticed any brackish taste yet?'

'No.'

'It'll come. Last year it came when the water level was about what it is now.'

'Was it this hot last year?'

Allan made an effort, but he could not remember last summer. Living in the city, he hadn't noticed changes in the weather much. Summers were usually warm, winters usually cold, and it rained now and again, or it was windy. That was how he saw it, and he had given it little thought. Now every sign of a change was hugely important. One good rainstorm would relieve the situation, it only temporarily.

'No, perhaps not quite so hot. It didn't start so early. But it was bad enough. And it'll be worse this year.'

They were in the shade of the poplars, and yet they were both dripping with sweat. The leaves at the top of the trees were turning yellow, but otherwise the drought had not affected the lushness of the garden. Rose shoots wound their way along hedges already choked by ivy, couch grass and other creeping plants. Amazing blooms spread heavy, musky scents and thick leaves down by the ground oozed sticky moisture.

Allan got down on his hands and knees and filled the second bucket himself. He had worked hard for this bucket, hauling over sixty kilos of old lead from batteries in the heat, as well as iron and copper and anything else Doc would take. Everything had been weighed and calculations made. It had taken him several days to investigate the wrecked cars on the Dump and in roadside ditches round about. More and more kept arriving. People drove them out at night, removed the number plates and left the cars hidden somewhere rather than pay to have them towed away once they were no longer roadworthy. The regulations were fierce.

But it took time to get the lead off old battery cases, and even longer to remove copper from a dynamo. He had laboured for weeks to ensure their water supply for the summer and the two buckets of brown water he fetched every other day were hard-earned.

Doc liked talking to him, liked telling Allan his thoughts and experiences from his earlier life. Doc had been an idealist, still was, though now in exile. He believed in systems, changing systems, even now when economic necessity had wiped out traditional political opposition and the government controlled all investments, prices and wages. Political activism in the traditional sense was limited to isolated groups of extremists that would never play an important part, but all the same, the authorities brutally persecuted and suppressed them.

Doc found it difficult to understand Allan's indifference when it came to such subjects. Doc felt something important had been lost in the course of recent decades. He was hoping developments would bring people to a point where they would stop and think, then turn round to look for what they had lost. Allan simply could not understand those concepts and could only connect rhetoric of that kind with his father telling him that everything had been so much better before the swallows (were the swallows an image of what had 'been lost' . . .?).

To Allan, life in Sweetwater had simply become impossible and change had *had* to come. They had packed up and moved without reflecting to any appreciable extent. They had sought new fields much like animals whose pastures or hunting grounds are threatened, without looking back to the old days afterwards, with no sense of loss or of having left anything precious behind. What they had left behind was chaos, a process gone too far for those involved – the victims – to be able to intervene and control it. The city had become a dangerous trap slowly closing in on them. They had escaped, so far. No one could know for sure what would happen when the trap finally snapped shut.

So Allan preferred talking about practical matters with Doc, seeking his advice, asking for information, exercises in the art of survival, which he knew he would have to master should the worst befall them.

'How does Lisa take the heat?' Doc asked. He often asked about Lisa.

'She's fine,' said Allan, though that was not entirely true. Lisa had been poorly recently, complaining of tiredness and itching rashes. But he also suffered from rashes and found the heat exhausting. They were not yet truly adapted to their changed conditions.

'Marta can't stand it,' said Doc. 'She says it makes her worse. She sweats, you see, sweats until she hasn't the energy to get up. It was bad enough last year and no doubt it'll be even worse this year. I don't know what to do to help her. Sometimes she doesn't seem to *want* to be helped. But I suppose she's getting old – we're both getting old.' Doc laughed briefly. 'So things are all right for you over there, then?'

'Sure. Lisa likes it. The boy does, too.'

'Make sure you get enough salt.'

'Salt?'

'Yes, it's important when you sweat a lot. Then you don't lose so much water and get so exhausted. Have you got any?'

'No.'

'Here. . . .' Doc dug into his pocket and gave Allan a handful of coarse grey grains. 'That's sea salt. I get it from Dos Manos. He's got a contact. Take a couple of grains occasionally, and make Lisa do that too.'

'Doesn't it make you thirsty?'

'Not if you don't take too much. Salt is supposed to keep the water in your body. Yes, another thing, try to drink as little as possible during the day. If you drink a lot, you sweat more and get more exhausted. Better to drink in the evening after the sun's gone down.'

Allan nodded, grateful for all these tips. He put the fistful of salt into his pocket, bent down and lifted the two buckets carefully, so as not spill any water. He had a tough trip ahead with the precious liquid.

'Thanks,' he said as he was about to leave.

The day's conversation was over.

Lisa was dozing on the mattress outside the camper. They had had to put up some protection from the sun, so Allan had dragged back some corrugated iron and cardboard boxes, empty sacks and fibreboards to make a roof on some ramshackle poles. The shade helped a little, but the flies were a torment and every gust of wind brought acrid smells over from the tipping places. The merciless sun was quite still over Paradise Bay, enclosed in a light but impenetrable sulphurous cocoon. The perpetual veil of yellow smog seemed to intensify the heat descending on the desolation of the Dump like hammer blows.

Lisa could see smoke from where she was, thin columns rising here and there and small clouds drifting low over the refuse heaps from the spontaneous fires caused by the heat. It had become a common sight and fires of that kind often went on burning for days.

She was thinking about what she had to do, troubled by the thought of the mess in the camper (it was *always* untidy in there, but she had made an effort before), the cooking and the washing. Without meaning to, she had let things slide recently, only doing what was absolutely necessary, and sometimes not even that. The cooking had increasingly been left to Allan because she simply couldn't find the energy. She was feeling unwell and listless, sleeping for long periods every day, but she was still tired. She itched and felt dirty, but even that no longer aroused any real distaste in her.

She yawned, stretched and waved away the flies. She was not feeling so bad now. She had been sick earlier on, but the nausea had gone, leaving her feeling almost pleasantly relaxed. She still hadn't told Allan she was pregnant, a fact that surprised even herself. She had meant to, had planned to several times over the last month, but something had held her back, a new and strange feeling of shyness, almost embarrassment towards him, a defence of what was happening to her body, a defence against all outsiders, even him, her husband.

This was quite new to her, the exact opposite of the feeling she had had the first time she had been pregnant. Then they had agreed from the very beginning, in an abstract, rather theoretical way. They had discussed it and weighed up the pros and cons matter of factly and soberly. Over-population was a problem, abortion a formality and they could decide for themselves. Pregnancy had given them something to talk about, a focus to their life in April Avenue far more important than simply increasing the family. That seemed to them quite alien, almost unreal, despite or perhaps because of all the information and books they had been given at the health centre. Pregnancy and its consequences were a problem to solve, a task to set about intellectually, together. It had been stimulating, although she had regretted their somewhat arrogant decision more than once when she saw how misshapen her slender body became as her condition advanced. Then she had not been prepared for the bundle that was her child, screaming and demanding things of her, nor did she know whether she had the strength.

But this time she was prepared and knew what it entailed – she had been through it all before. She and Allan were also much closer to each other in many ways than they had been before. Life in the camper impinged on them more and their whole existence meant they had to cooperate and were more dependent on each other. Although their situation brought them into closer physical contact and some inhibitions over their natural functions had gradually gone, she felt becoming pregnant again was primarily her concern.

She secretly watched him working. She had seen him labouring in the heat to provide them with immediate necessities. He worked hard. He had thinned down. Finding something to eat was harder now things rotted in a few hours. But they had a supply of hard bread they could soak and eat, or grind and fry, as well as cans of chocolate and whatever Allan bought in the kiosks with his wages. They had fruit, largely oranges from a damaged load Allan had come across. He had sorted them and brought them back, sweating, covered with fruit juice and surrounded by flies. Sometimes she hardly saw him all day when he went on exploration trips to distant parts of the Dump. He often came back exhausted and simply fell asleep. He had grown with his task, full of resolute energy and putting everything he had into making life as satisfactory as possible for them all. She had become stationary, largely occupied with elementary household chores in and around the camper, cooking, tidying (not her forte at any time) and keeping their clothes in some kind of order.

Their roles had become clearer on the Dump. The marked difference in skills, now further emphasized by her condition, created another kind of distance, a segregation between his life and hers. It had become so obvious, so *visible* what was her work and what was his, what was her responsibility and what his. Pregnancy and childbirth must definitely be *hers*. So she must have kept her condition from him almost instinctively, trying to behave normally, blaming the heat when she clearly felt weak and unwell. Like a sick dog, she lay beside him at night, swallowing, clenching her teeth when the nausea came, protecting her secret from his rough, demanding maleness.

Yet she would have liked to share it with him and she wanted to confide in someone. She knew she would have go on playing this game, lying, trying to distract his attention until it was no longer possible to keep it a secret. When she thought about it, about when she would just have to wait because there was nothing else she could do, then she felt all she could do now was to crawl away into a dark corner and hide, and not be a nuisance to anyone until it was over.

At the same she feared the loneliness and the pain. She remembered the great waiting room at the Central Hospital where she had been left struggling with terror and increasing pain for hours before she was finally moved into the crowded maternity ward. There she had been given an injection and had fallen into a miserable daze which was still nightmarish to her, something she never wanted to go through again. Then the time afterwards in the cramped draughty apartment in April Avenue — her thoughts scarcely touched on April Avenue without a shudder of horror — Boy's thin body, his weak constitution, his constant colds and earache, his accusing eyes. . . .

Where was he, for that matter? She hadn't seen him since the morning. Probably roaming around on the Dump, his new kingdom. He had been an anxious whining child before, never daring to take a step on his own, and now he was becoming a self-confident vagrant, guarded even to them, his parents. But that didn't worry her — she could see he was healthy and growing. He had become stronger and brown all over from the sun. So it couldn't be helped that they could never get out of him what he did during the day, where he had been, or get him to share his experiences with them.

She stretched out on the grubby mattress, put a thin, freckled brown arm across her eyes and placed her other hand on her lap, almost as a protection. She was wearing a shirt and panties. She didn't go around naked so much these days, anyhow not when *he* was anywhere near. Something warned her not to tempt him, excite him — he did as he pleased anyhow when his need arose. His hard male body sometimes made such demands on her that she had taken to tears. The very sight of him when he looked at her in that special way could fill her with a childish fear. She found him attractive — he was leaner, had thinned down, his hair had grown and he had stopped shaving, but his persistence usually came too suddenly for her. Although she nearly always liked it, she had to hold back, to defend it — her secret.

She sighed. She had quite forgotten Boy, forgotten even that she had thought about him a moment ago, almost worried about him because he was so turned in on himself, forgotten she had revived memories of April Avenue. She found it easy to forget and it was even easier in this heat. She closed her eyes and drew in the sharp smell of smoke in the air, then fell into a light, almost happy doze.

11

Boy came rushing over the mounds, slipped, fell, was up again and running, running for his life, anguish in his eyes, his mouth wide open in a scream which was nothing but his breath heaving in and out in a suppressed wail. A tall figure of a man was running at top speed behind him, heavy in thick boots, one arm out as if at any moment he would reach the boy and grab him and . . . he got closer, his long black overcoat flapping round his thin body, one hand fumbling inside it.

At that moment, Allan appeared on the path with the two buckets. When he saw his son and the pursuer some way away, he put down the buckets and started running in their direction, but soon realized the distance was too great. The black-clad man was closer now, and in three, four, five more strides his outstretched hand would be there. In the hand he had pulled out of the folds of the coat was a sharp glint of metal – a weapon? A knife? Allan shouted, yelling with all his might when he saw it, and he could feel in his sluggish legs, his aching chest, he would never get there until. . . . But Boy heard his shout and swung round, changed direction and came straight for him, apparently flying, unbelievably fast for a boy of five. His pursuer hesitated for a moment, enough for the boy to gain a little more on his lead, but then rushed after him with the knife held aloft. Allan ran as he had never run before, without a thought for how he was to overwhelm this tall attacker, who to crown everything was also armed. . . . If he got there – his throat ached, his chest was bursting for lack of breath, his eyes blurred, seeing nothing except that something else was happening in front of him, something unexpected, something which completely changed the situation.

Another stranger appeared, a short stout man moving with incredible speed. He came racing round from behind the towering pile of lumps of concrete to the left of the main in the coat and the boy. He was clearly trying to cut off the pursuer, and he shouted something, foreign words in commanding tones, an order, but with no effect. Then they collided. With a leap the stout man had locked his arm round the thin man's neck and shoulders and they fell to the ground, where they struggled in a heap until a short club appeared in the fat man's hand. It cut through the air.

The thin man let out a sharp, agonized shriek, then lay whimpering, his hands covering his face. The stout man got up and began calmly and deliberately brushing dust and soil off his clothes as if nothing unusual had happened. Neither seemed to bother about the weapon, a murderous double-edged hunting knife lying on the ground only a short distance away from them.

Allan took in the incredible scene only in glimpses as he comforted the sobbing, trembling Boy. He had lifted the child and was holding him close to him as he kept a watchful eye on every movement the two strangers made, ready to take up the fight again – or flee.

The plump man raised his head and looked at him, then took two or three steps towards them, walking slowly, almost cautiously, limping slightly. He was fastidiously dressed in shirt, tie and waistcoat under his jacket, a crease in his trousers, his shoes recently polished. The whole effect was utterly absurd, considering the place and the temperature and the fact that he had just knocked down a dangerous assailant. He stopped and waited, apparently neither aggressive nor hostile. His face was broad and pale and he had the beginnings of a double chin. His thinning hair was brushed back sharply from the sloping forehead and temples. A small moustache adorned his upper lip.

At a distance, he could have been taken for any ordinary businessman, but when Allan looked more closely, he saw the man's clothes were old and shabby, although relatively clean and in good repair, and the soles of his square-toed shoes were just parting from the uppers. But they were good shoes, Allan could see that, genuine leather and possible to repair. Allan was confused by the men's presence, but he also took a few steps forward to shorten the distance between them, still holding the boy and watching the other man intently. If he stopped too far away, the man would think he was frightened. If he got too near, he might consider that provocation, or nonchalance, even letting oneself in for something.

Allan could feel cold sweat trickling down his chest and his knees shaking, reaction after his sudden anguish and the wild chase. He felt weak, but knew that he would have to remain on guard, although for the moment there seemed to be little danger.

The man in front of him looked fairly unaffected, not even plagued by the heat. He bowed imperceptibly before speaking.

'I am sorry. . . .'

The words were deliberate and precise, the tone of voice odd. The three words he had pronounced told Allan he was a foreigner.

'I am sorry for what happened. It was a misunderstanding. My brother. . . .'

He nodded towards the other man, until then still on the same spot, but now beginning to move and get up.

'My brother misunderstands sometimes. The little boy came very inopportunely. . . .'

The stranger pronounced the words fastidiously, like a teacher, but his accent was unmistakable.

'My name is Felix,' he went on. 'This is my brother, Run-Run.'

The other man stood up, holding his head in both hands and rocking from side to side.

'My brother is very temperamental. The little boy came very inopportunely. . . .' He carefully repeated the phrase as if that entirely explained the man's murderous pursuit of Boy.

The other man came slowly towards them. He was tall, a good head taller than Allan, and very thin. The long dark overcoat swung round his body, his boots flapped and looked far too large for his feet, but Allan recalled the speed and litheness with which he been chasing Boy only a few minutes ago. His hair was thick, short and raggedly cut, his skin as brown as bark. Involuntarily, Allan took a step back and pressed his son close to him, prepared for anything, although there was nothing threatening about the dark man as he shuffled up. Felix raised his hand dismissively.

'No, no. Not dangerous. Not now.'

The man called Run-Run came right up to them and stopped beside his brother, staring at Allan and Boy. His face then suddenly broke into a broad smile, a grin revealing two rows of strong white teeth. Just as suddenly, he held out his hand, as if in greeting, but pulled it back before Allan had time to react.

'This is Run-Run,' said Felix. 'My poor brother. He can't speak. I speak for both of us.'

The smile on the brother's face did not alter. His mouth was large, but his head relatively small on a thin, sinewy neck protruding out of the overcoat that came down almost to his feet. His hands were long and supple, hanging straight at his sides. Allan noticed they came a long way down his thighs, and he also noticed the knife was no longer lying glinting on the ground. Run-Run must have retrieved it as he was struggling to his feet.

At last Allan got his voice back.

'When did you come here?'

The other men's behaviour, the natural way they made their way round in these surroundings, told him that they were also here on the Dump, presumably actually living lives there. That was their right and needed no explanation. But they owed each other some information if they were to live side by side.

'A while ago,' said Felix evasively. 'A while ago. We are foreigners, as you can hear,' he went on. 'We look for work but have not yet found any.'

'Where do you live?'

'Over there. . . .' The man called Felix pointed vaguely over the mounds. 'There are some crates there. Not bad. We have seen worse. No, not bad at all. Until we find work. Every day we look for work.'

He turned to Run-Run, who nodded his head vigorously, his grin even broader and his eyes gleaming almost unnaturally.

Boy started wriggling in Allan's arms, so Allan put him down. The danger was over. The anxiety he had felt faded, though he was still curious and watchful. He looked straight at the strangers.

'My name's Allan. This is my son Boy. I have a wife called Lisa. We live in a camping van over there.' He pointed. 'We have been here about twelve weeks. I have casual work at a petrol station out in the East Zone of the city.'

He stopped. No need to say anything more. Nor did he know anything more about them.

He could read nothing in the strangers' faces, but Felix bowed his head again, almost imperceptibly, before replying.

'I am glad to hear it.'

Run-Run's broad grin remained unaltered, like a mask, his magnificent teeth brilliant in his sunburnt face.

'I wish *I* could've met them, too,' said Lisa sulkily when Allan sat down beside her and told her briefly what had happened.

'You say they're harmless, only a couple of unfortunate immigrant workers. You could have asked them. . . .' But she stopped. She could see for herself it was not that simple to invite people back home. Friendly contact and hospitality meant something different there, and she had also taken in that at first one of the two strangers had behaved threateningly.

Boy sat beside them, his eyes gleaming with excitement. To him, the dramatic episode had already become an adventure.

'Did you see his knife, Dad?' he said. 'I saw he had it in his belt under his coat. Do you think he wanted to kill me, Dad?'

'Don't talk like that,' whispered Lisa. Allan said nothing. He had a lot to think about.

'Dad, he did want to kill me at first, didn't he?' the boy persisted.

'If they're that friendly, why go around with a knife?' said Lisa.

'Maybe to defend themselves. You never know what you'll come across. And they're foreign workers. They're often vulnerable, as things are. They're not exactly in a good position.'

'But they threatened Boy.'

'They didn't mean to. That's what the stout one said, anyhow. Felix.'

'And the other one, what was his name? The one who can't speak?'

'Run-Run.'

'What a funny name. Where do you think they come from?'

'No idea.'

'But how can anyone attack a five-year-old boy?'

Allan shook his head and stared at Boy. His child was clutching something in one hand and had been squeezing it all the time.

'Where did you meet them, Boy?' he said.

'Over there.' The boy pointed vaguely across the vast wilderness of the Dump.

'Where?'

'There.'

The stubborn, reluctant expression had returned.

'What've you got there?'

'Nothing.'

The boy hid his clenched fist behind his back.

'Show me what you've got there.'

Allan's hard tone made the child obey with a sullen look. He opened his hand. Two gilt buttons fell to the ground, identical to those they had found on the mattress in the camper that time.

'Where did you find these?'

'Don't know.'

The boy's face was closed as he stood looking down at the ground, as if he could scarcely hear what was said to him.

'You must tell me where you found them.'

The boy tightened his lips. Allan grabbed his arm and pulled him to him; his grip was perhaps harder that he had intended.

'Ow!'

'*Where* did you find them? Was it where you met those men?'

The boy shrugged. Allan hit him. Lisa got half-way up and tried to stop him, but he shoved her away. Boy rubbed his face but said nothing. Small and hard, he stood looking angrily down at the ground.

'Now listen,' said Allan savagely. 'You *must* tell us where you met them and what you were doing. It could mean anything!'

He tightened his grip on the thin arm. He had never consciously been brutal to his son before, but the unease he felt smothered his doubts. He *had* to know.

'Well?'

The boy wriggled, but said nothing. Allan struck him again and it sounded like the crack of a whip. The boy screamed and tried to wriggle over to Lisa, who was looking on in horror. But Allan held on to him.

'Well?'

The boy wept.

'Are you going to show me where it was? Or do you want another bash?'

The sobs rose to a wail.

'All right. Let's go.'

Allan got to his feet, still holding on to Boy's arm.

'You're to show me where it was.'

Boy started walking down the path without looking at either of them. He had stopped crying, but his narrow shoulders shook now and again and he kept wiping his nose on his hand. Allan drew a sigh of relief. He had won. With a glance at Lisa, he started after his son. He looked at the boy's slender neck beneath the filthy unkempt head, the fair hairs running into a point at the nape. His hand was stinging from the blows and he was already regretting losing his temper in anger, however necessary it had been.

He realized a new element had come into their lives that morning. That element was Danger. For a few short moments, he had been confronted with Danger, with mortal dread, for the first time in his life, those crazy moments when he had seen Run-Run raising the knife and had known he was too far away to intervene. His legs had turned to lead and yet he had known, sensed rather than seen that all was lost.

That had opened his eyes; his sense of impotence at that moment threatened his own reason, etched into him and left an ineradicable scar. The fear of death. Now he knew he had to be prepared to meet every danger, that the security they had felt during the first weeks

79

was only an aftermath of city life, the sense of being protected, protected by their anonymity, by statistics and light-hearted games of chance. It always happens to other people. But out here it would happen to them, and he had to be prepared to defend himself and his family against Danger. Finding out as much as he could about the strange brothers and their activities was one way of protecting himself, one feature in this struggle for life.

12

The corpse had swollen in the heat. The distended body was threatening to split the rotting material of the uniform. The face had gone, the fingers and feet eaten by animals and insects. But the shape was still human.

From a distance they had seen the flock of crows rising, then the smell had reached them, the foul stench of putrefying flesh – unlike anything else, even out there on the Dump. As they got closer, flies rose in great clouds, swarming over them before again settling on the dead body.

Allan stood a little way away, holding his hand over his nose and mouth as he wondered what he ought to do. But Boy went right up to the corpse, ignoring the flies and the smell and the ghastly hole the crows had left where the face had been. He had spotted a uniform button on the nearest sleeve round an arm and wrist of inhuman dimensions. Allan ran forward and grabbed him before he touched the stinking cadaver, nausea clutching at him and an aching lump coming into his throat. The boy resisted as he carried him back to where they had stopped. Allan tried to calm him down by speaking in a controlled voice, telling him how dangerous it was to go near dead animals – and people. He didn't really know much about it but could vaguely remember television news reels from disaster areas with pictures of dead animals and people lying in water and the commentator talking about epidemics. But the stench told him enough. Nothing that smelt like that could be harmless.

'. . . you could get infected, and die,' he said. 'It's dangerous to go near anything dead. Dead things have to buried at once or . . . or awful things can happen. Epidemics and. . . .'

Boy stared at him.

'What's epi–demics?'

'When lots of people get ill at the same time and the doctors can't help them.'

He could see Boy was taking no notice and he could feel the thin body tensing under his grip, trying to get free. His irritation mounted in time with the sense of impotence that had overcome him. Before he knew what was happening, he had grabbed the boy hard by both upper arms and was shaking him wildly.

'Listen to me, will you! This is serious! It's *dangerous* to go over there. If you don't stay here, you know what'll happen. You'll get another. . . .'

Boy stopped resisting and hung limply in Allan's hands, his eyes turned sullenly away. Allan knew he ought to be ashamed of losing his temper with the boy again, but other thoughts were occupying him. He sat the boy down and again looked at the dead man. The corpse was in a kind of military uniform, but blue-green in colour. It must be a policeman, or an officer in the Peacekeeping Force.

'Stay here. I must investigate something,' he said curtly to Boy.

He went over to the corpse, covering his face except his eyes with his arm. The stench seemed to press against his temples and to be more tangible than the heat. He fixed his eyes on the uniform tunic and tried to avoid looking elsewhere. The flies rose again in a repulsive, buzzing swarm. He waved them away furiously. With his free hand, he cautiously poked up the flap of the nearest top pocket, held his breath and fumbled with two fingers inside. Nothing. Cursing, he withdrew his hand. To reach the other pocket he would have to take a step nearer. Sweat was blinding him and the nausea made him feel faint, but he had to take one more step. One arm lay crookedly across the dead man's chest, covering the other pocket. It would have to be shifted. He cautiously gave it a push, but to no effect, then shuddered and tried again. The arm tipped away slowly and fell to one side. Allan acted as quickly as he could, knowing he couldn't stand this much longer. He could feel a flat contour inside the pocket and in a second he had fished out the little plastic folder. Ants were crawling over it and on to his hand, but one look was enough to see that he had found what he was looking for. The corner of the identification card protruded. He had the weapon he could use.

At that moment, something happened to the corpse. The movement of the arm and his own quick fumbling had ripped the buttonless tunic wide open and the distended corpse burst free from the rotting remnants of cloth. Paralysed by revulsion, Allan saw the swollen belly come into view in the gap between trouser waistband and what had once been an undershirt – grotesquely distended, it literally bulged out of the clothing, revealing more and more skin, putrefied skin, almost the colour of soot – and a wound, black with purple edges, a wide gash in the taut skin right below the navel, a slit, a long cut. . . . As he stood there, riveted and numbed, incapable of moving and horrified at what was happening, the gash widened and grew larger, second by second until the purple stomach simply split open along the crescent-shaped wound and emptied its rotting contents calmly out into the suffocating heat.

Tears rushed into his eyes, blinding him, and with great heaving sobs, his hands pressed to his stomach, Allan vomited.

On the way back, he kept feeling the plastic folder in his pocket, wondering how long Constable Joseph Bean had been dead. He knew very little about such matters, but reason told him that the process of decay was rapid in such heat. The man had probably been dead for a week, perhaps a little longer, perhaps not so long. But then Allan remembered that Boy had come back with the first buttons at least two months ago or more, and that meant. . . .

He suddenly noticed two figures some way away and before he could think, he had crouched down out of sight. As he turned to warn Boy to do the same, he saw the child had already hidden behind the wreck of a car. Had he seen them first? Were his senses sharper, more alert than his own?

Felix and Run-Run were walking in single file along the track up towards the main gate, Felix ahead, his steps calm and measured. He was now wearing a hat in addition to the clothes he had had on that morning and at a distance looked like any office worker or businessman. What about the dead Joseph Bean? thought Allan. What was the connection? For there must be one. Boy had taken buttons from the body and they had spotted him. Or Boy had surprised them as they had been doing something by the corpse. . . .

Run-Run was a few paces behind in his thick dark overcoat and boots, his hands swinging freely at his sides, strong, shapely, frighteningly clever hands, his steps springy despite the clumsy footwear. He was moving as lightly as an animal. Then Allan realized why the sight of Run-Run produced in him such fear – it was that suppleness, the natural way he moved, the physical control literally emanating from him and revealed in his every movement. It was inhuman, Allan decided, cat-like, an image of the 'wildness', the unpredictability he had felt, no, *knew* could take over when a man let his self-discipline go, when he gave in and lived impulsively and 'naturally' in 'natural' surroundings. Everything Run-Run did was 'natural', even raising a knife to strike. . . . Allan could not understand what frightened him, and that frightened him even more, because he could sense it in himself.

The sun was low as evening drew in. A breeze took the worst of the heat with it and carried it across the bay towards the city. Felix and Run-Run were marching purposefully along the deeply rutted track. Were they heading for the city? To find work? At this time of day? Allan wondered. Were there more corpses hidden behind those two?

It was Thursday. The second Thursday in June. In two days' time, he had to go to work in the city. He was suddenly horribly uneasy at the thought of leaving Boy and Lisa alone overnight. He wondered how he could neutralize the danger, or at least the element of uncertainty this mysterious pair of brothers represented.

13

He got the chance the very next day.

Even after they had got back and he had given Lisa a bare outline of what had happened, what they had found and his suspicions, he could not rid himself of the thought of the dead man. Lisa was frightened when he showed her the identity card and told her it would be evidence against whoever had killed the policeman. So he had hidden the card behind the wall panel in the camper, and impressed on her that should anything happen to him, she must take it to the authorities. She had stared at him in terror and nodded. 'The authorities' meant the police, the Peacekeeping Force. She did not like the police, and nor did he for that matter, but he hoped she had understood the seriousness of what he was saying, although he had no wish to state outright that their new neighbours were in all likelihood killers.

With that he dismissed the matter – he was not one to brood. After washing his hands thoroughly, he sat down to eat with them their usual meal of soaked bread, vegetable cheese, and coffee, but with no particular appetite. That night he dreamt of Joseph Bean's repulsive remains and woke in a cold sweat, the stench still in his nostrils. He simply *had* to do something about it. It couldn't just be left lying there. He could hear the rats rummaging around in some paper outside.

He set off at first light the next morning while Lisa and Boy were still asleep.

It was an effort of will to approach for a second time the place where the corpse lay, but the thought of what he had to do overcame his doubts and revulsion. The crows again rose flapping and squawking as he came closer, but this time he made a detour round the heap of broken concrete not far from where he had met the two brothers the day before. That already seemed a long time ago. Once there, he pulled a ragged towel out of his pocket and tied it round his mouth and nose. Then he collected two or three chunks of concrete no larger than he could take in his arms, and staggered over to the corpse. The same sight and the same stench as before almost finished him, but with the last shreds of determination, he went right up and dropped the lumps of concrete, one by one, on to the putrefying mass. Then, without looking back, he quickly went back and collected some more, as many as he could carry, and repeated the operation.

The sun was smouldering behind the yellow mist above Sweetwater. He was sweating so profusely he had to keep wringing out the undershirt he was wearing and he was soon covered with concrete dust. His back ached, but he persevered. The mound where the corpse had been slowly grew higher. Now and again he stopped and looked sharply round, but could neither see nor hear anything, apart from the crows circling round and occasionally settling on a nearby mound. And the flies. He went on.

An hour later, a cairn of rough lumps of concrete hid the place where the dead man had been. With some satisfaction, Allan straightened up in the increasing heat. The dead had to be buried for their own sake as well as for the sake of the living. The stench was still there, the flies still gorging on what the crows had left, but after a while, in a few days . . . he thought, shuddering as he considered the inhumanity of what had been there, the insanity of letting a dead man lie rotting. 'Wildness'. He looked at the cairn and drew a deep breath, as if he had saved them all from something menacing and had averted the danger.

They suddenly appeared there in front of him, a short distance away, without a sound or a movement to warn him – Felix first, Run-Run just behind him, no smile on his face this time. They were both looking serious, but otherwise just the same as the first time. He started when he saw them, not because he was frightened, but because it was so unexpected. He had reckoned they might hear him throwing stones on to the heap, for not many sounds broke the silence of the Dump and all sounds carried a long way. But this sudden confrontation had been unexpected, for if they had any ill intentions, they would have come from behind. He said nothing, just stood still calmly looking at them.

Felix cleared his throat and bowed slightly.

'You have been busy?'

'Yes. I had to cover something decaying. Otherwise we might all be infected.'

'You do not think things decaying should be allowed to stay there decaying?'

There was a touch of menace in Felix's courteous and formal words. Run-Run was standing behind him with his arms hanging down, apparently listening to every word.

'I don't know what you mean. . . .' Allan's reply was neither sympathetic nor unfriendly. 'Dead things spread infection. They have to be buried or covered with stones.'

He remembered even more clearly those television programmes he had seen over the years – a cholera epidemic somewhere, typhus somewhere else, influenza, smallpox . . . corpses left lying and infecting the drinking water. You could still see or read news items about 'misfortunes' of that kind, for they were always called 'misfortunes' when they had nothing to do with 'luck'. Even in areas not far from Sweetwater, alarm had been shown over the 'new' diseases for which there was as yet no cure, mutants of well-known viruses, and bacteria resistant to well-tried vaccines. New ones were being tried and worked on, but funding was a problem. Meanwhile foreign tourists were put in quarantine and the country's health authorities publicly praised for their efficiency.

'*Some* dead things should perhaps . . . be left lying? So that they can simply disappear. A grave always exists, can always be opened. Do you understand what I mean?'

A weight rather like sorrow lay behind Felix's words; his eyes glinted in his servile, almost apathetic face. Run-Run took a step forward, but Felix halted him almost without moving his hand, apparently not quite in control of the situation, as if he were testing it – and Allan – before deciding what had to be done.

'Perhaps you saw something you should not have seen? And that could be very . . . inopportune,' he went on. Sweat broke out all over his pale face and his voice had risen in his agitation.

'Listen,' said Allan abruptly. 'Listen to me before you think up any more foolishness. I'll tell you what I know. I know that the policeman was called Joseph Bean. I know his number was KQ 130007/59510, his blood group was A, and I know that information is all on his identity card, which I have taken and hidden somewhere where it will be found if anything happens to me. I know he had a long gash in the region of his stomach, presumably made with a knife, and I assume the shoes you have on –' he nodded at Felix's solid square-toed leather shoes, '– belonged to him.'

Allan shuddered involuntarily at the thought of those eaten-away feet.

'I also know,' he went on, 'that the death penalty has been brought in for the murder of members of the Peacekeeping Force. But I have no intention of reporting anyone or letting this information go any further. I am not interested in what you are doing. All I'm interested in is that we can have peace and quiet and as little unpleasantness as possible. Do you understand?'

His eyes had not left Felix's face as he made this long speech. He saw the colourless eyes narrow with anxiety and anger as they flickered from his own shoes over to the heap of stones and back to Allan's belt buckle. When Allan stopped talking, he bowed imperceptibly and spoke again quite calmly.

'Good. Then we understand each other. That business with him . . .' he nodded in the direction of the cairn, '. . . that was an unfortunate affair. Very inopportune. I shall explain. My brother and I were smuggled into this country. No papers, no work. The Aliens Police track us down. They don't like foreigners here. One of them happens to arrest my brother on the street. My brother tries to escape, but the policeman runs faster. My brother panics and. . . .'

He made a quick cut horizontally in the air with two fingers. Allan nodded. There was a slight pause before Felix went on.

'Rather than be arrested. My brother has a dangerous temperament. He does not want to be imprisoned. Very unfortunate. An accident. So inopportune. But rather than be arrested,' he repeated after a slight pause. Run-Run smiled and nodded.

'I see,' said Allan. None of this was either surprising or particularly shocking information. It was well known that the police, reorganized under the name of the Peacekeeping Force, were used to oppress minority groups called 'undesirable' on the pretext of upholding law and order. Immigrant workers were a group of that kind. Registration rules were strict and punishments severe for breaches of the law. The free legal aid at the disposal of the underprivileged had shrunk to almost nothing owing to lack of funding, and was so overloaded it had virtually ceased to function. The chances of anyone who considered himself persecuted to defend himself in the courts were nix, so to speak. Allan knew this because Doc had told him. So he at once understood why Run-Run had acted in panic, indeed, he even sympathized with the brothers' situation.

'How did you get him out here?' he said.

'By car. I rent a car with the last of my money. I drive him here one evening. Hide him here.'

Him and how many more? thought Allan. But he was no longer frightened because he understood, and the fact that he understood and left it at that made him an accessory. The only thing that worried him was the thought of Run-Run's 'wildness', and how much (or how little) it would take to activate it – and with what consequences.

'What do you live off, now you can't find work?'

'We run a business,' said Felix, and a small smile made the ends of his moustache rise. 'A small business. We sell a little and buy a little. We have contacts. My brother takes on some inopportunities. We manage. Until we find work. We manage.'

This remarkable conversation was taking place on the edge of a large city, a metropolis of between six and eight million inhabitants (official figures were no longer reliable, unregistered moves in and out a steadily increasing problem to the statisticians). The central zones of the city still showed signs of prosperity and growth, the large department stores still full of vast quantities of goods on display, a city where millions of people went to work every morning and back to their houses and apartments in the various residential areas in the evening, with no sign whatsoever that they were affected by the soaring prices, threatening unemployment, and increased rationing soon to come. This was a city in which, according to the official news agency, people 'knew how to keep their heads in a difficult situation'.

One example of this was that the government in power and the opposition had collaborated on a programme entailing public control of prices, wages and investments, to counteract the prevailing economic crisis. Opponents of this programme were persecuted and oppressed, for broad unity prevailed among the population as well: such a serious situation demanded drastic action. The Peacekeeping Force was given increased powers to secure the maintenance of law and order. This was a city which knew it had to sacrifice some of its comfort in a situation when temporary slumps in the market, shortages of raw materials and financial straits could easily create unease, which in its turn could spread and become unpredictable and dangerous. This was a city which knew it had to sacrifice 'normal conditions', in other words its own civilization and – most important of all – which had to be defended in a reassuring way, because it had staked all on preserving those conditions and that civilization.

But this city was also a place where two men, not noticeably different in appearance from many of those who waved goodbye to their wives every morning before going to work, were able to talk to each other in calm and controlled voices about the necessity for killing a policeman and hiding the body, just as naturally as they talked about acquiring food, a roof over their heads and other things relevant to survival. Kill or be killed in the fight for life. Jungle law ruled where prosperity and progress no longer struck the eye, where the architecture was crumbling, where weeds were growing in the cracks and widening them, a disintegration that was unstoppable, at first scarcely noticeable, like normal 'wear and tear'. But when looked at closer, all was dereliction, destruction, and decay, until it was no longer possible to see where the city ended and the refuse dump began. Here were two normal-looking men talking about the necessity to kill in order to stay alive, while a third, the killer, whose sharper instincts, whose fatal pattern of reaction had become a tool as much as a threat, stood alongside, smiling broadly.

Conditions were that abnormal.

14

Allan told Doc all about it when he went to fetch water the next afternoon. Doc listened without saying anything, nodding thoughtfully.

'Perhaps they didn't necessarily mean any harm, although they do sound a peculiar pair. Anyone can become dangerous if pressed hard enough. Immigrant workers are not having an easy time at the moment, that's for sure. They're finished if the authorities catch them.'

'The one called Felix said he ran a "business".'

'Well, who doesn't? Lots of illegal trading goes on in Sweetwater, more and more as the shortage of goods gets greater. Dos Manos tells me the black market is flourishing in Dock Road. Lots of stolen goods exchange hands. It's impossible to stop. And why should it be stopped? People can get hold of things they need there, things they can't get elsewhere.'

They were sitting at the table in Doc's room. It was hot and the door was open, the afternoon sun slanting in. Marta was not well and in bed. Outside, the lush vegetation was humming. As the scrub on the barren land along the shore slowly turned to dust in the drought, the steaming moisture simply nourished the wild growth in Doc's jungle-like garden. Leafy climbers hung over the windows, shutting out the view and letting in the dreamy, greenish light. From outside the house was almost invisible. Insects buzzed incessantly and it was easy to imagine wild animals lying in wait in the shade under the bushes – but in Doc's untamed garden there was no sense of the kind of 'wildness' that worried Allan. At Doc's place, conversation was what mattered. He always wanted to talk and always had something to discuss or to expound on. To Allan, conversation was a security, an awareness of there being concepts, definitions, *limits*. Time and time again he felt almost optimistic as they sat there, and he listened to Doc's concerns about the state of affairs, the injustices of the world and expressions of hope for a breakthrough of reason and a desire for a better life for everyone. It made him forget that everything Doc said seemed to come from an old book, his expressions and turns of phrase often hopelessly old-fashioned, and that no one talked or thought like that any more.

'What shall I say if they ask me where I get water from?' said Allan. He had no wish to withhold such important information when they were all in the same boat, but neither did he want to land Doc with any new 'customers'.

'You can tell them where you get it from and what it costs. There's still enough for us all, although it doesn't taste too good. We have to share what we have out here. If they're trading, maybe they can get hold of things we need.'

'But what if they cause you trouble?'

'I can defend myself,' said Doc calmly.

'Against two of them?'

'Oh, yes. Take a look this. . . .' Doc sounded almost cheerful. He got up and went across to the shelves along the opposite wall laden with books, his radio, some vases and other small objects. On the top shelf were two solid wooden boxes Allan had not noticed before. Doc took the lid off one of them and when he put his hand inside, Allan caught a glint of dark oiled metal. Then Doc Fischer was standing there with a heavy revolver in his hand.

'This,' he said good-naturedly, 'will come in handy in an emergency. I bartered for it some years ago, with five hundred cartridges. Firearms have been impossible to get hold of since they banned them.'

Both front and back of Doc's sleeveless undershirt were soaked with sweat and his arms looked fragile in relation to his sturdy body. The hands holding the gun looked clumsy and inexperienced, despite their sinewy, weatherbeaten strength.

'This could probably get me five years inside,' he said almost lovingly. 'But you never know if you're going to need it. The world will probably get worse before it gets better, and who knows how long they'll leave us in peace on the Dump?'

Allan said nothing. What he had heard both reassured him and made him uneasy. It reassured him that Doc Fischer could defend himself. He liked and trusted the old man and hoped no harm would come to him. But the existence of the gun made him uneasy, implying dramatic events, collapse, the worst. . . . He is old, he thought, and I am young. . . . His feelings towards Doc Fischer were nothing but friendly, and he looked up to him, partly because he was older and in many ways wiser – at least more knowledgeable than he was – but first and foremost because he had managed to create a life for himself on the Dump. Nevertheless, he now had to repeat to himself as if it were a natural law he must not forget: Doc is old, I am young, and if anything happens, then I know he is old and I am young. His eyes never left the gun.

As Allan got up to go, Doc again asked after Lisa, whether all was well with her. Allan told him she was not well and was feeling the heat.

'You must make sure she gets proper food, I mean nourishing food,' said Doc. 'Vitamins.'

'We eat all right,' said Allan. Fundamentally what they ate was little different from what they had been used to in April Avenue. Lisa had never been much of a cook, so they had largely had convenience food, tinned stuff and vegetable bacon, artificial jam, tasteless white bread and that eternal vegetable cheese, coffee, biscuits and chocolate.

'That's good. That's good.' Doc nodded as if satisfied. 'But diet easily gets one-sided out here. I know that from experience. Come over here. . . .'

He went on ahead through the door and down the path behind the shed to the well and kitchen garden. It was growing dark and they had talked for a long time. Over by the beds, Doc bent down and Allan heard him rustling in the vegetables he grew there.

'There . . .'

Doc rose and Allan suddenly found a bundle of cool green leaves in his hand.

'It's lettuce. Get her to eat it, and come back when you need some more. It grows well here despite the drought. I have more than I need.'

Allan was again ill at ease over the consideration Doc was showing for Lisa.

'You don't think there's anything wrong with her, do you? That she's sick or anything.'

'Oh, no,' said Doc. 'No, she's not sick. It's just that some people stand the heat better than others. You're strong and needn't worry. But Lisa is anaemic and has a weaker constitution. She needs good food, iron most of all, and she'll get that if she eats vegetables, anything green.'

Allan knew Lisa did not like vegetables. He thought about her as he went back with the buckets, the lettuce clamped between his thumb and forefinger – the way she lay about day after day, complaining of the heat, a headache, anything – like a child giving up the moment she felt out of sorts. He was annoyed – lettuce!

He stopped, put down the buckets and tore off a leaf and cautiously munched it. It tasted dark and bitter, dry in his mouth and reminded him of the guest house at Pleasure Cove, the peculiar food they had been given there, eggs with dirt on them – and the smell from the kitchen, the landlady's fat arms, the smell of sweat and the white head-cloth, cats playing, chasing each other through the tall grass. . . .

He flung the lettuce away. It tasted like grass and that upset him. Damned if they were going to eat grass, even if Doc thought it good for them, as long as they could get hold of ordinary food. Allan fought against the thought that they might be forced to eat anything to stay alive if a real shortage of food arose. He was trying to draw new boundaries for his life, though he had some idea he would be willing to do *anything* in a crisis. He felt he had that strength, a determination which drove him – the will to survive at any price.

He could hear the small waves falling on the shore and smell the brackish water mixed with the stench of the sludge washed up and lying in strips along the water's edge. The smell was strong, both fresh and polluted – it made him think of Lisa. He could see her asleep under the sun-roof in her worn nylon knickers and the leather shirt she had borrowed from him. He saw her in the camper, sweating, bending over to roll up the wide mattress and shove it into a corner so they had more room. He saw her crouching over the rusty washing bowl carrying out her rudimentary toilet, behind the van where she presumably hoped he couldn't see her.

His child-bride.

He grew hot as he thought about it. She had rejected him two nights ago, afraid of him. She had whimpered, as if asking to be left alone, then had curled up on the edge of the mattress with her back to him, making herself as small as possible, as if not to arouse him with her scarcely perceptible presence. It had puzzled and irritated him, because when he had noticed his increased desire for her, he had imagined she felt the same. She had also given him cause to think so. But now . . . her caprices irritated him so much more because he himself had begun to regard sex as less of a problem than before, almost something you did when desire and reason were there, without complications or afterthoughts. His early, rather furtive contriteness was now behind him and he was confident in his new sensuality. Occasionally he was exaggeratedly considerate to her and her slight physique. It was hard to believe she was capable of arousing a grown man's passion, far less satisfying it. His consideration perhaps stemmed from his qualms of conscience after their first night together, so very long ago. But now she was turning her back on him like a frightened animal . . . he felt cheated, as if he had been denied something that was his right. If she were sick, she should say so. He had had enough of her whining.

He felt desire rising in him as he went on in the cloying heat, sweat breaking out on his back and in his loins. He swore he would not let her reject him again. Not tonight, anyhow.

When Allan got down at the bus stop nearest the petrol station in Abbott Hill the following afternoon, he stopped involuntarily and stared over at the Park on the other side of the street, a cramped square of green with gnarled old trees which opened out behind into sparse ground, once a picnic area and a place for walks all the way to the foot of Abbott Hill. There had been a development plan for this area as well, almost untouched as it was, a wedge of vacant land in the built-up area between the skyscrapers, the inaccessible Abbott Hill, and the more scattered residential area round Abbott Hill Road. Plans had been drawn up a few years ago when housing had been a leading issue, but various actions by the inhabitants in the East Zone to preserve the recreation area had resulted in one delay after another. Then the economy had stagnated, the housing sector became partly paralysed and the project collapsed. There was nothing left but rough roadways slowly becoming overgrown, some beginnings of foundations of houses and abandoned materials and construction huts, ugly sores on this once deserted stretch of open space.

Paradoxically, in the period that followed fewer and fewer people had used the area as had been intended, for recreation, sports and walks. It was now neglected and apparently abandoned apart from this little park of grass and pathways between the apartment houses in Abbott Hill Road. They had the same ill-cared-for look and litter lay everywhere behind their iron fencing.

Only one kind of activity continued in some parts of the Park, and that was gardening. Part of it had for many years been allocated as allotments, strips of fenced and well-tended patches with benches and toolsheds, where the locals were able to grow flowers and vegetables or go for picnics on Sundays. Later, gardening had gone out of fashion and most of the plots had become overgrown, the sheds falling down and fences collapsing. But more recently some of the gardens had suddenly sprung into life again, new patches hastily dug over and planted with uneven rows of various vegetables. Allan neither knew their names nor even recognized them, for the simple reason that he had never seen them in their natural condition.

The 'bad times' had brought about this renewed interest in allotments, but the results were very different from the days when allotments were regarded as a hobby or recreation. Most of these new patches bore signs of haste, of impatience, and after being sown and planted, many of them had remained untended, as if those who had set about them from some kind of need had then forgotten them, or had had to give up and wait for slow natural growth and maturing. Or had left to find other solutions to their problems. Or worse, had simply succumbed. The people seen about were largely older, perhaps those who had previously had time and energy to grow roses alongside their vegetables and put up fences round their small plots, take sandwiches and coffee with them and spend the whole day out there, but had now been driven there out of need, shortages and soaring prices. There was something pathetic, almost tragic about these small, hastily dug beds, so often abandoned, or harvested too early. Though they were one small sign of life in this desolate zone.

Allan stood thinking about all this, regretting he had thrown away Doc's lettuce. He was aware Doc knew about that kind of thing. Perhaps he should go up into the Park to see if he could find anything? The taste of grass on his tongue still repelled him. He would have to buy a few tins of 'green-substitute' and a vitamin-cheese if vitamins were as important as Doc said. Most of the food he bought had had vitamins added anyhow. He was inclined to think all Doc's talk about vegetables and a nourishing diet was a leftover from a past era, like so much of what Doc did, even if he did talk about it well and engagingly. But Allan could not rid himself of the thought of that green lettuce leaf, its dry bitter taste he suddenly thought almost appetizing.

He walked slowly along the rough pavement, preparing himself for half an hour's complaining from Janson. Janson always had a lot of complaints by the end of the week, and Allan seemed to be the best person to heap them on to. It had been the same ever since he had gone to work at the PAC station, but recently Allan had noticed he found it difficult to follow what Janson was talking about. Janson's troubles seemed to be fading into the distance, no longer his, Allan's, concern. He finally found he simply couldn't understand what his employer meant as the words poured out of him. He had to make a huge effort to produce suitable comments in reply, as Janson expected, in fact the only reason why he repeated his moans and groans to Allan when he came to work on Saturday afternoon.

Today it was the air-conditioning that wasn't functioning and he couldn't afford to repair it. He had also decided to sell his rescue-vehicle, as it only stood there for months between each trip. The service area had long ceased functioning and the mechanic had been dismissed. ('People don't maintain their vehicles any longer. They just drive them into the ground.') Then the water shortage had meant a ban on car-washing, yet another source of income literally drying up. Finally, Janson had discovered someone had been at the stores door and had tried to break open the lock. Allan could see the marks, so it was true. But what could poor Janson do? He dared not go to the police again, as they would lock him up after his attempt to report Roy Indiana. Things were deteriorating fast and the business no longer paid. He would have to be satisfied with seeing the year out and then. . . . Janson looked to Allan for sympathy and understanding.

Allan listened to that voice repeating the same things over and over again, week after week, without really taking in what was being said. His eyes roamed over the shabbiness and decay everywhere, the flaking paintwork, the pot-holes in the concrete, the missing light bulbs, the unemptied rubbish bins, the weeds coming up along the wall where the tap was dripping, but in his mind, Allan was still on the Dump where problems like Janson's did not exist.

15

Early one morning when Allan went out, he thought he could hear something unusual, a voice . . . a voice from down by the shore, a human voice, a murmur, rising and falling.

He wondered what it was and started walking over in that direction, carefully avoiding making a noise. Each time he stopped to listen he could hear the murmuring, and as he got nearer, he thought he could make out individual words and some kind of rhythm, like a tune. A song. Someone was singing down on the shore. A low, monotonous voice . . . cautiously Allan crept up a mound and looked over.

At the water's edge, almost immediately below where he was crouching, a woman was standing knee-deep in the water, washing herself, throwing handfuls of water over her face and snorting and spitting. Her hair, neck and breasts were dripping wet and water was pouring down and soaking her brief skirt. Another piece of clothing, a blouse perhaps, had been flung down on the shore, alongside it a pair of sandals decorated with large red plastic roses.

She was tall, as tall as he was, perhaps even taller. Her skin was brown, her hair black, her body majestic, with strong legs and thick sturdy thighs. She was splashing about with pleasure in the water, accompanying herself with that hoarse tuneless song. Then she lifted her hands above her head and let water run down her arms into the glossy hair and on to her shoulders. The bright morning sunlight made the surfaces of her body glisten, her belly a gleaming sphere beneath the pointed breasts. Allan had never seen a belly like it and could not take his eyes off it, smooth and taut, but at the same time soft and elastic. Whenever she made a movement, it was transmitted to her stomach, undulating in a calming tempo, as if it did not quite belong to the rest of her body.

When she had come out of the water, pulled the blouse over her head and thrust her feet into the sandals, Allan thought the time had come to make himself known. He retreated a little, swung round and came down on to the shore a little way away, then turned and walked towards her as if he had just caught sight of her. She had also seen him and was waiting quite calmly for him, her lips parted in something half-way between a smile and a grin. She was peering at the sun.

'Hi,' he said, suddenly feeling foolish now he was faced with her. He had been right, she was an inch or two taller than he was.

' 'Morning.'

'Who are you?'

'Who are you?'

Her reply was neither friendly nor unfriendly, though guarded.

'Allan,' said Allan. 'I live here.' He pointed vaguely behind him.

'Oh, yes?'

'Yes.'

'Alone?'

'I have a wife and a small son.'

Then she smiled broadly, her mouth large and her strong teeth stained by tobacco. The skin on her chin and cheeks was marred by small round scars only noticeable at close quarters, otherwise it was olive-coloured, but the large nose and broad wide nostrils told him she was a mulatta. Her eyes made the greatest impression, large, oval and slanting, glowing as if wishing to draw his whole attention to them and away from her poor complexion. She had pulled back her hair so that it hung wet and straggly behind her ears and down her neck, soaking the neck of her blouse. The cold water had hardened her nipples and they were clearly visible through the thin material of her blouse. And that smooth round belly he had not been able to take his eyes off bulged over the waistband of her tight brown leather skirt. Her legs were muscular and brown, her feet broad and planted firmly into the sand, the nails painted pink. A line of yellow scum at the water's edge extended the whole length of the shore, dancing each time a wave crept up and touched it, then fell back again. He looked up straight into her smiling face.

'My name's Mary Diamond,' she said. 'I came yesterday with Smiley. You must come and meet Smiley. He'd be glad of some company. He likes talking.'

Mary Diamond and Smiley lived in a car, a heavy wide old station wagon, all nickel and rust on the outside, plastic and lost comfort inside, but it had deep wide seats and plenty of room for the little luggage they had.

Smiley was asleep when they finally arrived after Mary Diamond had lost her way once or twice. Allan had asked her whether Smiley was her husband and she had opened that broad mouth again before answering. 'Let's say he's my friend and protector.' The station wagon had been carelessly dumped some way beyond where the wheel-tracks ended. The driver had clearly wanted to get as far as he could and had driven it until a front wheel had sunk into a hole. The car was standing more or less on its nose, the bumper buried in a low bank of soil. Smiley was asleep, his feet outside the open door, flies huddling together in the searing heat on the inside of the windscreen.

'We'll be moving it to a better place,' said Mary Diamond. 'It was dark when we came last night. Smiley!' She called out, thumping her hand on the bonnet. 'Someone wants to meet you.'

A suspicious, bearded face, swollen and sweaty from sleep and the heat, peered up at them.

'Smiley . . .' she repeated amiably. 'Up you get. It's late in the day.'

Some crumpled clothing had been flung over the back of the seat and a plastic bag of toilet things lay on the floor, spilling out its contents in the dust and sand. On the back seat were some torn newspapers and a few battered paperbacks.

'This is Allan,' said Mary Diamond, as Smiley at last managed to fix his bloodshot eyes on their visitor. 'He lives here.'

'Hi, Allan,' said Smiley in a scarcely audible voice, his greeting immediately developing into a violent fit of coughing. When he finally recovered, he sat with his hands pressed to his temples.

'Mary, Mary . . . what did they give us to drink at that damned club of yours? Do they want to turn us all into alcoholic wrecks? Where's that bottle we bought?'

'In the glove compartment.'

Smiley lay back in the seat, reached out and pressed the button. When it didn't work first time, he thumped the dashboard with his fist and the glove compartment sprang open. The bottle fell out and he quickly and skilfully caught it, uncorked it and put it to his mouth with a long look at Allan. He took several great gulps, but then started coughing again. With one clenched fist against his mouth, he held the bottle out towards Allan.

'Here, have some. Guaranteed pure acid.'

Although he had no desire for a drink, particularly in this heat, Allan took the bottle as if a new sense of 'decorum' told him he ought to accept when someone offered him something with the best of intentions – that giving and receiving something here were actions with a more profound meaning, a symbol of a positive attitude, friendship, so very important on the Dump. To refuse would have been to show hostility and arrogance. That was how things should be where people around you were important. So he put the bottle to his mouth and cautiously took a sip of the clear liquid, but soon found his eyes watering. It seemed an eternity since he had last touched liquor.

Smiley sat up with a groan, his gaudy shirt dark with sweat and his light trousers dirty. His hair was fair with a reddish tinge and hung in long greasy wisps down the back of his neck and over his ears; it was shorter on top and brought down over his forehead and temples to hide his encroaching baldness. He could have been anything between thirty-five and forty, his eyes small and close together, his nose thin and slightly crooked, mouth small and teeth uneven. His chin vanished into a fold of skin well on its way to becoming a double chin. He had two or three days' stubble. Allan ignored the man's shabby appearance. He had been taken by a glint in those small, pale-blue eyes as they had looked him up and down – an ironic, but friendly look, revealing awareness, humour and intelligence, a challenging look. It aroused Allan's curiosity, at the same time making him wary, uncertain of what to expect of this battered, apparently alcoholic creature.

'So you're Allan?' That look again, searching, sarcastic, but not unfriendly. 'And you live here?'

Allan nodded.

'How long?'

'A while. A few months.'

'Uh-huh. . . .' Smiley ran his hand over his sweaty face as if to clear his mind. Mary Diamond had opened the rear door and was rummaging around among things in the back.

'What do you live on?'

'The Dump mostly, as much as possible, anyhow. But I've got a job two days a week. At a petrol station. As long as it lasts.'

'Part-timer, eh? . . .' said Smiley. 'Part-time job. Listen to that, Mary. We had part-time jobs, too,' he went on to Allan, laughing shrilly, quite without humour. 'Up until yesterday. We had to resign yesterday . . . isn't that so, Mary? Wasn't that it?'

'Maybe so,' she said, her head inside the car. Was there a touch of irritation in her voice?

'Yes, we had jobs,' sighed Smiley. 'That is, Mary had one. She performed at Roadside, sang a little, danced, entertained the guests. Right up until yesterday.'

He took a gulp from the bottle, then another. Allan began to understand. The Roadside Club was part of a relatively new motel complex by the Motorway, Roadside City, a gigantic recreation and service centre for motorists. It had everything, apart from the actual motel, everything from repair workshops to supermarkets, boutiques, restaurants, cinemas, discothèques and night-clubs. Shortly after it had opened, this new and very popular place soon had a reputation as a centre for illegal drug- and other dubious trafficking.

'We got news of a razzia,' Smiley went on. 'So we thought we'd better get out. Not that we've *done* anything, anyhow nothing specially illegal, but it's always best to keep well away from the patrol boys. They know beforehand what they're after, and they get it. It's that simple, and God help anyone looking on. Then they really have a party. So we thought we'd get out and this is where we ended up – on a rubbish tip. An appropriate place, don't you think, Mary?'

'Of course. Whatever you say, Smiley. You do the talking, you know. You decide.'

She came round from the back of the car carrying something that looked like bread. Was it? Thick white slices of French bread with a delicious brown crust. Allan suddenly remembered he had not eaten that morning.

'Here,' she said. 'Food. Do you want some? I've got ham, pâté, jam, real cheese. We managed to get a bit with us before we had to leave. Help yourself. It won't keep in this heat.' She was stuffing a piece of bread and some kind of fish – was it salmon? – topped with yellow mayonnaise into her mouth.

'Move over, Smiley. You're not the only one who'd like to sit down.'

She shoved in beside him and made room for Allan. There was plenty of space for all three of them on the wide front seat.

Allan ate the bread and ham slowly, almost ceremoniously. He could hardly remember having tasted anything so good before. Nor could he remember when he had last tasted real meat. Meat had been in short supply for several years. What was sold as 'meat' was manufactured from vegetable proteins with added colouring and flavouring. Only luxury class supermarkets sold meat and then at such prices, people with ordinary incomes couldn't even consider it. But the substitute meat did taste of meat, and it was healthy and filling, so no one suffered directly from the shortage.

He bit off small pieces, one at a time, and chewed well before swallowing. Even the crust of the French bread was fresh and crisp, the slice of ham, pink and delicious, overlapping the edges, the strip of fat touching his fingertips, making them glisten. He licked his fingers carefully as he reluctantly swallowed the last mouthful. It had all gone very quickly.

'Here, d'you want some more?'

Mary handed him another piece of bread, this time with some kind of red sausage with a spicy smell.

'Of course he wants some more,' said Smiley. 'Just look at the way he's wolfing it down! He'll soon be sweeping the crumbs up off the floor. No offence meant, my friend. It must have been hard living here on a rubbish tip for so long – stimulating for the appetite, just the opposite of what one would think.'

Allan was deaf to his sarcasm as he relished the smoked sausage. He played the same game again, munching slowly, savouring the sandwich, though he could hardly restrain himself from gobbling it down in one gulp. At the other end of the seat, Smiley was devouring smoked salmon and washing it down with great gulps from the bottle. Mary had the bread and cold cuts on a large piece of paper on her lap, and they helped themselves until there was nothing left.

'Pity we've nothing to cook on,' said Mary. 'I could have made coffee. We've got some real coffee.'

Real coffee . . . the flies buzzed round their ears.

'I'm really glad we came here. I like it here,' said Smiley, when they had finished and the bottle was empty.

'Got a smoke?' said Mary. He handed her the pack. She eased out a cigarette and stuck it between her lips, long and white against her olive skin and red mouth.

'Yes, sir, am I glad we came here,' said Smiley. 'Look at it. . . .' He gestured through the window, taking in the mounds of refuse. 'Did you ever see so much garbage? Our civilization. . . .' He laughed dryly. 'Look – there it is. You can actually enjoy more things here than back there. . . .' His waved his long, thin fingers roughly in the direction of Sweetwater. 'You can live off it here – back there you die of it.'

Mary lit her cigarette and blew smoke out through her nostrils.

'The city's dying,' Smiley went on. 'That's a fact. Planned far too much or too little. The point of cities was supposed to be that they grew, wasn't it? Now they're being crushed under their own success, seething in their own poison. No, I say I'm glad we came here, Mary, eh? Camping, but in all seriousness. We can sit here like the Latter Day Saints and watch our magnificent civilization go to hell. Out on the muckheap, the last place where our common and inevitable destiny will come and visit us. Cheers!'

Fascinated as well as alarmed. Allan listened to this torrent of words. What the man was saying touched on vague ideas he had juggled with when things were at their very worst in April Avenue, when the idea of moving, getting out, had first occurred to him. But the words the man was using sounded like something behind him, unimportant despite their provocative shrewdness. He felt he had *lived* what Smiley was saying. Talking about it was of no interest. Living it, *surviving* it from day to day really did mean something.

Mary Diamond leant back, propped her knees against the dashboard and sent clouds of cigarette smoke up at the roof of the car to disperse the flies. The car doors were open and all the windows down, the heat suffocating inside. Hot car, oil, rubber and petrol was a smell Allan knew only too well from the PAC station. Mary had closed her eyes and spoke as if neither of them existed.

'My God, the way you talk, Smiley,' she sighed. 'You just talk and talk.'

Her lipstick had stained the white cigarette. Her brown leather skirt was tight and she had varicose veins, but they did not spoil her strong legs. She was perhaps thirty-five, and her hands were broader than his, with short stubby fingers.

'Yes, indeed, I talk,' said Smiley. 'But I am no dumb animal. What I'm saying is just how clever it was to come here instead of trying to get in somewhere in Sweetwater, where everyone is dying anyhow, slowly but surely. There's more life along the Motorway after ten o'clock at night than there is in Silver Street. People stay at home in their little caves and just manage to pluck up the courage to get to work – if they have any – and back, and count themselves lucky every day they are not struck down on the way. Because they believe in the fairy-tale of this gangster world, the lawlessness in the streets, and cannot understand that it is the police who are the gangsters of our day. They control everything – even have men inside the syndicates – and leave the silly jobs, a robbery or two, a break-in here and there, to the poor, good old-fashioned villains, the druggies and drunks, crazy kids and bums, I mean. . . .'

'Like you.'

'Exactly.' He smiled indulgently. 'People like me. Though anyone who is to be robbed by me has to come here and ask nicely. I am too lazy, I'll have you know, just too easy-going to hit people over the head to get at their small change.'

'I'm sure you got other people to do the heavy for you whenever necessary.'

'Well, yes, let's put it that way. But I think you'd better watch your tongue so we don't frighten the life out of our friend Allan here. He must be wondering what kind of people we are and what we're up to.'

Although their words contained some hostility, the tone was subdued, almost indifferent, as if they always talked like this. Allan listened with attention, wondering faintly why they wasted their energy on anything so pointless, when there must have been things they ought to be doing. But he listened. He was curious. Not that what Smiley was up to (or wasn't up to), whether legal, illegal or somewhere in between, affected him, but it interested him to know what people did to *manage*. He could learn something from that, pick up a useful tip or two.

'Just now you said "unemployed for the moment" . . . do you take that back?' She wouldn't let him go, and picked up the thread where perhaps it should have been left lying.

'No, I just thought we should fill out the general picture, as we're neighbours now, so to speak. Eh?' He turned to Allan with a semi-drunken smile, the glint of irony still there.

'Allow me to introduce myself. Smiley. First name, surname, it doesn't matter. I've never been called anything else but Smiley. Profession: student. Ha, ha. That's true, actually. I have a student card from one of our institutions of higher education to prove it. Great if you want a cheap meal in the student canteen, if you're in those parts of the city. I'm also a poet, well, *used* to be, and essayist, with all of four titles behind me, four slim volumes – booklets let's say, brought out by a small, obscure but idealistic publishing house, of which I was also co-owner – it went bankrupt long ago. Artist, then. Yes, mostly sculpture, in the days when sculpture was popular. Sculptor . . . that sounds fine, doesn't it, Mary?'

'Yes, you ought to get some visiting cards printed.' Mary was gazing steadily through the cigarette smoke at the roof of the car, her strong, sinewy neck glistening.

'But first and foremost a past master of the difficult art of "landing on my feet". Regardless of the means . . . almost. . . .' He grinned. 'Hard round the edges, good at heart. Or shall we say the dry rot is beginning to get into the marrow, too, eh, Mary? No one lives as you and I have done and gets away with it.'

'What are you going to do here on the Dump?'

Allan at last managed to get a word in edgeways. Smiley looked at him as he had forgotten he existed.

'Hm . . . well, first of all, I don't suppose we'll be around here all that long, just until the dust settles after the razzia, if you know what I mean. Though who knows? Who knows whether we won't like it so much we decide to stay for a while? Perhaps even for good? In that case, Mary is sure to find herself another job. Don't you think so, Mary? Yes, I'm sure you will.'

Mary sighed, leant forward and stubbed her cigarette out on the top of the dashboard, leaving the butt there.

'I myself have thought of collecting scrap here. I love scrap – and philosophizing over the foolishness of mankind, watching Sweetwater sink into the sea – and when the Day of Judgement comes. . . .' He flung out his arm in a deliberately theatrical gesture. 'We'll clothe ourselves in rags, dig a dwelling in these mounds, eat discarded food, couple with rats and howl out our wretchedness into the impenetrable darkness of the night. But we shall survive, while the rest, those back there, will die. The rubbish tip, the saviour of aesthetics. Elevating the mind. Listen, Mary, I do believe our friend is no longer interested, I really do. From here it looks as if the hem of your skirt is more important to him at this moment than the apocalypse. I really do think our good friend Allan desires you,

Mary. What shall we do about that?' His hand slapped down on her broad thigh, but her expression did not change. Allan thought this was going too far. Of course he had looked at Mary Diamond. He couldn't help doing so. She was so large and was sitting so close to him he could smell her, her skin dark and glistening – it was lush, untamed nature both attracting and unsettling him. How could he not show that?

'Do you find our dear Mary's presence stimulating, Allan?'

'For God's sake, stop it, Smiley. Allan's all right. He's got a wife and child out here.'

Mary's voice was cold and contemptuous, but she made no attempt to remove his hand, now caressing her roughly, almost brutally.

'But Mary. . . .' The lazy voice sounded superior. 'Most of your admirers have had wives and children – you know that. . . . Don't be offended,' he went on, turning to Allan. 'No one's reproaching you. It's quite natural and I know that only too well. Mary often affects men that way . . . what *I'm* looking for is to encourage a feeling something like jealousy, you see. A man who is proud of his knowledge of life cannot be entirely unaware of the anguish of jealousy, can he? I look at you and think – yes, perhaps he could be used. He's attractive in a rather primitive, almost animal way – just like Mary here. . . .' His hand had moved right up to the edge of her skirt. She had leant back again and closed her eyes, as if paying no attention to either of them or to what they were saying.

'And,' Smiley went on, 'you're so obviously innocent – don't misunderstand me, I don't mean stupid, just naïve, inexperienced, unused. You're honest. When you say something, you mean it. When you undertake something, you take it seriously. I can see that in your eyes, which at this moment are filled with good old-fashioned desire for a good old-fashioned poke. And natural impulses of that kind, genuine rutting like that is not something you come across every day, I assure you. No, sex is not what it used to be, not so simple for most people any longer – perhaps that's due to the mercury in the food?'

His hand had slid right up between her thighs and was playing quite openly under her skirt. He looked as if his thoughts were elsewhere. Mary lay as if asleep, breathing deeply. It was hot in the car, all three of them sweating profusely.

'I must be off,' mumbled Allan. The scene and Smiley's mono-logue had begun to be unpleasant. He had no desire to listen any more, nor to start despising this new neighbour and his peculiar ideas so soon. Anyhow, time was getting on. He had a lot to do.

'No, don't go,' said Smiley in quite a different tone of voice. 'I didn't mean it like that – you didn't take it seriously, did you? Stay a bit longer – here, have a drink?'

'No, thanks,' said Allan. 'I must be off. Lisa'll be wondering where I am.'

'Yes, yes, of course. You have to give a thought to the wife now and again, too. . . .' Smiley's tone of voice had turned pompous and sarcastic again. His hand was working rhythmically under Mary's skirt and she was lying quite still, just as before. . . .

'See you, then,' said Allan, kicking the door wide open and sliding down off the creaking seat.

'Hey. . . .' Smiley called him back. 'Did you say you worked at a petrol station?'

'Yeah.'

'Do you know about cars? Can you repair them if they're falling to bits?'

'I'm not a mechanic, but I can fix minor things.'

'Great. This crate's just about to fall apart. If you'd have a look at it, then I could get you some goodies in exchange. Something good to eat? I saw you wolfing down your breakfast. It's been quite a while since you had any decent food, eh?'

'We don't have smoked ham every day, but we live quite. . . .'

'That's the spirit! I'll see what I can do. I've still got a contact or two. It's what's called natural housekeeping, isn't it? Exchange of goods and services. Best to get used to it from the start.'

'When do you want me to take a look at the car?'

'Come this afternoon – no, come tomorrow morning. This afternoon we'll have to get back on the wheels and see if we can find Mary some suitable employment. Tomorrow morning's fine if that's all right by you.'

'O.K., tomorrow morning.'

Allan glanced again at Smiley's unshaven face and Mary's head resting dreamily on the back of the seat, her strong teeth visible between her red lips. A landscape before the storm breaks, vibrant and full of scents and expectation . . . that was what it looked like to him.

He turned and strode away.

16

Lisa had made an attempt to tidy up round the camper. Paper and tins had been swept into a heap behind the stove and she had managed to get another support pole under the sun roof – it had been leaning precariously to one side. She was struggling to get the mattress back so that it no longer blocked the way into the van, feeling a little better now and not so sick as she had been the last two or three days. But she thought she had felt a swelling the morning before, and she secretly felt it now and again, a hard swelling big enough to fill her hand, just below her navel. She had put on a dress so he wouldn't notice and was glad he had already gone out when she had woken. But it was so hot she had had to take the dress off again and was now walking round as usual in knickers and shirt. She had wondered where Allan was, but had not been worried. He was often away for a long time and it was also a good idea to start early, so he had at least two hours before the worst heat descended. She had often gone with him before on these forays. They had got used to looking around and collecting things which might come in useful. They had accumulated a variety of objects in this disorganized manner. But since she had become pregnant, her desire for adventure had faded. She preferred to stay by the camper, not really minding where he went or what he did, and he more and more rarely told her where he was going or what his plans were.

Boy had run off early as usual and no doubt would not reappear until he was hungry.

She was munching on a piece of hard bread, gnawing off a bit and softening it in her mouth before swallowing it. She had watched her weight during her first pregnancy, careful of her figure and trying to follow the diet in the booklet she had been given. She no longer gave such things a thought, but ate when she felt like it, and she was well. The same had happened to them all – they came and went and ate whenever they felt like it. As their food was more or less the same every day, mealtimes were superfluous, and oddly enough even when all organization had ceased, they still ate at about the same times day after day, in fact rather more regularly than before, as if their bodies and activities regulated the new rhythm and made sure they kept to it. They usually had their evening meal together at dusk when Boy was sleepy. She put out bread and whatever there was to eat with it, and Allan made the coffee. Then Boy crept into bed in the camper while they stayed outside for a little longer, sipping their coffee and waiting for fatigue to come with the darkness. They sat there gazing over at the ceaseless stream of cars, a river of headlights flowing across the spans of the Motorway bridge towards Sweetwater.

She could hear Boy's voice and then saw him down on the path, but he was not alone. A tall dark figure in a long overcoat was beside him. She froze as she realized it was the dumb man with her son and remembered what Allan had told her. Even Allan had been shaken and frightened – she was wondering in some panic what she could do to frighten him off, or chase him away. But then she saw the way the two of them were coming towards her, quietly, side by side, Boy eagerly explaining something to his tall companion, and he seemed to be listening. Her fears faded and she was amazed at Boy's flow of words. He usually said little when with them, as if he had lost interest in expressing himself verbally – perhaps because they also talked less and less to each other, as if words had become almost superfluous and a nod, a movement or a brief order was usually enough. Boy was chattering away, gesticulating with his hands, and the silent Run-Run was walking close beside him, his head on one side as if listening to every word.

'Ma! He's taught me to fish,' Boy cried when he saw she had seen them. 'We've been fishing. Down there.'

He pointed at the bay, which had been polluted and lifeless for years.

'Have you now?' She wanted to encourage him, but didn't really know how to set about it. 'Did you get anything?'

It was ridiculous. Everyone knew about the bay.

'No, but we're sure to tomorrow or another day.'

'Yes, maybe you will.'

Boy had come up and flung himself down on the mattress, but Run-Run stayed some way away. It was impossible to see from his expression whether caution or timidity made him keep his distance. Lisa was startled, but then she beckoned to him. He took a few steps towards her, held out his hand, then rapidly took it back again and smiled. She smiled, too, unable to think of anything to say. She went over to the stove where the kitchen utensils were kept, fetched a cup, went to the water bucket in the shade of the camper, filled the cup and offered it to him. He took the cup in both hands and drank greedily, then handed it back with a broad grin. Flustered, all she could think of doing was to repeat the ritual, and Run-Run drank down the second cup in one draught. She gestured that he

107

should sit down, but he stayed where he was, almost without moving, his arms at his sides and the white teeth gleaming in his tanned face, his eyes intently following every little movement she made. Ill at ease, Lisa sat down by Boy and started talking to him.

'What else did you do beside fishing?'

'Lots. He showed me some leaves you can chew so it tastes sweet.'

'Really?' To her relief, she saw Allan coming down towards them from the other direction.

'He's got a fine knife, too,' the boy went on. 'When he throws it, he hits all sorts of things. He hit a lizard *far* away!' The boy pointed excitedly to show the distance to the imaginary sand lizard. 'He can do all sorts of things.' Boy looked with admiration across at Run-Run, who had also seen Allan coming.

'Everything all right?' said Allan, glancing from Lisa to Run-Run as he came up to them.

She nodded.

'Boy's been . . . with him.' She pointed. 'They've been fishing and. . . .'

She suddenly felt faint and started to sway. She closed her eyes and pressed one hand to her forehead, the other protectively over the little swelling.

'What's the matter?' she heard Allan say sharply.

'Nothing . . . nothing. . . .'

Clenching her teeth, she fought back the nausea. When the attack had passed and she opened her eyes again, she saw Run-Run had come a few steps nearer and was staring intently at her again. She looked down, and when she looked up again, he had disappeared.

'What on earth?'

Allan stood watching Run-Run go and shook his head. Boy was about to set off after him, but Allan stopped him.

'Stay here. He'll be back. Anyhow, perhaps it's just as well if you didn't. . . .'

He stopped. He had wanted to say 'if you didn't go around with someone who'd tried to kill you', but it sounded too brutal. He couldn't say that to a five-year-old. Yet the realities were so obvious, even a child should know about them, and if not understand them, at least learn to deal with them.

'There aren't any fish in Paradise Bay,' he said instead. 'The water's been polluted for at least twenty years.'

Boy stared defiantly at him.

'He *said* we'd get something. Maybe tomorrow.'

'How did he *say* it? He can't speak.' Allan's voice was sharp. Boy was lying.

'I *understand* what he wants to say, so there!'

'Uh-huh.'

There was no point in arguing with what went on in a five-year-old's imagination. Allan sighed. The heat was suffocating, swarms of flies buzzing, and the ground cracked from the drought. His whole body longed for a change in the weather.

'Where've you been?' said Lisa.

She was feeling better and was hoping he would forget it all.

'Two new people have come. I came across them this morning. An extraordinary guy, a sort of artist who never stops talking. He won't stick it for long. But his wife seems to have her feet on the ground. I liked her better. Their names are Smiley and Mary Diamond. They gave me breakfast.'

'Mary Diamond,' mused Lisa. 'What a nice name. What's she like?'

'Well . . . tall and dark. . . .'

Allan felt a jab of conscience, a reluctance to describe Mary Diamond to Lisa. He would rather not talk about her at all, but hide her and the impression she had made on him.

'Is she pretty?'

'No, not really pretty. A mulatta, I think. She's got scars on her face and her teeth are stained. Smokes too much.'

He found Lisa's questions pointless. He suddenly couldn't decide what 'ugly' or 'pretty' meant. Was Mary 'ugly' or 'pretty'? Was Lisa 'ugly' or 'pretty'? What he remembered of Mary Diamond's appearance was her dimensions, the monumental thighs and belly curving so invitingly, the tips of those small breasts, the cigarette between those thick red lips. What could he say to Lisa?

'She seems nice,' he said. 'You'll see when you meet her. They'll probably stay for a while. They have to keep under cover here . . . they seem to have been up to something or other. . . .'

'Oh.'

Boy had heard Run-Run before either of them. The ungainly figure appeared between two mounds with something like a bunch of twigs in his hand. He nodded and smiled as he came closer, then went straight over to Lisa and handed them to her.

Surprised, she took the bunch of stems and spiky green leaves in her hand and sat down with them, not knowing what to do.

Run-Run sniffed.

'He wants you to smell them,' said Boy.

She sniffed at them cautiously – a sweetish, spicy scent, not at all unpleasant. Another smell wafted in her direction, the salty, pungent smell of the man who had given her the plants, an animal smell which made her flush.

'Nice,' she said. 'Rather strange.'

Run-Run smiled, patted his stomach and nodded.

'What does he mean? Why is he giving me these?' asked Lisa, looking at Allan. He shook his head.

'Perhaps it's a compliment?' he said. 'Perhaps he thinks you're pretty.'

'In our country, it is a custom to give rosemary to a pregnant woman,' a voice said behind them, and there was Felix a short distance away, as immaculate, formal and courteous as usual.

'It brings luck to her and the child.'

Allan stared from him to the smiling Run-Run, then at Lisa, who had bowed her head as if expecting a blow.

'I hope my brother has not been – inopportune?' said Felix apologetically, bowing slightly.

PART TWO

17

She didn't say a word on the bus in to Sweetwater, just clung to his arm. He could feel her grip tightening each time one of the passengers stared or happened to look their way. He was used to curious glances and ignored them and they didn't happen all *that* often. People who had to travel by bus probably had enough troubles of their own and huddled in their seats as if they needed sleep and had to steal some whenever they could, or stared blankly ahead of them. Their position was worst of all, cowed people obliged to use public transport, people in the same category as himself.

However, that situation was also changing as traffic density, costs and severe fuel rationing made private transport more complicated and less viable. There had been a noticeable increase in the use of public transport even among those who had always sworn by private cars in the past. Gradually the marked change in transport patterns impinged on the authorities. But they went on with their long-term plans for cuts and rationing, while buses to the commercial districts, from the satellite towns and back became overcrowded and timetables chaotic owing to lack of materials and flexible planning.

More recently Allan had become aware of more obvious glances on the buses and occasional abuse, though he largely ignored them. The new category of passenger seemed no different from any other. Had he lost the ability to distinguish people by appearance?

Allan and Lisa had seats, and people were also standing. Despite the open ventilators, it was incredibly hot and faces were swollen and red, shirts and blouses sticky with sweat – and that was not the only smell.

As they got out at the bus station surrounded by high-rises into the inferno of heat and dust and crowds hurrying by, Lisa staggered and he wondered whether she was going to have another fainting fit. He held on to her, but it turned out to be her shoes. She had insisted she had to look smart to go into the city, but now she found the unfamiliar high heels difficult.

They made their way along the littered pavement, Lisa holding his arm and keeping as close to him as she could. She jumped at every unexpected sound in the cacophony of the rush hour – a car horn, or a police whistle. The five streets to the Social Services building seemed endless.

Social Services took up an entire street and was ten storeys high. The old building looked dignified and intimidating as well as shabby. It had once housed an import-export company, but that had been nationalized with other key industries and the authorities had taken it over. The entrance hall smelt of urine and inside the walls were covered with graffiti, political slogans and obscenities. A chilly musty draught prevailed in the long corridors, the sour gust of ill-health from the social administration itself.

In reception, people were waiting on long benches, wooden chairs and stools, others wandering restlessly up and down, or sitting apathetically, staring ahead as if they had been there all day, perhaps several days with no hope of stating their case. Mothers hushed their impatient small children. Officials set behind thick plate glass in the harsh electric light, expressionless, filling in forms, telephoning or going through heaps of papers. They all wore identical brown jackets with gilt buttons, the emblem of the state embroidered on the top pocket. Occasionally loudspeakers summoned names to the numbered openings as the air-conditioning ground on noisily. Waste-paper baskets were overflowing and the floor was strewn with cigarette ends, paper and crumpled forms.

Lisa found a seat in the back row next to a man with a long, unkempt beard. He was sound asleep, a plastic bag under his head and, despite the heat, wearing a thick overcoat. Lisa sat as still as she could so as not to disturb him while Allan went to find out where they should go.

'Yes?' said the woman behind the information desk, without looking up. Her hair was smooth, dark and cut short, parted down the middle, her face blank, her features regular. Red and green lights flashed on a panel beside her and a circular screen showed rows of figures, and codified dots and dashes.

'It's about hospital . . .' Allan began. 'My wife is pregnant. I would like to know . . . I would like to register her for. . . .'

'Aren't you registered?' The expressionless eyes sharpened and looked him up and down.

'No. That is, yes. But. . . .'

'*Everyone* is registered,' said the woman.

'Well. . . .'

Allan found he was quite incapable of asking the question in the way expected of him. He had to find out how Lisa could get to hospital to have the baby. That was all. He had to get her registered somehow or other, to book a bed.

'First child?' The receptionist did not look up.

'No. We already have one.'

The man behind him in the queue started coughing violently.

'Room 709. Lift at the end of the corridor on the left.'

'Thank you.'

As Allan left, the man behind him grasped the counter and started coughing, heaving and gasping between coughs, saliva running down his chin. Allan shuddered. Every time someone came in through the swing-doors, a gust of clammy heat and the deafening noise from the street swept in.

The lift rose creaking to the seventh floor and in the glaring light the mirror reflected how pale they were despite their sunburn, how shabby their clothes, and how wretched they looked, although they had no sense of being any different from the crowd down in reception. The building was old and so was the lift. Glass reinforced with wire had great white patches where someone had kicked it or hit it. Obscenities had been scribbled or crudely drawn on the yellowed walls between floors.

They marched to the end of yet another long corridor. Here the ceilings were lower and the rooms hotter, the smell of dust more evident. Room 709 was large and brightly lit, full of more long queues, mostly women, some obviously pregnant. The heat was oppressive. Enquiries were dealt with in a row of booths along one wall. The numbering system was a slow process, with long waits between numbers coming up on the screen. Some people were wiping their eyes miserably as they came away from the booths. This department dealt with family support, child allowances and adoption. If a woman had more than two children, benefit was withdrawn if she did not agree to adoption or abortion. Population growth had to be limited – one of the milder forms of coercion brought in during the state of emergency.

Allan leant against the wall, holding the numbered ticket he had been allocated. He was thirsty. Lisa had found a vacant chair and had her eyes closed. There was a drinking fountain and a stack of paper mugs in one corner; crushed mugs littered the floor. Allan kicked some away and tried the water. It was as tepid as out on the Dump, but also tasted of chemicals and chlorine. He took a few gulps, then filled a mug for Lisa. People pulled their legs in as he passed and looked away. They all waited for their numbers to come up.

Inside the booths, the air was even closer than outside. Air-fresheners made little difference. Each booth had a glass wall with a 'speaker-slot', dividing the space into two. In their booth was a dark-haired woman rather like the receptionist downstairs, except that she had one arm in a sling. A metal plate on her chest stated she was M. Goddess.

There was only one chair in the booth and Allan led Lisa to it; she moved like a sleepwalker, exhausted by all the waiting. He remained standing, his head almost touching the ceiling.

The young woman looked from him to Lisa and nodded encouragingly. Allan began:

'My wife is pregnant and we need help . . . when the time comes.'

'Have you any other children?'

'Yes. A son.'

'Name?'

'Lisa and Allan Ung.'

The woman wrote it down.

'Number?'

'What?'

'Your identity number?'

'Number? I . . . I don't really remember . . . do you, Lisa?'

Lisa didn't seem to have heard. She shook her head without looking up.

'Haven't you got it written down somewhere? Identity card? Work registration card? You know you're supposed to have your number on you?'

Allan fumbled through his pockets.

'No.'

'Oh, well. We'll soon find out.'

She swiftly tapped on a keyboard with her good hand. A moment later, letters and figures came up on a screen just like the one he had seen down in reception. Allan couldn't take his eyes off the injured arm in the sling, a blinding white bandage right up to her elbow, as she worked with her other hand as easily if her handicap didn't exist.

'Here's your number. You really ought to write it down somewhere so you don't lose it.'

She wrote the number down on a pad, tore off the sheet and pushed it to him through a narrow vertical crack in the glass.

'Thank you.'

'You live at 845, April Avenue?'

'No. Not any longer.'

'Where do you live, then? You haven't informed us you have moved?'

Allan shook his head. He had not expected to be questioned. Irritation rose in him and he wanted to get out, away from this absurd situation, but at the same time he knew he was dependent on the help this woman could give him.

'You must have an address. You must live somewhere.'

'No. We have no address at the moment.'

'Have you registered with the Housing Department?'

'No, not yet.'

'You ought to do that as soon as possible. You're obliged to, you know.'

'Yes, but this is about admission to a maternity ward.'

'If you're under thirty-five and it's a second child, you get maternity help at home, unless medical reasons make it absolutely necessary to be admitted. We have mobile teams who deliver this service. Every necessary assistance is available, both at the actual birth and for a period immediately before and after. That relieves the pressure on our overcrowded clinics and maternity wards.'

'Uh-huh. . . .'

'So I can only help you if you can give me an address. You ought to tell them at the Housing Department as soon as possible, then come back when that's arranged. In your situation, it should be a pure formality. They always have a number of apartments free for those in need.'

'I see.'

The young woman turned to Lisa, whose eyes were closed, her head leaning on one hand.

'Aren't you feeling well?' she said.

'She's tired. We've come a long way,' Allan said. He was feeling claustrophobic himself.

'I'll give you some vitamins. And something to perk you up.' The woman wrote something down and passed the sheet of paper through the slit in the glass.

'There's a dispensary in the building on the ground floor, on the corner of Transport Road. You'll get what you need there. It costs nothing when you hand in that paper. They're open day and night. When you come back with an address, I'll arrange for you to have professional attention.'

Lisa nodded dumbly. She took the sheet of paper and stared at it. She had tried to keep her unruly curls in order by tying them back with a ribbon. Allan could see the nape of her neck now, slim and white where the sun never reached it, and he suddenly felt he had to protect her against the inhumanity of this apparatus they were forced to turn to for help.

'Otherwise,' the woman went on in a neutral voice, 'I suppose you know you can contact us if you find you don't wish to have this child. We can arrange an immediate abortion, and also . . .' – for the first time there was a change in that cool, correct tone of voice and she sounded almost eager – '. . . and I can also tell you that I represent a society which arranges adoptions. Sterility is a problem in many marriages, you know, and the lists of people wanting to adopt babies are long. So if you were thinking of having the baby adopted directly after its birth, that can easily be arranged. Of course, it's all done in a perfectly proper way: only candidates with spotless records and sufficient income and status are approved as applicants in our society. And sometimes it includes free admission to a private clinic and the very best treatment. There's also an adoption fee paid on signature of the papers. That could actually be arranged quite soon if you were interested.'

'No. No, thank you.' Lisa's voice was scarcely audible. 'We want to keep the child.'

'All right, then. Here's a card with the telephone number, should you change your mind.'

Again, as if the woman did not miss her bandaged hand at all, she tapped away with the sound hand. She noticed Allan looking.

'A road accident last Sunday,' she explained . 'I was lucky to get away with only losing two fingers. Over twenty killed. Perhaps you saw it on the television?'

A slight intimation of a smile trembled in the corners of her mouth.

There was a queue in the dispensary, a number system there, too. Tired, shabbily dressed people, mostly men, were waiting patiently along the long counter, some of them clearly drunk. Colourful posters on the walls provided information on contraceptive techniques, sexual hygiene and abortions.

Lisa was given a jar of large vitamin tablets and a tube of small reddish tablets in exchange for her prescription.

'Pinkies,' she giggled, when they were out on the street again. 'Fancy being given pinkies for pregnancy depression!' She laughed a small helpless laugh.

'Allan, I'm so hungry. Where can we get something to eat? Have we any money?'

'A little.'

They wandered aimlessly down the pavement, newspapers flapping round their legs. People were covering their mouths and noses against the gusts swirling through the street, as they might against the cold in winter. But it was midsummer and hot, and even on the shady side the gusts were hot against their faces. Dust swirled, making them sneeze and clear their throats – they, too, were driven to covering their noses and mouths to protect themselves from the very air they were breathing.

They had two hours before the bus left and they were both hungry. They stopped outside a huge department store and looked at the plethora of luxury articles in the window, all at reduced prices.

'Where there's a Glitza store, there's always a cafeteria.'

Allan had to shout above the noise of the traffic. People pushed past them as they stood there. They were jolted, pushed and shoved, and even had their toes trodden on by people who never even noticed, or looked up, but just hurried on.

'Isn't it expensive?'

She looked up at the big building, the steel and glass entrance, the ostentatious window display. The whole dazzling brilliance frightened her and made her wish she was far away, away from the city and the crush, its frenzy and filth.

'It's a chain of cheap stores,' said Allan. 'They mostly sell dumped goods. The cheap stores are the only ones surviving now.'

The cafeteria was long and narrow, the tables in two rows, one along the wall and the other below panes of frosted glass. Climbing pot-plants wound their way up an artificial, imitation antique balustrade which extended the whole length. Dark red walls were decorated with metal mosaics in variations of the letter 'G' and every table had a small lamp with a shade throwing a reddish circle of light on to the plastic table top, bright neon lights above. But the air-conditioning was working and the sudden transition from the heat outside made them catch their breath in the dry, cold air blowing into their faces. The place was empty apart from the girl at the end of the counter staring at a television screen mounted in front of her. She only had to lower her eyes slightly to look at the cash register and her customer. She made no sign whatsoever of having noticed them.

Allan read the menu and suggested 'meat dish à la Glitza', largely because it said salad was served with it.

'Doc said you were to eat salads.'

Lisa didn't mind as long as she had something to eat. Now they were actually inside, she was pleased to be eating in such a grand place.

Allan chose crème caramel for dessert.

'Dessert, too!' whispered Lisa.

The girl behind the counter entered the sum on the cash register. Allan undid his shirt and pulled out the leather pouch of money, then put the coins down one by one on the plastic shelf. The girl picked them up and dropped them into the drawer without looking at them, her attention now back on whatever was flickering on the screen. Her eye make-up glistened. She had already forgotten them.

The meat dish à la Glitza was an oblong fried slab of something in a pool of brown taste-additive. Fried cubes of potato concentrate were served in a bowl and the salad consisted of a mass of boiled vegetables with a sticky dressing on top.

They ate with keen appetites, for it was good. The meat substitute tasted of nothing in particular, neither pleasant nor unpleasant, nor was there much difference between the different brands. Taste was provided by using different types of additives as 'sauce'.

'What shall we do, Allan?' said Lisa when they had finished the meat dish. 'What shall we do when the baby comes?'

They had both been thinking the same. Of course. What else at this time? Fragments of what had been said came back to him. They had to have a registered address in Sweetwater if they were to get any help. That was impossible. With a sinking feeling, almost fear, he realized they would have to manage on their own.

'I don't want to have it adopted.'

'No.'

He was surprised at the determination in her voice. They had considered adoption for Boy, that and abortion. In principle he had nothing against either, but he had begun to think rather differently. To him, a child meant more work, more responsibility, a heavier burden, but also that life would go on, that they were both healthy individuals. He realized no one thought like that in an over-populated city in an over-populated country, where limitation of the population was a matter for the health authorities. But it had grown into an unshakeable feeling ever since he had known Lisa was pregnant again. He *wanted* his family to grow, to continue. Life went on.

He was touched by her trust in him. He didn't know what reason she might have for desiring this child. She probably had little idea what hard work it would be, presuming all went well during the actual birth. That both pleased and amazed him, but he couldn't bring himself to ask her to explain. The months they had spent with fewer and fewer words between them had created a distance as well as limits to what was her field and what his. This pregnancy, which she had also kept from him, was her affair, something she did not have to account for. They both wanted this child and that was what mattered most.

'We'll have to talk to Doc,' he said. 'Maybe he knows already. Maybe that's why he went on about you eating greens.'

'Yes, let's go to Doc tomorrow.'

Her face was white in the reddish light and although she had dark rings of fatigue under her eyes, she managed to produce a smile.

For dessert, they ate the sweet crème caramel shaped in a 'G' with red sugar additive. She liked it. She liked all sweet things and ate a great deal of chocolate when hunger overcame her, sometimes even digging deeply into the next week's ration. When they were to leave, Allan tucked the cutlery into his shirt. They needed it back in the van.

The ride back was even hotter and more unpleasant than the trip in. It was so late, many people were on their way back home from work and the bus was crammed with sweating humanity. As they got caught in the perpetual traffic jams, the sun struck fiercely through the filthy windows.

Allan stared out at the suburbs they were going through, monotonous buildings lining the roads, with occasional gaps where houses had been or were being demolished. New houses were rarities these days and the vacant plots simply accumulated rubbish and a rich growth of weeds.

Lisa tried to get some fresh air from the window in front which was open a crack. Her feet had swollen and were painful, and she leant her head against the window with tears of exhaustion and anxiety pouring pour down her cheeks.

18

'You're perfectly all right,' said Doc. 'All in order. I should say you're in the fifth month. Have you felt any movement yet?'

Lisa shook her head and dried her eyes, trying to smile. He had been both considerate and discreet. But the whole situation had suddenly seemed degrading, lying with her legs in the air on Doc's rickety old sofa while he gently examined her, squeezing her stomach, pushing a broad finger right up inside her and rummaging around . . . and the buckled washing bowl on the table by the dish of ordinary soap, a ragged towel, clean but . . . the flies . . . it had all suddenly become too much, added to her memories of the first time. She sniffed as she adjusted her clothes.

'It'll be fine. The second time is usually much easier than the first. Nothing to be afraid of.' Doc was talking calmly as he washed his hands.

'No. . . .'

All she could remember of her first childbirth was the anguish. The taxi ride to the clinic, Allan pale and loud-mouthed from anxiety and anger when the driver didn't know the way. The waiting. The first pains. Then the injection and the suffocating paralysis creeping through her, the feeling of being choked. Then convalescence for five days in the great overcrowded ward where she had watched the nurses bathing and feeding the ugly wrinkled creature they said was her son. Allan, pale and nervous on the stool by her bed, for the permitted few minutes. Flowers in sealed plastic packs. She had become seized by a desire to do something. She had suddenly felt a fierce responsibility for the baby and insisted on feeding him, giving him her breast although the doctor said she was too young and that her milk glands were underdeveloped ('It'll

120

probably be better next time. . . .') Then home with a carton of artificial baby milk provided by the social services.

'You must be sure to take the vitamins they gave you. Then we'll try to get some more when they've all gone. And you must remember to eat well. You're far too thin.'

Doc looked at her through his thick lenses. She was so fragile, a child in need of protection, and he wondered whether she received enough. Ever since he had first seen her, his paternal instinct had been aroused and he had felt a need to care for this young creature, this appealing child. And now chance, or Allan's carelessness – he gave an unfavourable thought to his neighbour – had more or less delivered her to him. He had been moved at the sight of her on his faded sofa, quite still, her eyes closed, her faced turned away with discontented, almost defiant lines on her smooth forehead when he had felt the slim body. It had been a long time since he had had any reason to practise what in thoughtful moments he still considered his medical skills. When she came to him for his professional advice, or what was left of his knowledge after all these years, he had remembered the desire to *help* which had driven him in the past and which could still be drawn out of him, although he could see all round him where it had led him – this self-inflicted isolation from a society which had rejected his idealism and threatened him with persecution and punishment. But Doc's idealism persisted, regardless of external factors and the fact that he had to endure a pitiful existence on the city's garbage tip. They had in fact taken up several of his radical ideas, but gone so far that most of his humanistic ideals now appeared completely meaningless. Doc's idealism had merged with his protest against the forces against him, which had defeated him and produced a tough, untiring egoism, the vital driving force in his life. He had preserved it, so it could be aroused again in the almost unchanged form of a young girl who trusted him, who had asked for his help. He was ready to do as best he could, although he was worried. It would not be easy to assist at a birth out here where there were no aids whatsoever.

'Will it hurt?'

She was doing her best to stop crying, annoyed with herself for being so stupid and childish.

'The second time is always easier.'

'But I didn't feel anything the first time. I was just given an injection and then it was all over.'

'I know. That's what they do in the public clinics, to save time.

Otherwise it can take ages, you see. Especially the first time.'

'I'm sure it'll hurt when I can't have an injection.'

She started crying again, largely out of relief to be able to sit and talk like this, to express the fears at the thought of what lay ahead of her. She couldn't talk to Allan.

'There, there,' he said. He didn't really know what to do, so put things away and tidied up. 'You said you wanted this child.'

'Ye—es.'

'It's too late for an abortion. That would be dangerous. But there's a chance of having it adopted.'

'I know. They told us at that awful office. But I'm never going back there. Never! We want the baby. It's just that there's so much . . . so much to think about.'

She sat on the edge of the sofa with her face in her hands, her tears wetting her grubby fingers. He sat down beside her. The tired springs creaked and he put an arm round her shoulders.

'You must take it easy,' he said. 'It'll all go well. You must trust me, trust us all. We'll help as best we can. It'll be all right.'

He could feel the delicate bone structure, and when he had examined her he had noted her narrow pelvis. He knew it was not going to be easy.

Again he thought reproachfully about Allan. He liked the man and knew he was reliable. Doc kept himself to himself and did not interfere – after so many years in isolation, all his dealings with human beings had become something of a problem. He wanted contact, but soon tired of people. He considered Allan hard, almost brutal, and lacking in imagination, almost primitive in his view of life, although he was certainly not unintelligent. Allan set himself a course and followed it. Doc was familiar with that. He himself had had to overcome external difficulties and inner weakness by mobilizing his strength and his ability to come to terms with himself. He had also had to harden himself in order to survive. But he had concealed his dreams, his hopes, his visions. Allan's intentions were in the here and now – survival from one day to the next in his own way, according to his own abilities, no matter how that affected those around him.

Doc patted Lisa's arm. He could not understand how Allan had got them into this situation. He felt weak in her presence, as if the fondness he felt for her were making cracks in his determination, weakening the driving force within him and making him indifferent. They belonged to a different generation, these two young people, to another era. In his eyes they were a hopeless lot, with the city as their only yardstick. They knew no dimension except the artificial landscape of the city, but also no other limitation except its destructiveness.

Lisa was sitting quite still, sunk in her thoughts, her eyes dry now; Doc, beside her, was wondering about this generation's arrival on the Dump. He knew new people had come and it worried him. The real problems would now begin to appear.

'Come back in a few weeks' time,' he said. 'And we'll see how things are going. If you feel unwell or have any pain, you must come at once.' He was oddly embarrassed saying what had once been an automatic statement to all his patients, and when he thought about his embarrassment, he was ashamed, for what pleased him was the thought of the next consultation and this intimate contact with her again.

19

The very thought of water was apt to become an obsession in the heat.

Lisa was resting. It was Sunday and Allan would not be back until the evening. She was exhausted and would have liked to sleep, but she was thirsty. She had promised Allan she would be careful with the water, and she had promised herself to keep that promise. They rationed it now. One bucket every other day was all they had. Try not to drink in the daytime, Doc had said. You sweat more and get even thirstier. But it was not easy when Lisa felt her tongue growing in her mouth. She had a child's craving for having her needs immediately satisfied.

The level of water in Doc's well had begun to be dangerously low, and it never occurred to any of them to complain about the rationing he had instigated, although Allan had been bringing scrap metal to Doc's house for weeks in advance payment for their water supply. Their method of payment, so much water for so many kilos of metal, had more or less ceased and had gradually become only a symbol of mutual goodwill. Little water in the well was their joint problem. But Lisa found it difficult to believe a well could be empty. Wells belonged in the realm of fantasy. A well *had* to be inexhaustible, otherwise it was not a well, only a hole in the ground with water in it. But she would not go behind the camper and steal a cupful.

She would *not*. She had taken in that the situation was serious and had asked him whether he couldn't bring a can back with him from the petrol station. But he had told her rationing in the city was now even stricter and water usage strictly controlled, with huge fines for anyone exceeding the quota. Janson read the water meter each time he was on duty. Taking water now would be as good as risking his job. And mineral water was no longer available.

The bucket behind the camper was now nearly empty despite her good intentions. Lisa's tongue seemed to stick to the roof of her mouth as she thought about the wonderful water that must exist everywhere, in glasses, carafes, bottles, taps, showers, bath tubs . . . she had loved having baths and showering when she was a little girl. She could stand for hours under the jets, feeling that she was being dissolved and flowing away with the water, drop by drop through the drain in the floor, washing away her sense of uncleanness at her first period. Her mother's cool explanations had not helped.

It was surprising how often the thought of her parents had come to her recently. Only a short time before, she had never really given them a thought, could hardly remember. . . . But now she had even felt she would like to contact them and had thought of writing to them, just a card. But Lisa could not write. She knew the letters of the alphabet and had been able to put together words and short sentences, but at that her interest had faded at school, and the teaching methods had meant she could hide her ignorance and never needed to catch up on what had been neglected. She mostly truanted in her last years before she had finally abandoned it all and joined Allan.

The thought of her parents, particularly her mother, kept coming and going. It depressed her. When she had first left home, she had telephoned them occasionally so that they would know she was all right, but her mother's reproaches, tears and beseeching her to come home had made her give it up. She and Allan had gone to see them after Boy was born, an impulse on her part. They had gone by bus to the deadly satellite town her parents lived in, rows of pre-fabricated houses with patches of ready-made lawn, picture windows and bubble glass. Allan had stood by the gate while she had rung the bell, the baby on her arm. But they wouldn't let her in, not the way she looked, not with husband and child, not this creature who was no longer their little girl. More tears and explanations, pleading, reproaches and a noisy departure. But she thought about them now she was pregnant again and considered sending a letter to tell them about herself, how things were, what she thought of her life now. But she couldn't write. There was also the thought that they had probably moved to another house in another part of the city – people moved so often in Sweetwater – and she would never track them down. In a few years' time they would end up in a communal old people's home and she would never hear from them again.

Lisa heard a sound and looked up to see Mary Diamond walking along the track towards the camper. She had seen Mary once before at a distance, one afternoon when she had been out looking for something she could use for a bed for the new baby. She had searched with an enthusiasm that had surprised even herself. Then she had seen her walking, no, *striding* up the path along the hardened wheel-tracks in the direction of the main gate, all in black: black leather skirt, tight black blouse, but with a flaring green wig that looked great against all that black and her skin glistening in the heat. Lisa thought she was the most beautiful woman she had ever seen. Her heart in her mouth, she had watched as Mary had tripped and stumbled so that one plastic sandal came off. But she at once regained her balance, fished up the sandal and put it back on (green nail varnish and green eyelids!) with the air of a queen.

Now Lisa was staring with the same admiration at this big, dark-skinned woman walking calmly right up to her.

'Hullo,' she said.

'Hi.'

'My name's Mary Diamond.'

'I know, Allan told me. I'm Lisa.'

'I wondered whether you had any water. We've run out.'

Lisa shook her head.

'No . . . no, we won't have any more until tomorrow.'

She had not lied because she didn't want to help, but in self-defence. She couldn't bring herself to give away any of their precious water just because a stranger came and asked.

'Damn!'

Mary Diamond put her hands on her hips and glared fiercely out over the scorched, disintegrating landscape.

'Is Allan here?'

'No, he works every weekend.'

'Of course. . . .'

She bit her thick lower lip.

'Does he work at Abbott Hill?'

'Yes, Abbott Hill Road. A bit out. Where the drive-in cinema used to be.'

'Yes, I know the place well. You see, Smiley can't get the car going, so can't get into the city. He's run out of booze. And I'm damned if I'm *walking* in to the city to fix his liquor for him. Allan fixed the car a couple of weeks ago, so I thought. . . .'

'He'll be back this evening. I'm sure he can do it for you tomorrow.'

'Yeah, fine, but what shall I do with Smiley in the meantime? He's already complaining, and in this heat. . . .'

The flies kept settling on Mary's shirt hanging outside her skirt and open right down to her waist. The short skirt emphasized those great thighs. How lovely she is, Lisa thought. So large and splendid.

'Is Smiley your husband?'

'Well, let's put it that way. Anyhow, we've been together for some years, to our mutual benefit, and a bit of satisfaction in between.'

'Where do you come from?'

Lisa had overcome her reserve, her curiosity getting the better of her. She thought Mary's voice sounded strange, crude, and her choice of words coarse, quite different from what she was used to.

'From the Palisade.'

Of course! She ought to have known from the way she spoke as well as her whole manner. The Palisade was the largest and most infamous of the shanty towns that had grown up north and west of Sweetwater along the Sandy River and up the barren slopes called Desert Hills. The scum lived there, the tens of thousands of unemployed who over the years had come in from the country districts, most of them with their families, to find casual work in the factories in Saragossa when the season and competition created a shortage of labour. That had been when there was work for most people, when Sweetwater was flourishing on the last wave of technical and economic progress, when the need for extra labour was so great, firms put up the first huts – provisionally, until they speeded up building projects to house people in an acceptable manner – because there was no housing for incomers seeking work. But the last 'golden age' became even shorter than those that had gone before. 'The miracle' hoped for never materialized and the shanty towns became permanent, soon to decay into scandalous slums, a headache and a swiftly growing burden on the hard-pressed authorities. The stream of incomers continued despite unemployment and all attempts to regulate the growth of the shanty towns. Families were moved out to new housing during various slum-clearance programmes and demolition began. But that changed nothing. Funds were continually restricted, priorities changed, work stopped and more people kept moving in where others had moved out, or they built new 'houses' out of second-hand materials, corrugated iron and metal sheeting they found or stole from the numerous demolition sites.

They came from the mountains where the means of making a living were poor, or from distant villages where changes in agricultural policies had put tens of thousands of farm workers out of work. Or they came from the shadier parts of the city, the asocial, the poor and the persecuted, seeking a hiding place in the increasingly uncontrollable, officially non-existent huddle of shanty slums.

Changes in this growing and varied population meant all attempts to register and regulate it were doomed to failure. The unfortunates who ended up there seemed to have instinctively resisted the city's attempts to incorporate them into its system. Most people did not even bother to draw benefit, but that could not be confirmed as there were no reliable census rolls. Work was seldom sought through official channels, and only few people seemed interested in acquiring new housing. The education opportunities started for children and adults were effectively sabotaged by truancy and apathy. What people lived off was an open question. Some grew vegetables and fruit on the narrow trampled strips of ground between the houses, some had domestic animals, goats and pigs running free and often infected with diseases. Illegal distilling of moonshine, a corn liquor typical of that part of the country, was a common occupation, along with theft, receiving stolen property, prostitution and abuse of the many different social services. Aside from the social problems, the shanty towns were also a health risk. Overcrowded and insanitary as they were, disease flourished in the fly-infested hell of heat and drought in the summer, and in winter, leaking, draughty, badly-heated homes, unprotected from rain and biting winds from the river.

Infant mortality was high, although the health authorities said they were doing what they could, but to vaccinate everyone against even the most common epidemic diseases was not that successful in view of the lack of co-operation from the inhabitants of the shanty towns – where planning and organization were wasted, where neither good times nor bad existed, where misery was endemic. A powerless welfare programme that was supposed to patch up the worst inequalities functioned only for a few, was cheated and exploited by many more. The urban 'order' so carefully constructed was decaying from within, a reflection of Sweetwater's own stagnation and slow dissolution.

'Are you going to have a child?'

Mary Diamond squatted down and stared straight at Lisa.

'Heavens, can you see?'

Although it was now an accepted fact, she had not lost the instinct to hide what was going on inside her. Yet she was calmed by Mary's presence and would have liked to have talked to her, to a woman, about her condition.

'I sensed it. I know the signs. I had four sisters. Two of them – well, it killed them. The youngest, Rosa, was not even as old as you. She didn't want the child and she bled to death. But that's nothing to go on about, not now. It was long ago. Now, now, don't cry.'

She put her arms round Lisa, who had suddenly thrown herself at her and was sobbing into her neck – unable to stop herself. What Mary had said sounded so horrible, it had been the last straw.

'There, there,' said Mary. 'No need for you to think about such things. You're perfectly all right, you know that. You're just too thin and anaemic, that's all. You must remember to eat greens. Eat all the green leaves you can find. They won't do you any harm, even if they don't taste nice. In the Palisade, we were given grass to eat when we were kids. Mother said it was good for us, and we never got the diseases lots of the others kids did.'

Her voice rose and fell in a slow melodious rhythm as she held Lisa in her arms and comforted her. Lisa pressed against her, taking in the heavy scents of salt, sweat and cheap perfume coming from this big woman, and gradually she calmed down.

'I'm so afraid it'll hurt,' she said. 'Out here, where I can't get any anaesthetics or anything. I can't think how I can possibly have a child in there.'

She nodded towards the camping van and bit her lip.

20

The fan above his head was rotating. The door was open, the heat shimmering over the forecourt. Allan was sitting on a chair behind the office counter, eating. There was not much to do at the PAC station on Sunday mornings. Rationing had put an end to Sunday outings and those who could still stand the price rises and official references to saving fuel kept to the Motorway.

He had tipped his chair back and was sitting with his feet on the counter, his head resting on an old calender advertising synthetic-rubber tyres. The fan in the roof was going round and round. The air-cooler was irreparable. He ate dutifully, without excitement or appetite. Impossible to have an appetite for anything in this heat. He had bought a packet of sweet biscuits and a soft drink over at the kiosk, and with a bar of chocolate and a tube of spread, that was his midday meal. The choice in J.C. Sweetness' kiosk had grown sparser, too, fat Sweetness himself swelling over the low stool inside and throwing up his hands – he had got hold of what he could. He was suffering just as much, his business. . . .

Most of what they needed for the next week had to be bought at the small supermarket by the East Terminal, where he had to wait up to three quarters of an hour for his connection. Shortages were noticeable there as well, empty shelves gaping at customers where a profusion of special offers had been before. But there was no lack of chocolate, biscuits and cigarettes, substitute coffee or synthetic spreads.

The creaking fan was almost giving up its attempt to get some air circulating. The air-cooling apparatus had been Janson's great pride and before leaving the day before, he had brought it up again. Repairs to it would have to come out of Allan's own pocket, as things were . . . now Janson was talking about the heat. He couldn't stand it, couldn't sleep. People weren't even allowed to use their own bath-tubs any longer to cool off in. In the worst of the heat, Janson always used to spend half an hour in a tepid bath and then go straight to bed. Nothing cooled you as well as a tepid bath, he said. But with this damned rationing of everything, even water. . . . Heat waves before had also been different, not so hot, not lasting so long. No wonder older people were dying like flies. Allan must know more old people died of pneumonia in the summer than in winter, whether in old people's homes or on their own in rented rooms or tiny flats, hardly daring to go out to the shops? If it wasn't pneumonia, it was some kind of 'flu there was no cure for, because the bacteria (as Janson called them) had got so used to all the medicines people were pumped full of from the day they were born. Ordinary clap couldn't be cured any longer, regardless of how much antibiotic they injected. Perhaps Allan didn't believe him? Perhaps he didn't believe old people lay dead in their apartments for weeks, yes, months if neighbours didn't notice the smell? Not surprising, because people weren't told what was happening any more. Information was withheld and news agencies had become a farce dictated by the 'necessities' of the crisis. Facts were always being withheld from the common man. . . . Janson's dentures clattered, his expression grim, but almost with pleasure, he put his hand on the spot just below his ribs, as if he could feel the outline of his ulcer. He muttered on, grey and stooped, as he stumped off across the hot asphalt, leaving Allan's money on the counter, two or three notes and some coins, payment for the week's work. No payslip, no bookkeeping. Allan worked 'on the side' for wages far lower than the prescribed minimum, but he did not pay tax. Then Janson was free at weekends and escaped paying national insurance. Minor illegalities of that kind kept Sweetwater going.

Allan ate the biscuits and cheese spread, swilling it down with a soft drink he reckoned made him even thirstier and left a taste in his mouth he never seemed to able to get rid of. He stared out of the open door at the row of houses on the other side of the street. Old four- or five-storey buildings. Some of the ground floor shop windows were nailed up. The windows on the upper floors belonged to flats, curtains in some of them, but no sign of life.

It suddenly struck Allan that perhaps they were all empty, had simply been left, but how long ago? When had he last seen anyone going in or out? When *had* he . . .? He had worked there for over four years and had never spoken to anyone who lived across the road. Of course, *something* must have gone on opposite when the shops were still open. When had they closed? What kind of shops had they been? He knew, of course he knew – it was on the tip of his tongue. But his memory seemed to fail him as numerous changes slowly undermined everything, re-creating houses and streets, blocks and whole districts becoming different from what they had been; at first imperceptibly, then noticeably but without it making much impression on him, until the once familiar surroundings became unrecognizable, as if the *content* was slowly being filtered out and replaced by something new, a cold and hostile strangeness. On Sunday morning it was as quiet in Abbott Hill Road, once a main artery, as it was out on the Dump.

Allan started involuntarily at the sound of a car, not from fear, but because the actual noise had broken into the thoughts he had been so absorbed in. A long, low nickel-plated vehicle, an expensive private car, an old model, came gliding along, slowed down but did not stop, and simply swung off the road and bowled slowly, almost soundlessly up to the pumps and past them, the faces inside blank, summing up the premises. Youths. Pale faces and dark glasses behind the smoked glass windows. Allan opened the cash-register drawer slightly. Inside he had a gas pistol and two screwdrivers. Possessing weapons was prohibited, but gas was recommended for self-defence and a screwdriver was just as effective as a knife, so no one could accuse him of possessing a weapon. Petrol stations were favourite spots for robbers. But the car speeded up again and disappeared with a piercing screech. Allan thought for a moment he recognized one of the faces, but then dismissed the idea. Who had he ever known who might drive around in that kind of car? No one.

Although it was not like him to bother about an episode of that kind, he felt a restlessness as the car drove away and the Sunday quiet again settled on Abbott Hill Road. He looked at the clock on the wall. Nothing more to do. He got up, locked the door and went out into the misty heat past the pumps and their flashing lights. He walked straight across the pavement and on to the street, his hands in his pockets; he looked both ways. Nothing. Not a person. Not a car, nor a sound apart from the faint wail of a patrol car far away. Even Sweetness' kiosk was closed in the oppressive Sunday heat. Sunday emptiness. He stood there — an angular, untidy figure in overalls, undershirt and home-made sandals, his hair and beard unkempt — he felt defenceless between the menacing, deathly quiet rows of houses.

Nothing but the gateposts was left of the once proud entrance to the park when he got there. The cast-iron gateway and actual gates had gone, stolen no doubt by someone needing iron for repairs. Or a dealer. Scrap metal prices had risen, Doc had told him. Sometimes they saw people out at the Dump hunting for parts of cars and other saleable objects, but they never came near where they had settled, so it didn't worry them.

Inside the park entrance he soon saw that any order in the once well-maintained park was crumbling fast. The long grass was brown and dry and weeds proliferated across the neglected gravel paths. The air was heavy with the scent of dead flowers and two

131

mongrels ran off as he approached. Not a human being in sight.

His sandals stepped on heaps of dry brown petals under a large rhododendron. Had he walked in the park before? He must have done. He found it all vaguely familiar and seemed to know what it looked like. But when? And for what reason? He couldn't remember. He kept finding it more and more difficult to remember anything of his life before he had moved out to the Dump. When he tried, random images floated through his mind uncontrollably. He saw his mother, tired and irritable, sitting at the end of the table by the stove in the cramped kitchen they always used to eat in. 'Eat up your vegetables, Allan. Go on, eat up your carrots.' He had detested vegetables, and still did, whatever Doc said, but the memory of that dish of steaming carrots (the *worst*) remained with him. The smell of them was there, nor was it entirely unappetizing – a hunger for 'something' gnawing at him after sweet biscuits and synthetic food.

Where the formal beds opened up into a scorched brown area of grass that had been for picnics and walking, he could see the first gardens, largely dug-over patches, some with rickety fencing of planks and wire round them. Most of the plots were neglected, scorched and overgrown, though in between, a few had been weeded and obviously watered. Further on, where the grass sloped up to the first low hill, fences round the gardens were higher, more solid and he could see the small sheds and huts of traditional allotment areas. The cultivated patches were larger and there were ornamental shrubs and trees in some of them, the plots symmetrical with old footpaths leading between the fences to gates, some of which had not been opened for a long time. Only a few of the plots had been regularly tended and the whole area had an air of neglect, anarchy, almost 'wildness'.

He walked along looking at the vegetables he could see in among the wilderness of weeds, but none told him anything. He knew nothing about growing things. He had noted Doc's enthusiasm for his kitchen garden with a kind of 'hunger', an appetite for 'something' inside him, making him more observant. He also noticed that he was automatically thinking: Is that edible? Or that? It surprised him, even worried him a little, as he did not favour the idea of eating grass. But the scents reinforced his appetite for what was lacking in him, driving him restlessly on. He wanted to fill that need, yet hesitated, didn't dare, didn't know *what* was edible in this green wilderness.

He stopped at an overgrown tangle of tall bushes with branches hanging over the path. They had large red berries on them, some so ripe they were almost purple. He hesitated, at first inclined to pick and eat them, but then he remembered dimly the warnings he had been given not to eat things he found. Overripe fruit rotting on the ground gave off a tempting sweetish smell. A small grey bird with dark brown marks on its head and wings flew down and landed a little way away from him. He looked at it, recalling Doc's enthusiasm for greenfinches. Doc knew. The bird hopped about picking up seeds – or whatever – out of the gravel. When it came to fallen berries, it at once set about them and Allan watched with interest. If this bird could eat them without coming to any harm, then . . .?

He cautiously picked one. The bird flew away as he moved and he almost changed his mind. He felt the soft berry, then squashed it between his fingers. The red juice ran out and dripped to the ground. The smell was fresh and sweet. He licked off some of the juice. It was sourer than he had imagined, but not unpleasant. He put the berry into his mouth, munched and swallowed it. Then he picked some more, and some more. He was soon eating greedily, using both hands and snatching the berries off the branches and gobbling them down in handfuls, the juice running down his chin, almost as if he couldn't stop himself. He couldn't remember ever having tasted anything so refreshing and delicious and wished he could just stay there until his hunger was stilled. He leant over the fencing to reach some higher up . . . there were more inside, many more, redder, juicier. He was so busy eating he failed to notice a cloud covering the sun and then he heard a rumble in the distance. Thunder, forecasting rain, the first rain in Sweetwater for almost four months.

'What lovely shoes,' said Mary. 'Are they real leather?'

She had looked into the camper and seen Lisa's high-heeled shoes.

'I think so,' said Lisa. 'I bought them some time ago. Before rationing.'

'Jesus, they're really smart,' said Mary. 'You can't get them like that any longer. Unless you have some damned good contacts.'

'They're too small for you.'

Lisa looked at Mary's broad feet in the pink sandals. She would like to do something for her new friend and would have given her the black shoes she would anyhow have no further use for – they reminded her of that dreadful trip into the city, but they looked ridiculously small, dangling on thin straps from Mary's stubby fingers and dirty fingernails.

'Do you think so? My feet aren't as big as they look.'

She propped one hand against the camper, kicked off one sandal and hooked her big toe into the narrow shoe, then tried it on. After several dogged attempts and some swearing, she succeeded. The other shoe was easier. Delighted, she strutted round determinedly, though somewhat unsteadily on the uneven ground.

'See – they aren't too small.'

The straps bit deep into the soft flesh of her ankles and heels. Her whole body, her feet too, looked softly upholstered and lush. What a beautiful woman, Lisa thought again as she lay back, following every movement Mary made, her grey-blue eyes hungry, her hand running dreamily over her stomach. What a lot of men must desire such a woman. She wondered whether Allan . . .? With no trace of jealousy, she fantasized as Mary took some joyful dancing steps out in the sunlight.

'Can I borrow them? You see, where I work, we have to be a little sort of, sort of . . . elegant.'

'You can have them.'

'Have them? Buy them, you mean. I could get you something for them.'

'No, you can have them. I don't want them. I'm tired of them.'

She said that to excuse her generosity. Her eyes were filled with this woman in front of her, an expression of astonishment on her face. She felt like a child wanting protection and she could hardly resist the temptation to creep up into Mary, into oblivion, away from who she was and how she was and what was happening to her. Anguish of that kind often came over her these days, in between periods of listlessness and well-being, the contradictions of pregnancy.

'But Baby. . . .'

Mary Diamond knelt down beside her on the mattress.

'Baby, you can't just give perfectly good shoes away. Shoes you can't get hold of any longer. I can get you something for them . . . vitamins perhaps. You'll probably need them. Smiley has contacts.'

But Lisa had no desire to profit from her generosity.

'No, no . . . no, thank you,' she whispered, as if ashamed. 'You needn't. I don't need anything special. But if . . . if you could. . . .'

She shook her head when she realized she was going to cry again, her emotions overcoming her unexpectedly, without her being able to do anything about it.

Mary pressed her cheek against Lisa's and took her into her strong arms.

'There, there, Baby,' she whispered. 'There, there. I'll come over and see you sometimes, I promise you. You mustn't be frightened. It'll be fine. In the Palisade children come into the world on the bare floor in some places. I've seen it many a time, straight on to the ground, naked as skinned rabbits. I had eight brothers and sisters. They're scattered all over the place now, and two are dead, but they came into the world in our little hut in the Palisade, every one of them. And were they any the worse for that? I'll tell you a little about what it was like.'

She was speaking in a warm low voice. She smelt of sweat, soap and strong scent, of earth. She knelt on Lisa's grubby mattress and rocked her in her arms as if rocking a baby to sleep.

'When Father was sacked from the factory, he became a bait-digger to support us. I don't suppose you've ever seen a bait-digger, but they waded in the mud at ebb tide in the shallows below the Saragossa banks and dug sandworms. Then they sold them to holiday fishermen. Sandworms are the best bait in the world, or were . . . when there were fish to catch. He dug with his hands, as deeply as he could, his arm right in up to the elbow, turning the mud over to find those white maggots, one every third or fourth time he shoved his arm into the mud. It wasn't bad and kept us going. We had a few chickens. Mother took in washing. We collected green plants and my sister pretended to have fits to get sick benefit. That's what it was like, until pollution killed the worms and everything else, and salt and acid took the skin off Father's legs. But my brothers were twelve and thirteen by then and used go into Sweetwater with the gangs of youths. They always brought something back with them. You could always get jobs no one else wanted. One of my sisters started walking the streets outside the offices in the city zone. It may sound wretched and we weren't happy, but we managed, we survived and *that* was what was mattered.'

She flowed quietly on and to Lisa her words seemed to be full of understanding and consolation, words whispered from one woman to another.

A cooler wind wafted over them and the sky above the ravaged Dump darkened as a cloud covered the sun. Then heavy drops of rain splashed on to the tin roof and Lisa pressed her hand to her stomach.

'I think it's moving!'

She stared out into space with an absent but none the less concentrated gaze.

'Yes, I'm sure. It moved!'

21

The first rain brought relief, mild and refreshing as it poured down on the heaps of refuse, softening things, dispersing contours, laying a blessed veil over the crumbling expanse of Sweetwater. Hard objects sank into the mud, the cadavers of abandoned technical aids still keeping their shape and in places even their pride, their right to exist and becoming more and more at one with their surroundings, shadows, ghost-like and unreal, not so glaringly obvious as they had been in the bright sunlight. The remains of more personal articles, clothes, furniture, the first to disintegrate and disappear, were now only fleeting outlines, almost spectres of those who had once left them there to be consumed by time and the forces of nature – those who were themselves now being consumed, and heading for their own destruction under the great city's dream of progress and growth.

With its healing, almost imperceptible act of re-creation, the rain seemed to be penetrating the actual structure of what had been created by man and there completed its quiet work of demolition. The Dump's great mounds of broken bricks, shattered concrete slabs which should have been houses, offices, shops and human dwellings – all absorbed the moisture after the long drought, until shapes disintegrated and again became sand and soil. Metal, too. Metal plates, girders, rods and pipes, left in tortured shapes protruding from the earth, shrieking their raging pain, groaning under the weight of stored heat from the sun – all were soaked, and soaked again, the rain washing away layers of flaking rust, until they again stood out, scrubbed clean and stripped by the downpour, centuries of year-rings exposed, the nervous system of their structures bearing the weight of time, now worn thinner and slowly reverting to undisturbed symbiosis with the soil.

The rain softened the strange divisions mankind's efforts had erected between nature and culture, revealing that the city and the Dump were essentially identical and that mankind's existence in both places could easily become just that, stagnant, reactive, driven down to levels of pitiful primitiveness.

The dust now settled, loose paper, refuse and dirt laid to rest in a layer of fine mud on the ground like sweat coming from the earth itself – the earth that had lain lifeless, scarred, cracked and exhausted after the long drought, and now in the sudden change was suffering from attacks of fever, steaming before again coming to life.

Allan and Lisa collected rainwater in saucepans and vessels, in everything that would contain it, however little. It was a game, a relaxation. They didn't really need it, for Doc's well would soon be full again, but they felt a childish delight in collecting the precious drops and then wasting them. For it went on and on, pouring down, with no sign of clearing. But nothing could take away the joy of being outside and feeling the rain drumming on their hot skin, soaking their clothes, and with none of the unpleasantness associated with wetting yourself in childhood.

Lisa had taken off her dress and was leaning over the washing bowl rubbing the last remains of a cake of soap into her hair. Allan sat in the doorway watching her, the rain rattling on the tin roof. She had put on weight. Pregnancy rounded her and he was pleased to see she had swelled considerably in only two or three weeks. He liked seeing the physical changes which had worried, even repelled him before and were now somehow attractive. He could already see the curve below her waist, her fuller breasts and the slow flow of all her movements, of her whole body, and he found it exciting, captivating, essentially feminine.

She straightened up and emptied the bowl over her head, tipping the soapy water over her face and shoulders, breast and back. She bent down and poured some clean water out of the bucket and repeated the process, enjoying herself. Mary had been washing herself like that in the bay when he had first seen her that morning – large, olive-skinned, her nipples like leather buttons.

Lisa had hair all over her face, so did not see the look in his eyes, but there was no mistaking his tone of voice as he called over to her.

'Come on over!'

She shrank, all enjoyment gone from her first bath for many weeks, the water cold now – she put her hand down as if trying to hide her genitals from his gaze.

'Come on. . . .'

His voice was commanding. She looked across at him, at the long dark hair and wild brown beard framing his big face and emphasizing his impatience. She had learnt to evade him, not to arouse him during her pregnancy. But sometimes he commanded, and then she obeyed, although reluctantly.

'Mm,' she mumbled without looking at him. 'I must just rinse out the soap.'

She was outside and standing in the rain, bare-legged in the mud, her feet and legs grimy. When she bent down again to fill the bowl, her ribs could clearly be seen, but her position also emphasized the swelling and again he thought about Mary Diamond.

'I'm going in,' he said with a last glance at Lisa, her body glistening in the rain. 'Are you coming?'

'Yes,' she said, staring down into the battered enamel bowl in her hands.

She knew then she was frightened of him. Sometimes, without any warning, she would suddenly feel his hand on her stomach when she had been doing something, and to her it was almost an assault – those strong fingers seeking, searching. No longer at night, as so often in April Avenue, when those fingers caressed her until she woke. He would be half-asleep, as if he could only reach her when his affection was slumbering in the darkness, in the shelter of dreams behind his tightly closed eyes. Now he took her in broad daylight, often while the child was looking on – that no longer bothered them. At night he slept heavily without moving, without dreaming? She presumed so, because of his calm breathing, almost inaudible as he lay curled up on his corner of the mattress, his arm across his face.

She shivered as she poured more water over her head, partly from the cold, but also the resistance rising in her at the thought of the rough treatment to come. It often hurt and she was scared. Couldn't he leave her alone at this time? Couldn't he wait until she was all right again? Three or four months soon passed.

She would talk to Doc Fischer, ask him if it did any harm. She would ask him to speak to Allan and explain about the pain. She liked Doc. He was a friend. She would take the two little boxes with her and show them to him. He would like that. He had a lot of odd little things of his own. He would surely help her.

A towel hung on the open door of the camper. She slowly started drying herself, although the towel was already wet and not much use. Her hair would not dry and was still hanging round her face, trickling water down her body. She heard him rummaging about inside, getting ready. She struggled with her hair, not liking it half-dry, not wanting sex just then, when Boy might be back at any moment. He was with Run-Run as usual. They had become inseparable. But this was about the time of day when Felix and his brother went into Sweetwater 'to look for work'. Always in the evening. Never in the daytime. Sometimes she had seen them coming back long into the following morning.

Boy might appear at any moment. Her pale lips trembled. She did not want to, did *not want to*. Then she took the decision, turned round and went back out into the rain, pulled on her wet dress and half-ran down the path, away from him. That was the first time she had disobeyed him, defied him, but she had to. Everything told her so. She was soon soaked through again, scared, worrying about his anger, but she had no regrets. She would go to Doc. She wanted to do that. She could find consolation and protection from him.

Through a crack in the wall behind her back, Marta could see everything Doc and Lisa did. She could see him examining her, his bronzed hands feeling her belly, her hips, the loins of that young girl, and she shuddered, almost as if in pain, for she could not forget his activities in his consulting room in Park Road, the lovely secluded house with its large sheltered garden. She suffered physically at the thought of this girl who had become pregnant in this misery, the fabric of her own last days on earth. Marta had once believed in God, believed in some *meaning* in life, that everyone given a life had a responsibility to live it respectfully, properly, a *worthy* life. But that was an ideal, a privilege denied her, destroyed for her by *his* criminal acts, an assault on her, on the government, beyond all forgiveness.

But was it not some consolation that a child was to be born out here, and that Doc, the abortion doctor himself, was to assist at the birth? For some reason, the thought upset her even more. Would the conflict between her growing desire for revenge and this hope swelling inside Lisa turn Doc's action into something positive again – was it that causing her this agitation, almost rage one moment, and despair the next? Or was it a kind of jealousy of their increasing intimacy, not the physical intimacy of his examining her – that simply aroused unpleasant memories in her. Worse was the childish communication they indulged in, a 'game' between them Marta did not understand, but which she thought was perverse. It had started by Lisa bringing small objects with her to consultations, little boxes, ornaments, games as far as she could see. And he, an old man, looked with interest at what she had brought, also took out things he had hidden, a piece of jewellery or parts of something he had found, some marbles, pearls of coloured glass, trinkets. He had collected things over the years, things he liked because they were pretty, or perhaps might come in useful some time. He never gave up hope of everything coming in useful one day, and she despised him for that, because *she* knew that in spite of all his fine theories, his grandiose visions, his old-fashioned need to oppose, his escape into misery to preserve his 'integrity', it was the *past* he collected and hid, as if hoping the past would come back one day and offer him a place in it. She despised him, because *she* was the one who had had faith and good intentions, had been satisfied with life as it was, not wishing it to be otherwise, and who in the end had been betrayed. Now it was *she* who realized that the good times were over and everything would get worse, that they were lost and would soon die out there.

She suffered. She suffered in the rain just as much as from the heat. The heat had been bad enough, as if the source of life in her were slowly running out, drying up, listless days with no strength, days of burning, cracking skin and insatiable thirst. All he said was that they had to be sparing with water because they had to share it with the others – they were all in the same boat. She had cursed him, begged, even wept, as she eked out their last drops, degrading herself. But he had principles and was adamant, maintaining that it was not good for her to drink so much and leaving her while he exchanged profundities with that Allan who came every other day to fetch buckets of their precious water as if that were the most natural thing in the world.

But with rain came the damp and that was even worse, turning the whole house musty, the furniture and the bedclothes acquiring a grey mould – everywhere, even on clothes and the woodwork. The damp seemed to penetrate right into her, torturing her arthritic joints and bringing even more pain and insomnia. She hated him for that, though she knew he was not responsible and had done everything he could to get pain-killers for her. That strange pale man in a black hat had brought something recently, he and his horrible dumb companion. They had been paid well. Razor blades, perfume and two cigarette lighters, things high on the list in Sweetwater. He had promised more. He had good contacts and the pills had worked. She had slept soundly for the first time for God knows how long and dreamt of two horrible creatures in hats and suits constantly merging and becoming one, then separating before merging yet again.

In pain, she lay with her eye to the crack, watching Doc and Lisa at their games with stones, pieces of glass and coloured boxes. She could hear fragments of their conversation, mostly childish, and their laughter. She didn't know which pained her most, their affectations or their laughter. She saw the girl lean over towards him and whisper something into his ear, as if too shy to say it aloud. They looked like father and daughter.

Marta had had no children and had grieved over it, though the memory of her loss had long since faded. But the emptiness she had borne all these years seemed to turn into jealousy, even hatred of Lisa, the girl who had obtruded upon their lives, disturbing the equilibrium of bitterness with her innocence, her importunate, pathetic fertility, and who had got him to take up his medical activities again, changing this stage of his life and giving him indulgence for his past sins, making him – the old fool – laugh. . . . At the same time, Marta's frozen old heart trembled at the thought of the new life entrusted to him.

'Does it hurt much? Does it hurt every time?' she could hear Doc saying.

The girl nodded. 'Yes. I wondered if . . . whether it could do any harm?'

'You poor thing. . . .' He put his hand on to hers and reassured her in the same calming, almost ingratiating voice. 'I'll have a little talk with that man of yours, so he doesn't go on being naughty to our little girl.'

He smiled and stroked her cheek. Rain was dripping into sauce-pans he had put out, and the windows also let in the rain, making pools along the window-sills.

It was all too much for Marta. She sank back, her hands over her eyes, moaning as memories returned to her. The heavy drops of rain streaking down the cracked panes – they reminded her of the circular stained-glass window in Magdalena Church that grey, wet day in May when she had married Doc Fischer, heavy drops running from red to blue to green, the blurred condensation high up under the concrete arches, black iron rods protruding from them, all part of the 'sober' architectural dictates of the day. She had been in white, young and happy, and it had been a celebration, despite the taped music and the fact that no one else was there apart from them, their parents, the witnesses and the priest. The priest was their age and had recently been appointed to her parents' parish, in the church where she had been baptized and confirmed, a dark, serious youth. He had agreed to come to the modest reception afterwards – Henry Dos Manos, the theologian whom the bad times, curtailments of funds, closing churches and general godlessness had turned into a travelling scrap-dealer, who came on his rounds to see them every other week, their only contact with the city and the life she missed so much, longed for every minute of her present life. She refused to see Dos Manos or talk to him when he came. But she occasionally looked through the crack in the wall when she knew he was there. She had seen how his fine-featured face had now aged, its grimace rigid, as if in surprise at the trick life had played on him. She saw the slim hands which had made the sign of the cross over them now holding a glass of the home-brewed maize wine Doc kept for special occasions, and she heard the cracked dry voice which had once read the gospels like the sweetest of songs, now complaining.

She couldn't bear it. She groaned, twisting and turning, the damp bedclothes like fire on her aching limbs. Her thick rich hair, once her pride and joy, was now matted and sweaty, falling over her eyes. Why should she suffer so? She had had faith, a husband, a home, security, sufficient income and a life for which she was grateful. Now she was on a rubbish tip, old, sick and smelly, waiting with longing and terror for death, with nothing but a foetus inside a young girl to fix her hopes on, her hope of salvation.

Those voices. The pain was so great, she knew she would have to ask him for a pill, although it was not yet time, although there were not many left, although she hated asking him for anything. She would wait five minutes, then she would call. No, not that long. She couldn't endure it. She despised him, but he was not to forget she was in pain. She would count to a hundred, slowly, concentrating on that to forget the pain. No, why slowly? Why should *she* always have to restrain herself? Ten-twenty-thirty-forty . . . her jaws were working. Laughter again. Serve him right! Serve him right! He was having a good time . . . she closed her eyes and called out as loudly as she could.

'*Doc!*'

22

The rain had turned the neglected allotments into a wild tangle. Every weekend, Allan took a large sack with him to work and filled it with anything edible he could find. His weekly trips provided them with a welcome change in their diet. He had asked Doc's advice about the most important plants, but still found it safest to get Doc to check the ones he was not sure of. The old man had once or twice tried to use those occasions to bring up other subjects concerning Allan's and Lisa's sex life, but Allan had interrupted. He was reluctant to discuss his private life and annoyed with Lisa for complaining about something to Doc, about things nothing to do with anyone except themselves.

But it must have made some impression on him, because he became more considerate in his demands on Lisa, and it also dawned on him that it was important to be able to control his sexual impulses. He had noticed her avoiding him and heard her crying, quietly so as not to disturb him after he had crawled off her and lay staring out into the pitch dark of the Dump, feeling that sleepy satisfaction filling his body. But it had affected him, filling him with melancholy, almost grief, although he did not really know what was wrong.

He climbed over fences, scratched by brambles and stung by nettles. The proliferation on the allotments amazed him, as they were clearly reverting to their 'natural state', regardless of the concrete buildings all around. He felt the same strange attraction mixed with fear that sometimes came over him in Doc's unruly jungle garden, as if he had come into contact with a subtle but overwhelming process drawing its strength from the actual mystery of life. It could teach him to live, to *survive*, if only he could absorb the secret signs of its process, once he could see beyond this tenacious growth as an obstacle to his main aim, to find food.

He took anything he considered edible, some vegetables recognizable from the once well-stocked supermarkets, others he instinctively felt were appetizing, and he often used his sense of smell. A smell could make him pull up plants and brood over them, insignificant plants he would not have been able to distinguish from grass before.

Back on the Dump, they ate as many raw vegetables as they could and made a kind of soup with the rest. It tasted good and stilled their hunger, at least for a while. Run-Run had eaten with them once, appearing with Boy, his arms full of green plants he and the child had collected on the Dump and along the shore. Lisa had just started preparing their meal. Run-Run had made a sign and Boy had explained that what they had brought should go into the soup. None of them knew what kind of plants they were, but the soup seemed more filling, and they could chew on the stems and roots so that both the taste and the sense of being full lasted longer.

Run-Run had sat cross-legged and upright on the hard ground, solemnly eating, his bowl cupped in his hands as he slurped in small mouthfuls, his eyes half-closed, even his perpetual smile gone. An animal smell came from him, and his movements were measured and precise, as if eating were a ritual from which under no circumstances whatsoever was he going to be diverted. It had never occurred to them that it was inopportune of him to appear just as they were to eat, and the unease Lisa had previously felt whenever he was present had worn off after the incident with the bunch of rosemary. She occasionally shivered at the thought that he was a dangerous man, a killer, but he had shown an interest in her as a person with much more attention and understanding than Allan had. Boy sat beside him with his cup of soup, looking up admiringly at his large, silent friend.

Slowly Allan's sack filled with anything he considered might be edible. A patch of flowering cauliflower had attracted his attention and he had also discovered carrots under the soil below unrecognizable tufts of green. Most of the vegetables had seeded themselves over several summers, so there was no order and many of the plants bore little resemblance to their cultivated versions. Allan went from patch to patch, making the most of it between showers, his back bent, his fingers black with earth, pulling up whatever he recognized and thought might be useful. It was important to take a lot, for it was much more difficult to find food on the Dump in wet weather. Fortunately the kiosk was still open, but the selection there had become even more limited. Allan was sick of Sweetness apologizing feebly every time something was 'sold out'. Some goods were in chronic short supply, especially foodstuffs, but cheap 'luxury goods' were plentiful at reasonable prices – what could a kiosk do? Allan knew there was supposed to be some kind of quota system to ensure all shopkeepers had a minimum stock of basic goods, but he suspected Sweetness of selling his quota on the flourishing black market. What could he say?

'Next week . . .' the fat man had said. 'Perhaps I can get some vegetable cheese next week. Then you'll fill up my tank, won't you? Eh?'

It was Saturday, a quiet Saturday afternoon beneath a grey sky threatening rain, and Allan was gasping under the weight of his sack. He was pleased with his haul, but then he realized time had run away with him and he had been away from the station too long. He heard an occasional noise down on the road, weekend motorists passing the 'Closed' sign he had put up. If Janson knew, his job wouldn't last much longer. He must be careful, for he was none too sure of Janson. The old man had started muttering about the weekend takings gradually becoming more and more meagre. He might come to check to see if everything was all right. He might do anything.

Allan hurried down to the gateway to see whether anyone was waiting at the pumps, or whether he had been 'found out'. His sudden anxiety at having done something wrong made him start running. He was still dependent on the job and the money it brought in, still uncertain whether he could manage without it. But it wouldn't be long now.

He found himself gasping for breath. A brisk run had never taken it out of him like this before. He had always kept himself reasonably fit, although he had put on some weight before moving out on to the Dump. Their poor diet had now removed the surplus. He fumbled blindly in the sack, found a carrot and stuffed it into his mouth, munching hungrily on it as he stumbled on, sucking the juice. Sweet and good. He hit a branch and a shower of raindrops fell on him. He licked them off the back of his hand and found it sharp but refreshing.

Then back behind the counter, his feet up and his chair tipped back against the shelves of auto parts behind him. It had been a very quiet afternoon, only six or seven customers (Janson would as usual go on about how only a year ago ten times the number would have produced a reasonable return), and someone wanting a tyre, presumably to have in reserve. But tyres had long since been unavailable and their small stock had sold out soon after rationing started. The man had resignedly shrugged his shoulders and left in his battered pick-up truck. Another black marketeer, no doubt.

Autumn had come. Rain spattered on the pane of glass in the door and red and green neon lights played on the four still-functioning pumps. A single fluorescent light swung precariously in the wind, throwing a harsh white light on to the wet forecourt. The road was dark and empty of traffic, only two or three lights visible in windows on the other side of the road. Most people were saving their electricity quotas for cooking and heating – the evenings were beginning to get colder. If those flats were inhabited at all . . .?

A gust of wind made the thin door rattle and the light swerve across the deserted forecourt. He could see the rain splashing up against the wall, on the windows, in the litter round the overflowing bins, merging with the oily mud into a shiny, glistening layer on everything outside. He could see the pumps under their glass fibre umbrella, the stand of boxes, engine oil, plastic buckets, cans and window-cleaning gear, the pressure gun and its cable coiled on a hook, and the rain on the posters on the hoarding proclaiming PINK-PAC . . . PAC-ACE . . . ECO-PAC to the traveller – now tattered, dirty and torn by the wind and rain. Snakes of red and green light up and down, up and down, like the dots on an electronic screen, scattering and coming together again . . . steered by the whims of the weather.

Apple Blossom Time.

This was the scene he had once found so attractive, even beautiful. The symmetry between pumps, the sun-and-rain-roof, the entrance and exit, the office, stores and toilets, the flaking wall, the posters and their slogans, offers and crude typography, to him had had a beauty, as if this desolate, soulless landscape, now exposed beneath the harsh light and bathed in dirty rain, had been a reflection of the landscape of his emotions, symbolizing just what he had seen as the outside world.

But no longer. He sat looking out through the glass in the door and felt utterly alien in this cocoon of concrete, metal and artificial light. The smooth shape of the petrol station seemed to irritate his very optic nerve, the earlier hypnotic effect now gone, and he suddenly felt exposed and threatened. The smell on his fingers, the chemical smell of oily mud, had become repulsive, irritating his skin, and when he crossed the forecourt, his soles slapped against the concrete, sending shooting pains up his legs. The world of the petrol station was hostile, its qualities no longer suited to his body. He knew it would not be long now.

The wind struck the door and the lamp swayed, the light catching something else on the edge of his field of vision, a fleeting glitter across the asphalt. No. Then the pavement was in darkness again. But at that moment he heard a sound through the patter of the rain on the windows – a cry? His first instinct was to stay still – it could be someone trying to lure him out and finish him off in the dark, a not unusual occurrence at petrol stations – people were wounded or killed and robbed for small sums of money. He opened the drawer with the gas pistol in it – how could he defend himself with such a toy against armed thieves? He sat quite still, alert to the slightest sound or movement that might tell him something, prepare him for what to expect, prepare him for action. Then he heard another cry, or an exclamation, closer and clearer. Reluctantly, he got half-way out of his chair. The sound seemed to strike a chord in him, making him react against all reason.

He got up, went across to the door and peered beyond the pumps, his hand still on the doorhandle. That voice . . . Then he saw her, a swaying, stumbling figure staggering into the circle of light. A second was enough and he was sure, already outside, the wind and rain in his face, racing towards that figure, that voice he had recognized. He reached her just as she fell against a pump, grabbed her as she fell, and held her upright.

'Mary!'

She was as tall, no, taller than he. He stared into her battered face.

'Mary, Mary, what's happened?'

'Hi, Allan.'

Although she could scarcely speak, she managed to twist her battered mouth into a smile. 'Thought I'd never find you.'

'What's happened?'

He was holding her upper arms as hard as he could. Her whole body was shaking, her legs bare. She was soaking wet and blood was trickling out of cuts and grazes, mostly on her face. Her lips were swollen. She had a large graze on her forehead and one eye was swollen and red.

'What's happened?' he repeated helplessly.

'Oh, nothing special, Allan. Nothing special.'

She managed to produce another small smile, but her eyes were dull and she was shuddering all over as if about to faint.

147

'Come on,' he said, leading her towards the office, using all his strength to hold her up. He was shivering himself – not with cold, but with excitement.

'The bastards beat me up and took my money,' said Mary. She had washed, but her face was swollen and long shudders still occasionally ran through her as she sat curled up on one of the customers' chairs, wrapped in a car rug.

'Who?'

'The police, of course. Who else?'

'*The police*?'

'Yes, the *po-lice*,' she mimicked scornfully. She had got some of her strength back now, her eyes had cleared and she was speaking quite distinctly through her bruised mouth. 'The cops. They're involved in the girlie traffic themselves, most of them. They can't stand freelancers like me.'

At last it dawned on Allan.

'So you're a . . .'

'Too right!' The old irony had come back. 'I work the Motorway. Surely you knew that? Or was it a great shock to you?'

Her sarcasm had a touch of defensiveness so was not as effective as it should have been. He thought that meant she liked him, and a strange delight rose in him in the middle of this unexpected drama. He had been sitting there only too aware, all the time, of the plump legs she had drawn up under her in the chair; beside her was a wobbly table with tattered auto magazines, an ashtray full of Janson's cigarette ends and bottle-tops on it.

'Of course not. . . .'

There was a pause.

He felt she had done him an injustice. It was nothing to do with him what she did for a living and nor had he anything against prostitutes. On the contrary, those he had gone with before Lisa had moved in had been nice girls, pretty, and good lovers. He had enjoyed doing it that way, with no introductory play-acting to lure girls up to his flat and then perpetuating the masquerade until it was over, even longer if the situation demanded it – silly flattery, caresses, perhaps even half-hearted repetitions of various tricks in bed, when all he wanted to do was to sleep and forget the girl he had struggled to bring to orgasm, forget it all. It was more real with whores. They made no demands, expected nothing, knew what it was all about and were usually attractive and clean, anyhow those with health certificates. And some of them had also been warm women, whatever people said – if they had been acting, then they had managed to fool him.

'And Smiley?' he said, although he knew the answer. Maybe he asked just to get her to go on talking about herself. He liked that. It excited him, not the fact that she worked the Motorway, but that she had revealed herself. His attraction to this large, dark woman was powerful and unmistakable.

'Yes, Smiley.' She managed a smile. 'Poor Smiley is my impresario, my great protector. My consolation and my burden. He picked me up out of the gutter – as he likes to express it – and sent me out on to the Motorway. But that was promotion, a step up the ladder. Don't think anything else. Better than working the side-streets and the disco cafés in the North West Zone, or outside the chemical factories in Saragossa where the boys go nuts from all the muck they breathe and *have* to have a little. . . . Smiley and I have been together for four or five years now. It's been good, and not so good, but it's been all right.'

She ran her finger cautiously over the swelling on her eye, now the colour of raw meat.

'Actually, it's not so tough working the Motorway as most people think. Motoring clients are not so interested in the good old-fashioned 'trip round the world' any longer. A poke in the old way is too much effort and takes too long. Most of them now want a 'speedway massage'. As they stamp on the accelerator, I tickle their G-strings a little, and when we get up to a hundred and eighty it's usually over and they have a wet patch on their ties. Lots of them find it difficult to get it up at all these days. Most manage it best that way. Just like poor Smiley.'

Allan burst out laughing, her directness delighting him and her knees hypnotizing him. She smiled herself, but was still clearly exhausted.

'Say, have you any coffee?'

'Coffee? Yes . . . yes, of course.'

He had a packet of substitute. It would mean short rations for them all in the week to come, he thought dutifully. But he had decided. He was elated, almost happy, in a better mood than for a long time, just because Mary Diamond was sitting there talking to him, exciting him with her chubby knees and hairy legs.

'It's only substitute,' he said as he poured the steaming brew into

149

two mugs. He had heated it up on the electric plate inside the stores. He put her mug down on the table beside the ashtray.

'That's pretty good,' she said. 'When you make coffee with bark and leaves and burnt nutshells, then you can talk about ersatz. That's what most people in the Palisade do.'

She thrust her hand inside the car rug and pulled out a flat flask.

'Here, something to strengthen us. They didn't find this, the bastards.'

She poured out a goodly helping into each mug.

'The only kind of liquor you can get hold of. I sometimes take a bottle in part-payment. Poor Smiley will have to manage without tomorrow. Cheers.'

She drank and winced as the strong liquid touched her sore lips, then swallowed and started to cough, clearing her throat with her hand in front of her mouth and spitting on the floor.

'Christ!' she gasped between two fits of coughing. 'You should see what those bastards have done to me.'

The fit passed and she struggled for breath.

'I've been lucky, actually. This is the first time they've gone for me. I know girls who've been totally wrecked after they've been done over. Some just disappear.'

'What did they do?'

'Oh, they came in a car, an unmarked car, of course, and stopped at the exit road where I was standing. By the time I saw they were the cops, it was too late to get away. One got out and asked for my health certificate. While I pretended to be looking for it, two more got out, grabbed me and hauled me into the car. I fought them off as best I could, but that wasn't much use. There were three of them. I think I tidied up one of them a bit, though.' With a wry smile she took another gulp from her mug.

'Then we drove up the hill.' She waved towards Abbott Hill. 'Two of them set about me while the third one held me. That is, one held me, another hit me and the third tried to have a poke while the jokers were at it, but that clearly didn't go all that well, so he started bashing me, too. In the end my head was singing. I came to when the car stopped and I heard them discussing what to do with me. It ended by them just tipping me out of the car. They took my bag. I lost my shoes, too, my lovely shoes.'

For the first time she showed signs of breaking. Her lips trembled and she was breathing heavily, but she went on.

'Things got even worse then. I at last got my head together and could start finding out where I was and getting down to the road, to some house or other. I thought I'd try to get someone to help me. I knocked on doors, but no one would open. Those that did just chased me away and some threatened to send for the police. I knew I was up the hill, but didn't know where. I asked them to tell me where I was and where I could get a cab, but they slammed the door in my face and shouted at me to go away. One had two great dogs. He said he he would set on me if I didn't shift. It was bloody awful.'

She was crying now, her head bowed and tears falling on to the rug.

'There's a mattress in the stores,' he said.

It was a little later and she had calmed down and been given another mug of coffee. He reckoned she was feeling better.

'And some blankets. You can sleep there tonight if you like.'

He had not even considered the pros and cons. He was quite sure, as sure as he had ever been of anything. She would spend the night with him.

'Great. Thanks, Allan.'

He had been certain she would accept. He had felt it coming all the time without having willed it, as if he had walked round her in decreasing circles since that first morning on the shore when he had seen her in the water, naked, arms up, glistening in the sun and water. His initial guardedness, given his fascination and the difficult situation it would create on the Dump with Smiley and Lisa, had restrained him. But that had gone now. He was only delighted by the attraction he felt for her, her fearless, almost brutal femininity, however battered and bruised at this moment. There was no doubt about it. She would stay with him that night.

As if she had been thinking along the same lines, she suddenly exclaimed: 'Allan, I *am* glad I found you! I don't know what I would've done if I hadn't got indoors. Left dying in a ditch, I suppose. When I saw I was on Abbott Hill Road, I had a faint hope. Lisa told me you worked here. But, God Almighty, what a long way it was to walk.'

They had finished their coffee and half emptied the bottle. The scratches on her face were red and inflamed and one eye was quite closed now, but she seemed to have got over the shock of her incident with the police.

'There are buses from here to the East Terminal in the morning,' he said. 'If you're lucky, you can get a connection.'

'Oh, I always get a lift.' She smiled, showing her stained teeth, then stretched. 'The bastards went off with my cigarettes. I suppose you haven't got any?'

'No. I can look, but I don't think. . . .'

'It's all right, look. . . .' She rummaged in the ashtray with her finger. 'Here's a long butt. I suppose you've got matches?'

Janson had a gas lighter in the top drawer of the counter. She leant forward as he lit it for her, then inhaled deeply.

'Ah. I feel almost human again. God, I'm tired, flaked out. Where did you say that mattress was?'

He looked at the clock on the wall. He was supposed to stay open until half past eleven. It was only half past nine. He went across and turned off three switches. The lights in the pumps and the lamp outside went out. He turned the key in the door.

'What are you doing?'

'Shutting up shop. Bedtime.'

She got up, the same height as him in her bare feet, and she smiled.

'Sorry to take your bed, Allan.'

'Maybe we can solve that problem.'

It was a naïve little game they were playing, as if both were impatient after the first physical contact, as if they wanted to make the transition from the old strangeness to this new closeness as quick as possible, as if neither of them had any time to lose. He quickly secured the drawer of ration coupons and badges and locked the cash register while she stood watching him. She knew and she was still smiling, although her weariness was like a stiff mask under the golden skin, subduing the lively dark eyes.

'My God, you're keen,' she said. 'You're the randiest man I've met for a long, long time. I've seen it all along, since that very first day, you know? It shows on you. Men don't react like you these days. The Lord of Creation has to have pills and massage to get it nowadays. But you . . . you sizzle in that good old way.'

Allan pulled the blind down over the door with a bang. He smiled at her. He knew that what she had said was true. He knew Sweetwater had not destroyed everything, not in him. He had felt his vital force growing stronger all the time they had been on the Dump, despite the bad food, hard work and the monotony. And he had never felt stronger than now when he was close to Mary Diamond.

23

Allan soon noticed that Smiley had begun to follow him around, and he was sure it was because of Mary and their relationship, although nothing was ever said.

Smiley's attention was not really either threatening or hostile. Basically, life went on as before. He and Smiley met more or less by chance and talked together, Smiley embroidering on his cynical philosophy of life and asking Allan for advice on various practical matters. Just before the rains started, the station wagon had heaved a last sigh, and with joint efforts, they had moved it to a place nearer to the camper where it was more concealed from any possible passers-by. Allan had also helped put up a ramshackle lean-to of corrugated iron to give them a place in the dry outside the car. That had finally done away with Smiley's loud-voiced illusion that his and Mary's stay on the Dump was of an ordinary nature. His earlier fear of 'being stuck in the muck' had become an acceptance of the fact. 'The first roof over my head I've been able to call my own – my first real home,' he declared, nodding at the lean-to at the back of the station wagon. So they became almost neighbours, and to start with Allan had not found it peculiar that Smiley kept appearing on some pretext or other, or with a question, or by 'chance' for a bit of company.

But after a while Allan began to see there was something else, a strange intensity, a mixture of curiosity, aggression and impotent fumbling behind Smiley's seeking contact.

He assumed that Smiley knew all about him and Mary. For all he knew, Mary herself might have told him, or anyhow admitted it if he had happened to ask. But although nothing had been said in so many words, it was as if what had happened and was happening between him and Mary had brought about a change in him, a change affecting everything he said and did, making itself known in every fibre of his own body. They must all have noticed. That could be due to only one thing . . . out there, where they were so close to each other, where one person concerned them all whether they thought so or not, it was not possible to keep anything of importance secret.

He knew Lisa had sensed it. She had seen and heard him discussing with Mary and Smiley the possibility of getting the station wagon going again, one evening when they had gone down to the camping van and were all sitting round the stove. She had realized

153

then, with some trepidation. She had seen it in his movements, his expressions, in his angular body every time he was close to Mary. Mary played it down, unaffected and neutral, but still in an aura of dreamy mystery which complemented his noisy cockiness. Lisa had been so sure she had asked him straight out that evening. 'You like Mary, don't you?' she had said, as if establishing a fact. He had replied 'Yes', without bothering to enlarge now that it was out in the open.

'So do I.'

No reproaches, no hysterical outburst. To Allan, she seemed almost relieved.

'I gave her my patent leather shoes. She was so pleased. She was so nice. She said she would come and see me, and help me when the baby comes. She's so elegant, so large and plump and dark. Don't you think so?'

'Yes.'

Nothing more was said between them, but he saw her occasionally looking anxiously at him when he had been over to see Smiley or had just been out looking for something – anxious and relieved, as if she feared he had been with Mary and was glad he had after all come back to her. It was true that he did sometimes waylay Mary on the Dump and beg or threaten her to pull her skirt up. She would look at him sideways, laugh scornfully and call him a guttersnipe, never satisfied. But she nonetheless agreed, gave in to him, warming him with the fire below her tiredness and boredom with all familiar things she had to do with him, a fire that brightened her eyes and put a sting in the bites she rewarded him with as they lay in a wreck of a bus. He had found a foam rubber mat in a corner, and the place was well suited to their activities, despite the rain trickling in on them through the leaking roof. Oddly enough, it was not easy to find a place to get together, if only for half an hour. Everything on the Dump had a kind of logic, objects as well as moods, guided by a transparent continuity, whether just waiting, resting, eating or sleeping.

But if Lisa's fears were that Allan was going to leave her, they were quite unfounded, for Allan's obsession with Mary was not such that he was willing to change his way of life. It worked quite well and in general he found it satisfactory, measuring his physical hunger according to Mary's generous contributions. At this stage there was no real conflict between the lives they all lived on the Dump, the stability so necessary to them, co-operation, the most necessary of all, and his sudden sexual whim. He had not given much thought to what his relationship with Mary might lead to. When he was close to her, the attraction was a stronger factor than considerations of reason. When he was away from her, the absence of her firm body often distracted him. But he had no clear alternative. They had to go on in this way out of necessity, and although he knew perfectly well his carelessness was putting their peaceful relations in danger, he found it impossible to fight against it. He could do nothing against the laws of nature.

Oddly, a new kind of tenderness grew in him towards Lisa and the burden she was carrying, once he had begun to satisfy his sexual desires elsewhere. He looked at her with a pride of possession, and the knowledge that he was to be a father again, the head of a growing family, a clan, filled him with something almost like intoxication, although he knew it would mean more work and greater responsibility. His delight was spontaneous and unreserved, just as his world of ideas had gradually lost subtlety and become almost primitive as it was gradually muddied with dirt and vermin, the task of finding their daily bread, the grey monotony which was their life in the camper. He saw the small movements of the foetus sharply outlined on Lisa's taut, white skin and in his simple, increasingly concrete world of ideas, he regarded that as a miracle.

'I talked to that old criminal quack,' said Smiley. 'But he hadn't anything he thought might be used to repair the pump. The old fox, he's sitting on a whole heap of spare parts, and he's damned if he's going let any of them go.'

Smiley was always dropping in for a chat, asking for advice or help with something, as if he could in that way keep an eye on Allan. Allan had suddenly become interesting as a person, even fascinating to him, although he never missed an opportunity to make him the target of his cynical sarcasm. Smiley had probably become less self-satisfied when it was clear Allan and Mary got together the moment an opportunity arose, but in exchange he had become more loquacious.

'The question is,' he went on, thumping his fist on the rusty bonnet, 'the question is, whether it's even worth considering. It would probably be possible to get it to go, sure – with the help of my gifted neighbour's technical skills, but how far and for how long? Presumably from here up to the Motorway – then crash bang,

boiling over and all cylinders cracked. That wouldn't be particularly desirable, my dear Allan, would it now? I, who am so bashful
when it comes to the cops. And also, this damned weather is taking
the last spark out of the battery.'

He was still dreaming about getting his old crate going again,
although Allan had told him numerous times it was not just the oil
pump. Smiley kept maintaining it was the only ideal justification
for being on the Dump and living in and off society's garbage, once
one was a freeloader, and there was no ideological alternative after
'theories' had 'collapsed under the weight of the actual collapse of
society'. He called himself an idealist, an aesthete and artist. He
wished to 'sit at a safe distance watching Rome burn', and turn the
sight into impressions in the excrement of technological civilization
he found around him (he *had* actually once started to work with a
'sculptor', but the job of collecting materials had proved too much
of an effort, so he had decided instead to proclaim the Dump as a
whole as the 'total work of art of the last epoch'). He went around
clearly feeling ill at the thought of his highly conventional means of
communication with the 'stinking old world of cadavers' having
broken down.

Allan listened as long as he could stand it. As far as he was
concerned their conversations usually ended in boredom and contempt for Smiley. Although Smiley had read a lot, was quick-witted
and always had a ready comment on anything, his tirades were
meaningless, had no content, a liturgy he threw himself into to
maintain all those lost illusions of power and self-respect by making
his fellow human beings uncertain and fearful – this untrustworthy,
impotent wreck of a man who sent his woman up on to the Motorway to earn his keep, who just talked and talked and could never *do*
anything.

They were leaning against the hard cold metal of the body of the
stationary vehicle, staring out into the rain.

Smiley's voice bleated on.

'He's got a lot of funny ideas, the old man. Crazy, of course, but
you have to admire him. Still an idealist after having lived for so
long on the tip. He believes in the alternative society. He thinks you
can opt out, begin again, get something *new* to grow. I think he
thinks it'll start out here on the Dump. With *us*.' Smiley burst into a
fit of convulsive, cackling laughter.

'What's so crazy about that?' said Allan. What Smiley had said
corresponded faintly with his own vague ideas on a continuation of

this life. They survived, despite everything. Co-operation had come about, a kind of understanding between the very different and individual people who had sought refuge there. Thinking like that produced optimism, gave him courage.

'Yes, didn't I think that,' said Smiley, rolling up his eyes. 'You're also one of those who believe it will go well, one of the faithful in the herd. You see,' he began, his malicious little eyes flickering from Allan's heavy features to the dirty earth floor of the corrugated iron shed, then out into the desolate grey of the rain still pouring down, 'you see, you can't escape what you're dependent on. You wouldn't survive many days if Sweetwater weren't there.' He pointed out into the mist. 'Supplying you with work, things you have to buy, the garbage we live off out here. D'you see? You're as dependent on Sweetwater as fleas are on a dog's back.'

'No.'

Allan had to think hard. What Smiley had said was true up to a point, but not entirely.

'No,' he repeated. 'Maybe it was like that to start with, but it's changing. We buy less and less because there's so little to be had. There's less and less to find on the Dump, because nearly everything edible gets ruined by the rain. We live mostly on vegetables I get from the allotments. Like the ones Doc grows. We'll soon be living on nothing else *but* things we can find for ourselves. We're becoming less and less dependent.'

'Do you really think you'll get away with it?' said Smiley. 'You haven't a hope, unless you go right back to the caveman stage. Well, perhaps we'll all end up there. Let's look at that possibility. Let's call it a primitive society, shall we? A tribe. OK? A primitive society also has its own structure. It has to have a certain number of members, a minimum of a few hundred or so, I think, so the work burden is shared – and anyhow enough to defend themselves against enemies – primitive societies have a great many enemies – to prevent inbreeding and degeneration, enough to prevent fighting over the women. . . .'

He grinned. 'And so on. You can't tell me you seriously mean to create a "society" with eight or nine people, two old people, a deaf-mute idiot who also happens to be dangerous, and a little girl half-dead from pregnancy.'

Allan clenched his teeth. Smiley's grin broadened. He knew he had him now.

'And,' he went on, 'people like you and me, not to mention the others, are unsuited to creating any kind of society. We are marked by the mortally sick society we come from, I'll have you know. We *represent it* with the mark of death on our foreheads. We are the *distillation* of what has gone wrong in society. How could we create anything new and different?'

'Oh, shut up, for Christ's sake.'

He couldn't stand any more of this sermonizing, this mixture of self-satisfaction and self-contempt. Everything Smiley said made much less impression on him than it had before. He had heard it all before. It was nothing new and no longer frightening. Smiley's talk was his way of looking on life. The more he went on about their dismal outlook, the more he laid it on thick about the fears to come when the 'apocalypse' arrived, the more peculiar, theoretical and harmless his talk seemed to be. Allan admitted he was right in some respects. His prognoses were based on intelligent observation and knowledge, but he also managed to reduce everything to a subject of conversation, his apocalypse becoming an exhibit, relative and measurable, which could be regarded from this or that angle, his attitude to it presuming *something afterwards*, a condition not unlike the one they were in, in which theories and arguments could be checked. It presumed that *nothing* happened – not in reality – at all. Smiley's cynical pessimism was camouflage for superficiality, for lacking a grasp of what was *really* happening.

The opposite applied to Allan. He felt it in him. He felt decay to be a process threatening him physically and mentally. He could feel the dissolution of society threatening the very nerve of his life. Without reflecting on it, he had seen degeneration affecting most people's forms of life together and creating crippled mutations in human nature. Degradation, simplification and brutalization had become part of the life expected in Sweetwater. He had seen it, noting it almost intuitively and acting accordingly. He had moved out to the Dump. That had turned out to be possible. They lived primitively and wretchedly. They were gradually losing the thin shell of 'civilization', more sophisticated skills little by little wearing off, but it was possible to live there, while it was no longer possible to live in Sweetwater. He felt the will to win in himself, to survive in any conditions, with no outlook or hope beyond living from day to day. *That* was the difference between him and Smiley.

'So the child of nature does not like being reminded of nature's unpredictable odds against the individual?'

Smiley was enjoying provoking Allan out of his usual torpor. He knew Allan also knew he talked mostly for the sake of talking, to keep his unease and thoughts of the impossible at bay, but he went on because it stimulated him to try to disturb the sluggishness like protective armour round his taciturn neighbour, immunizing him against their terrible conditions, the boredom, the stench, the rats, the wretched food. Though he shouldn't complain. Mary often brought back delicacies which the others had to do without, if they even knew they existed. But that made no difference. Did Allan have the diarrhoea, he wondered, which had plagued him ever since he had come out there?

And now the rain, pouring down day in and day out, only occasionally letting up, the great clouds apparently welding earth and sky together into a sticky grey dough soaking up more and more moisture, making the paths impassable – all things which drove Smiley to despair and certainly would have broken him if he hadn't had the possibility of 'strengthening himself', as he so arrogantly called it. So it cheered him up, for instance, to be able to rock the equilibrium of this stubborn, silent man.

'To survive, or not to survive,' Smiley declaimed, as if feeling his way, trying to find out whether the situation could take another push. 'Does it really matter? The best don't necessarily survive, you know. The best die in battle if they're not too intelligent to fight at all. Perhaps they don't care and are the first to go under in the dog fight? No, the best don't survive, but the next best do, and the third best.'

'Oh, shut up, Smiley.' Allan waved his hand, as if Smiley's talk caused him physical discomfort, and when he spoke it was almost reluctantly, as if arguing with Smiley took all his strength away.

'You're just as scared as the rest of them, Smiley. You don't deceive anyone. You think it helps jawing away about defeat and catastrophe, while in reality you're pissing in your pants with terror. If the worst comes to the worst, you'll lie there drinking to stay alive just like the rest of us. If you think about it, you know you're a coward, Smiley. Aren't I right? You aren't even a bloody man. So you're scared to death. So you have to keep on preaching. You haven't it in you, Smiley, and you know it.'

Then he knew he had gone too far. His irritation, the contempt that had suddenly welled up in him, had made him say too much, bringing what really lay fermenting between them into the open. He shouldn't have brought Smiley's manhood into the argument. Not that he feared he would be defeated in open confrontation with Smiley, but something told him that that must not happen yet, not now when neither of them could foresee the extent of the consequences, now when they all needed the equilibrium that had been built up between them on the Dump.

But Smiley let it go. He feared physical violence more than anything. His flickering mind turned rage and hurt pride into irony, a crushing sarcasm, and his vengeful scorn could make long detours before striking again in camouflaged counter-attacks. He knew Mary slept with Allan and in itself that did not worry him, but it irritated him that she went with Allan for nothing, free, like a lovesick schoolgirl, and the thought that she might have talked to him about private matters, which the kind of reference Allan had just made indicated, infuriated him. With tremendous force, he flung the iron bolt he had been fingering, and the crash as it hit a tin can echoed back at them through the rain. But there was no other sign of Smiley's rage. He just sighed, grinned and scratched his stubble.

'No,' he said. 'It's not easy to be a hero these days, if that's what you mean. Neither in bed, nor anywhere else.' He laughed shrilly, peering suspiciously at an empty bottle between his legs. He saw Allan had relaxed, so slowly and carefully he began his reprisal. He yawned, stretched and rubbed his hands.

'Oh, if only a man had something to strengthen himself with. . . .' He kicked angrily at the bottle. 'Not even any bloody booze here. By the way, Mary's over with that huckster with a bowler hat, Felix. Isn't that his name? To get some stuff. Last week he had Deep Purple, first class goods. God knows where he gets hold of it.'

'Does Felix deal in that kind of stuff?'

Allan had never really fathomed what kind of 'business' Felix ran. He occasionally saw him trudging towards the gate in the evening, always with Run-Run a few steps behind him, and sometimes he met them in the morning on their way back, often carrying goods of various kinds. He guessed it was largely foodstuffs, in boxes and plastic bags. But what Felix actually did in Sweetwater at night he had never found out. The information about drugs surprised him because he knew Deep Purple was one of the most sought-after and therefore the most expensive of the lot, and that it was very difficult to get hold of. If Felix could get Deep Purple, he could get anything.

'Of course. The guy's a mobile apothecary. Didn't you know? Or perhaps it doesn't mean anything to you when you don't touch such dangerous substances?'

Smiley grinned. Allan's temperance was also a source of amusement to him.

'What does he take in payment?'

The question was automatic. It was all largely a matter of getting hold of things, things they needed, where one could get hold of what, and what it cost. But Smiley's malicious grin told him that he shouldn't have asked the question.

'Guess.'

Smiley could hardly restrain his laughter, his slanting little eyes watering with amusement and derision.

'I don't know.'

Allan shook his broad shoulders and looked away, the answer at last dawning on him. Smiley licked his lips.

'What do you think my capital consists of, Allan, eh? My policy in life, my long-term investment? Do I have to write it large for you? You must have realized that it is our Mary who is my method of payment in this contemptible world. That's what it's come to. Shocking, isn't it? Life can turn out that villainous, and that's how you have to take it, at arm's length, if you're to have a chance.'

Mary, Mary Diamond lay like an unexplored landscape between them, tempting on the one side, threatening on the other, with her swelling corpus, smell of artificial rosewater and sweet sweat. They preferred not to talk about her as they circled round each other, growling and snarling, but not really wanting to measure up each other's strength. But Smiley was excited now, and his crazy mind, his perverted jealousy made him go on.

'I really do think you're looking quite cross, Allan, old man. Thinking I'm a bastard, eh, using Mary like that? Thinking perhaps it's a wicked shame, exploiting and abusing the girl in that way? But your conventional little mind is wrong, I'm afraid. On the contrary, she's enormously indebted to me. Listen to me now. I found her five or six years ago out in the West Zone. She was washing up and scrubbing floors in a dance café in North West Avenue, and in between she was freely sharing her treasures, if you understand what I mean – I'm sure you do – generously between motor bike mobs, lorry drivers and anything bumming around North West Avenue.'

He glanced at Allan as he spoke, as if to make sure his story was having the required effect.

161

'Mary, yes. At the time she was nothing but a dirty little tart. I'll never forget the first time I saw her, on a motor bike, bent over the petrol tank going at top speed down North West Avenue, her skirt up under her arms and tail up on the nose of the man driving. I followed in the old rattletrap – her great buttocks were glowing in the sunset! Her friend was standing up in the stirrups poking away – some kind of sport they were carrying on – faster and faster – they drove like madmen out towards the Desert Hills. I lost them. Nothing can keep up with a heavy bike on a good road. But I couldn't forget what I'd seen. Then I met her by chance one day in the cafeteria. I offered her a job and she took it on. She was my model. I was an "artist" at the time. In between she kept my bed warm and cooked and cleaned the place. Then the art began to go to hell, so we got more and more into photography, specialist stuff for advanced tastes, you know . . . and then finally we took the step and moved out to Roadside City, where I had a contact. That's how it went, Comrade Allan. If I hadn't picked her up, she'd still be scrubbing café floors and fucking for small change. If abortions hadn't finished her off. A girl with that background can't improve her situation, you see. She's got a lot to thank me for, Mary has. I'm the one who's made her what she is, perhaps nothing all that marvellous, but a good deal better than what she was. I provide her with a fixed point in her life, a certain security, kindness when required, love to the extent that my deplorable physical constitution permits. She doesn't need anything else. She knows nothing else. It binds her to me for good or evil, "for better, for worse" – isn't that how it goes?'

He glanced at Allan's sullen face. Self-deprecation was Smiley's most effective weapon and it pleased him to take a dig at his rival's reserve, which he was sure included a moralistic attitude. Despite his jealousy, Smiley seemed immensely cheered at the thought that Allan had perhaps gone and *fallen in love* with Mary, so he *had* to run her and himself and their relationship down as much as possible, in order to get at Allan, too.

Allan got up off the box he had been sitting on so abruptly, he tipped it over.

'You're a creep, Smiley. A loathsome toad. Do you know that?'

'Now, now, old boy. . . .'

Smiley had started at Allan's abrupt movement, and the fury in those sharp eyes, the indignation in the feeble accusation made him wonder if he had gone too far – but he couldn't stop himself or hide the snicker behind his words.

'Take it easy, man. Surely you don't want our cultivated little chat to end in a degrading physical brawl? Fisticuffs over the right of the strongest to say what he wants to say? Do you? Surely you don't want barbarity let loose in this little paradise, do you? It's rather old-fashioned to fight with bare fists over the honour of a woman, don't you think? And think of the consequences. What do you think you'll achieve by bringing a dictatorship of muscle power to the Dump? You'd just hasten your own defeat, my dear chap. If you once let that demon loose, there'll always be another enemy after *you*, lying in wait behind the next mound of rubbish. And so on. The shell of civilization is very thin these days, you know. It has enough cracks in it out here as it is. I'll have to keep an eye on you all so that we don't revert back to the Stone Age or even further. Before time. . . .'

Smiley's flabby, unwashed face was glistening, sweat pouring off it and running down his neck. His face could not really tolerate daylight. It seemed to be dissolving into obesity, filth and sweat, its shape more and more indeterminate every day. So he persisted with his tirades, touching on things firmer and harder than himself, something which would define him, even if it had to be confrontation. Reconciliation had crept into his voice now. He had performed his number and had taken his revenge. He was afraid Allan would leave him alone for a long grey afternoon. His helplessness was now clearly visible, an attraction to his rival, his dependency on his solidity, on security, the strength visible under that slow, taciturn manner.

'Not going yet, are you, old man? Not going to let all this chatter of mine deprive you of the good atmosphere, are you?'

But the joke fizzled. Allan could no longer be bothered to look at him.

'You talk too much, Smiley,' he said. 'You should get on and do something instead. You'll rot away if you stay here talking your head off. See you. . . .'

He stepped out into the rain as if it were an effort to drag himself away from Smiley's company, as if he realized he had to watch out so as not to sink into the clutches of this weakling trying to make him stay.

24

Smiley's talk changed nothing in Allan's attitude to his new woman. She came to him almost every weekend, and they spent the night together on the mattress in the store. She said she came because he asked her to, and because she had to be on her way relatively early the next morning for the Sunday exodus, so the PAC station was a practical stopover for her, and he never pressed her to make any special concessions for him. It was enough that she came and stayed the night with him. It was enough that his hunger was stilled, at least to start with. Then he gradually realized the longing for her he had first regarded as exclusively sexual encompassed her whole presence there, everything they did together, everything they discussed, although they never talked much. Details he had scarcely noticed before suddenly became significant, her actual presence making the job he was gradually beginning to loathe reasonably bearable. Her physicality, her smell, her voice, the way she carried herself and did things all soothed him, the semi-derelict PAC station almost becoming a pleasant environment where he liked to be.

They were well suited to each other, sexually, too. He had never before been with anyone who answered better to his idea of what a woman should be, so fleshy, so robust. She would match him tempestuously, whatever he thought up. She could even take the initiative in moments of enthusiasm, overwhelming him with special desires, enjoyable arts her life had not managed to spoil. She knew much more than he did – he was more unimaginative, only violent when desire came over him – he could only pull out all the stops together with her. Yet it made him uncertain and uneasy when afterthoughts came and put what they were doing into larger contexts. There was nothing 'wild' or 'animal' in what he and Mary did together. He had no regrets over having let it 'go too far', as he often had when he had hungered for Lisa in the days before she became pregnant and retreated from him. With Mary, everything seemed to happen in harmony, from their very depths – it *couldn't* go 'wrong'. She affected everything around her with her sensuality, and satisfying himself in her embrace was only part of a continuity, an expression of a state both before and after their climax, expressed in other ways. He had never been so satisfied with anyone before, and although she had in no way committed herself to their relationship, apart from being unwilling to take any payment from him, although he had offered it, her warmth and generosity were the only confirmation he needed. She was his woman. Nothing could change that.

Nonetheless, he took care of Lisa in his clumsy way, as if no conflict existed between his life as husband and as Mary's lover from Saturday evening to Sunday afternoon. He was as considerate as possible to his wife, though that became more and more difficult as her pregnancy advanced. Every week he filled up the petrol tank of Sweetness' old car without registering the sale in exchange for foodstuffs. He took back all the vegetables he could find and also managed to get a jar of vitamin pills on the black market in return for various car accessories he stole from what was left in the stores.

He had conferred with Doc to reassure himself all was well with Lisa, but Doc stressed that she was anaemic and that she must not exert herself in the weeks to come. Doc knew about his double life and Allan thought he heard a note of reproach in the old man's voice when they touched on the subject. But he ignored it. To the extent that he could understand, he considered Doc's moral attitudes old-fashioned and inapplicable in their situation.

But the care Doc took of Lisa comforted him. The old man and Lisa seemed to have become more intimate recently, since Doc had become aware of his unfaithfulness. Their growing friendship relieved Allan of some responsibility. As things grew more difficult and the danger to her health and the unborn child's grew greater, he found it more and more difficult to behave as the situation demanded. He could be considerate up to a point, but then impatience took over. He was unable to overlook aspects of Lisa's condition, or even the thought of illness or impairment as a whole. It irritated him, and that made him feel inadequate, even guilty. A whole evening in the cramped camper, now even more cramped because she was *there* most of the time, her questioning, reproachful looks, her pathetic little requests for various meaningless things, for help with this and that, were all enough to put him in state of feverish, even aggressive restlessness. Fortunately Doc made sure she had most of what she needed and that lightened this uncomfortable burden.

Allan did not really think of himself as living a double life, largely because it had never really been a secret that he and Mary went together. He looked on it as the result of inevitable development – a fact no one could overlook, but nor did anyone comment. Apart from Lisa's anxious references at times when she was feeling lost and helpless, and Smiley's harangues, this tacit agreement was accepted. To him, he simply had another wife, and it seemed natural for him to be able to meet Mary regularly to feel 'complete'.

165

A bus still ran past the Dump into the East Terminal and he took it every Saturday. But it was becoming more and more irregular and no one knew whether it was going to be cancelled, like so many others. The crush and suffocating atmosphere had grown worse, as had the terminal, the waiting, the change of bus and then the long, dreary trip through the suburbs out to Abbott Hill Road. The route went through the area of newer high-rises and older houses due for demolition, gaps, building sites and barren land. From there he could see the Motorway swooping up towards the sky and disappearing behind Abbott Hill, then appearing again and curving across the bay. He knew the route inside out now, every minute of it, every wretched metre.

Allan still reckoned people kept their distance from him, even in the crowded bus. Perhaps it was his smell, but they smelt, too, of sweat, cheap soap, fusty flats and unclean clothing. But he smelt of the Dump and that was different. However much he washed and tidied his hair and beard before leaving so as not to attract attention, there was something about him, something suspicious, which made people shy away from him. He kept away from them and they kept away from him. Fragments of conversations he overheard seemed more and more meaningless and became a kind of mental torture, reminding him of what he had had to bear in his previous life in Sweetwater.

Thinking about Mary and what they would do shortened the journey, though that didn't vary much. There weren't many opportunities at the PAC station. But he liked it that way, pleased with the order it entailed, something he could grasp. His life seemed to have been simplified and now required that. He found it impossible to follow up possibilities, even unthinkable to adapt to the shapelessness of city life again. He thought of the delights to come and felt warmth rising in him.

Autumn had come and it was colder at night, but he left the electric plate on full blast in the stores to warm it up. The waste of electricity would be found out one day, but he did not care. Nor did he care about the free petrol to Sweetness, or the car rugs he had taken from the stores and then back to the Dump for the winter. Anyhow, he knew he would not be at the station much longer.

At the terminal a plump whore glanced suspiciously at him as he sat alone on a bench waiting for his connection. Her bottom bobbed under her cheap skirt and excited him into a state of expectation. Mary's buttocks. He saw them in front of him, golden and majestic, folds of fat and furrows as she bent over the counter and let him in when he wanted it that way.

Dirty grey daylight was trickling down on to him through the vast, transparent plastic dome of the terminal. A queue had formed over by the loading bay of one of the supermarkets, mostly elderly, shabby people. It was Saturday afternoon and some of the shops were already closed. They were probably waiting for the rubbish bins put out after closing time in the hope of finding something they could sell, or eat, among the remains. . . .

He got off at the usual place. For the last stretch he had been the only passenger, and the weary driver let him out with a glance in the rear mirror. He still had a short walk to the PAC and found it good to use his legs, although the hard pavement seemed uncomfortable and unnatural to walk on.

The rain had stopped and the fresh cool wind made him wonder if autumn had come for good. Doc reckoned Lisa was due in the second week in December, and although she was not very good at working it out herself, the moment was approaching.

A car came towards him and went straight on, a low, fast limousine, well kept and glittering, an older model. He glanced at it, his mind full of the change in the weather. It was full of young men and for a moment he thought he recognized a face behind large sunglasses. But the vehicle accelerated and roared down the empty street, the roar of the engine echoing against the silent houses, and Allan soon forgot it once it was out of sight and the noise had subsided. He turned his head to the wind and sniffed the spicy smell of autumn, or was it smoke? Any change was enlivening after the weeks and weeks of rain. He could also see gaps in the heavy clouds in the west – a reddish patch on the dark horizon above Saragossa. Was it going to clear up?

Suddenly there was an explosion, a dull boom, so near that for a moment he was blinded by the dazzling light, and the pressure of the wind took his breath away. A great black cloud of smoke rose and flames flickered up only two or three streets away. Then he knew, and he ran towards the fire as fast as he could, sensing that it was already too late and dangerous to go near if any petrol was still in the tanks. But he ran all the same, the smell of burning in his nostrils and the crackle and deafening roar of flames drowning everything else, even the sound of his own footsteps.

The station was a mass of flames soaring out of the twisted remains of the pumps. The explosion had blown out the front of the office building, which was now a gigantic bonfire. Broken glass crunched under his feet, and bits of melted plastic from the roof, which had exploded into a thousand pieces, were now melting on the pavement and sticking to the soles of his shoes. There was no one in sight except a man hurrying away up the street. Another man hastily retreated into a doorway as Allan raced past. Then he was suddenly faced with Sweetness barring his way, grabbing him and trying to say something, his jaws trembling as he repeated something over and over again.

'Dead. He's dead. Nothing to be done. Dead. Blown to bits. Nothing to be done. Quite dead.' Sweetness went on and on, his eyes rolling as if he had gone mad. . . .

Allan pushed the man aside, then he ran over to the figure behind the ruined rubbish bins under an advertisement for odour-free, smoke-free PINK-PAC. The plastic paint on it was bubbling, hissing and cracking. Janson was badly hurt, his face bleeding from cuts, his hands, arms and chest burnt, his hair and most of his clothing burnt away. The heat scorched Allan's eyeballs as he grabbed Janson's ruined hands and started pulling him away from the fire on to the pavement. At least he would be relatively safe there for a moment. The effort after all that running was great, but terror gave him the strength. After about fifty metres down the street, he could go no further and he heaved the lifeless old man into an entrance, praying that the fire had not yet got to the main tank. He could see faces in some windows, but no one on the street. The roar of the fire followed them into the narrow entrance, the light reddish and darkened by drifting clouds of smoke. It had started to drizzle again.

His head was now spinning. He dragged the unconscious Janson in towards the courtyard and put him down so that the rain fell on his face, then waited, his heart thumping and throat aching. Janson couldn't be dead, could he? A rattling groan came from those ruined lips and a moment later the eyes opened and Janson was looking wildly at Allan, crazed with pain. Then he opened his mouth slightly and let out a howl like an animal in agony. Frightened, Allan put his hand over the mouth and pressed the head down.

'It's Allan!' he shouted into the old man's ear. 'It's Allan! Tell me what happened. I'll get help.'

Far away he could hear the wail of sirens.

Allan was trembling all over. He had no idea why he had risked his life to save the old man, and his mind was full of questions. What had happened? He *had* to find out. If he gave up and ran off, as every impulse told him to do – more and more so as the seconds ticked by – that would be accepting that 'fate' shaped his life just as it does an animal's. The accident and the fire had nothing to do with him and there was no reason for him to run blindly away as his instinct told him to, but what human pride still remained in him told him to *stay*, stay until he *knew*, until he *understood*, then act accordingly. He wanted to raise the alarm, get help for the old man, but he hesitated, sensing that he had to be careful, that he was in danger, although Janson was dying in front of his eyes. He *had* to find out what had happened first.

'What happened?' he shouted again. Janson crumpled, apparently lifeless. Allan shook him cautiously, then moistened the palms of his hands and put them on Janson's forehead. The old man's face was battered and horribly burnt down one side, almost unrecognizable. Allan could feel his own teeth chattering.

Janson groaned again, but his eyes did not open as he struggled to say something.

'Allan . . .' he at last managed to say, 'Allan, is that you?'

'Yes! Yes, it's me.'

'You must get away, Allan.' The voice rose and it took a few moments before the old man could find the strength to go on.

'You must go . . . if the cops find you. . . .'

'But what happened? You must tell me.'

'Roy Indiana,' groaned Janson. 'Roy Indiana and his buddies. They came. . . .' The pain seemed gradually to lift from his body and his voice was clearer, but Janson kept his eyes closed, as if able to fight back better that way and hold on to whatever spark of life he had left.

'They came in a car . . . they beat me up. They all hit me . . . hit and kicked me . . . then they must have set the place alight. They left me there. I had to drag myself out, but I couldn't put it out. Then it blew up. . . .'

Allan was lying across Janson with his ear to the old man's mouth. Roy Indiana. So it *was* him he had seen in the car, today as well as a few months back. The same car. The same gang. But he hadn't thought about it before. Roy had come to take his revenge, robbing and murdering a defenceless old man.

'You must go, Allan,' Janson wheezed. But Allan stayed. He wanted to assure him, to say help was on the way and everything would be all right, but he knew it was useless. Janson's voice was now almost inaudible as he started slipping into unconsciousness.

'Get away!' The old man managed to put real urgency into the warning. 'If they find you here, you'll get the blame for everything. No use talking to the cops. If they find you, you're finished. They'll make you confess to anything. The swine! Go now. I'm finished anyhow.'

Allan could hear sirens coming closer and someone running along the street. Perhaps the fire was spreading? Perhaps people were escaping from houses round about?

'Away . . .' mumbled Janson. 'Hurry . . . the bastards. . . .'

Allan hesitated, then he wrenched his eyes away from the disfigured face and ran.

He ran through into the back and climbed over the high fence between two buildings, to land in a pool of mud and dirt which had once been a garden bed, some cabbage stalks protruding out of the puddles. He was across the garden in a couple of strides, over another fence and found himself on open ground, the fire roaring on his left. He ran gasping in a great detour, trampling over dumps and abandoned sites, the sirens wailing nearby now. But he was well away. He raced clear of the high-rises, heading blindly, by instinct for the hill and the Motorway. He fell into a foul-smelling stream and crawled along it until he thought he was safely clear of the fire. Then he was faced with a wire netting fence round a garden, a little hut and low fences to right and left. He realized where he was – the allotments. He could breathe more easily and his fear receded. He ran on.

25

Allan decided he ought to teach Boy to read. After the fire it was a relief to think about spending time and energy on something of that kind. He had always intended to take on the boy's schooling and he was nearly old enough now. Allan was also troubled about the way Boy withdrew more and more from them both and spent more and more time with Run-Run.

He had found some old magazines he thought he would use at first. They were full of brightly coloured pictures, the print easy to read, both the headings and in the many advertisements.

But it did not go as well as he had hoped. Boy was restless and resistant, and Allan himself found it almost impossible to concentrate for any length of time. He expected far too much and couldn't understand why Boy couldn't even learn the letters of the alphabet or even string a few simple words together. He realized he was not good at explaining. He kept repeating what he had said before, when it was obvious the boy had not understood. Even when he applied himself, the words and sentences he used were awkward and clumsy, and made no impression on the sullen little boy. Allan grew more and more impatient and irritable as he persisted.

It was no better when he tried to get the boy interested by reading aloud to him from the magazines. He found that he himself read very badly, and then the total meaninglessness of what he was reading soon reduced him to silence. The brightly coloured pictures of handsome houses, lovely white towns, unrecognizable people, blue seas and skies in unimaginable far countries made him feel ill at ease. The pictures of scantily dressed women – quite unlike women, in unnaturally contorted positions and with blank smiling faces – also gave him a feeling of unreality, as well as a tiresome erection.

The lessons usually ended with him losing his temper, shouting at the boy and sending his totally unaffected and probably grateful pupil back to his secret pursuits elsewhere.

It sometimes weighed heavily on Allan that yet another chance of contact with his son had been lost, but it never occurred to him that the lack of communication between him and Lisa might be the reason. For long periods, their conversations were reduced to one syllable words and grunts and gestures, signs they both understood because the monotony of their way of life meant that there was no need for anything else.

With Run-Run, Boy picked up skills with enthusiasm and showed an impressive ability to absorb them. He and the dumb man had become inseparable and went all over the Dump looking for edible plants or useful articles. Allan was often amazed how practical the boy's knowledge was. He had learnt to make fire with the metal rods that could be found everywhere. He lit fires with the synthetic upholstery material and there was always furniture to be found, in all stages of disrepair.

He could tell the difference between half a dozen edible plants and knew where to find them. They dried the leaves up on the camper roof to make tea or to put in soups. They chewed on roots and stems which were tasty and stilled their hunger. The juice of a small cactus even produced a slightly alcoholic effect, while other plants gave off strong scents, and he also knew which were poisonous.

Boy had also made himself a pair of shoes when the sandals Allan had made for him had rotted on his feet in the wet. He had cut rubber from an old tyre, flattened and softened it, then sewed them together with thongs, all under Run-Run's supervision.

Otherwise they went fishing and set snares for birds, but Allan said that was a waste of time for there were no fish in the bay and everyone knew it. The only birds they ever saw were the crows always flapping and shrieking above the tips. And who wanted to catch crows?

He was surprised how clever and quick to learn his previously backward son turned out to be, and the understanding between him and Run-Run seemed excellent, as if words were superfluous between them. Perhaps the reason why the boy did not want to communicate with them was because companionship with the dumb man was instructive and productive enough?

Within a week, the weather had cleared sufficiently for them to go out on to the fields between the end of Doc's garden and the foundations of the Motorway. Maize grew wild over the old service road right up to the semi-derelict or demolished huts on the sites of the old houses. The maize had seeded itself year after year and become a wilderness of stiff, shoulder-high stems bearing fist-sized maize cobs.

They took with them as many sacks as they could find as they trampled a path through the hard maize stems, Doc, Run-Run, Boy and Allan. Smiley had also joined them, not, as he said, to participate in their agricultural day-dream, but to collect enough to make himself a keg of maize beer. They picked what they could find, following Doc's advice and leaving some cobs so there would be some the following year. Doc showed them how the fields were growing smaller each year, the undergrowth slowly covering the open ground. They ought perhaps to clear some of it, he said, raising his voice almost to a shout to make himself heard above the noise from the Motorway.

Although the maize cobs were not all that plentiful, there was more than they could carry back in one day, so they went back the next day, all except Smiley, who was totally exhausted and complaining of blisters and a bad back.

'Oh, no, let me live as it says somewhere "like the lilies in the field",' he moaned. 'Why on earth did I get involved in this madness? I'm useless at gathering and hunting. Anyhow it's bad to eat those things growing under the Motorway. The damned stuff must have a lead content as great as lead shot.'

They quite often scared small birds away from the ripe maize and Doc noticed there were more of them that year.

'I think they're on the increase,' he said. 'That means the pollution content is lower than when they reckoned it was unprofitable to grow things here. And there's less traffic too.'

He still had to shout to be heard.

Allan thought Doc's concern for small birds sentimental and time-consuming, a luxury. Food had become harder to find on the Dump, but whenever he had found nests, he had destroyed them, although they were deserted at that time of year.

A hare might leap up in front of them on those mornings and Run-Run's lightning hand at once dived for his knife, but by then the hare had already vanished into the tall grass.

'Perhaps all for the best,' said Doc. 'It may have been a female with young. Then there'll be more next year.'

Run-Run grinned and nodded his agreement, his fingers up in the air — ten-twenty-thirty.

'It's our only hope.' Doc had stopped to rest and to look across what was now virgin territory. 'Our best hope is that the wilderness will take back this area right up to Abbott Hill and further. Building has stopped in the East Zone for the time being and people are getting out of the city, anyhow those that can. Grass and bushes will soon grow through the asphalt and we'll have the wilderness right up to the harbour area, to the East Terminal.'

'He's a romantic old fool!' snapped Smiley, when Allan told him this. Day-dreams of that kind had existed fifty years ago. Breaking new land out in the 'wilderness'. Alternative living in harmony with the elements, far away from destructive civilization and its technology and filth. 'Yeah, that's an old story. Don't you know it takes a third of an acre to cover the *needs* of every *single* person if you *really* want to be self-sufficient? Do you know how many people live in Sweetwater? Then work out just what acreage is required so that *everyone* could have the luxury of living off the land and nothing

173

else. Do you know how many inhabitants this country has? Do you know what the total acreage is? Do you know how much is culti-vated? Do you know how much of it is *cultivatable*? No. Well, I can tell you the figures are interesting. And nor can you tell me what we are to do with the nine-tenths of the population there simply won't be room for in this natural paradise. Eh? We haven't a hope in heaven, my boy. Nature spat us out a hundred years or so ago when we became her enemy. Things have got worse and worse ever since. We are totally dependent on things going on as they are, on tech-nology, on mass production and intensive farming and all the rest. That's the grisly truth. For us just as it is for all other wretches.'

Then he reverted to his usual grin and looked at Allan.

'Well, speech over. That was Smiley the speaker of the truth, the autodidactic sociologist, ecologist and historian Smiley, letting off steam, the amateur student Smiley, who at one time spent a lot of time in libraries because they were warm. Ha. Meanwhile, we can be pleased we are *here* and not *there*, with some chance of surviving a *little* longer than that lot in the vale of tears. So one can allow oneself the pleasure of reflecting on the state of the nation, and perhaps hope the plague will dispose of the nine-tenths. Or that they will start cutting each other's throats. You never know. These corn cobs taste good with salt and a bit of fat, provided you haven't dug into our winter store yet. I'm eating mine now. Who knows if I'll live long enough to enjoy them later.'

Felix stayed discreetly in the background as always, but his part in the small community on the Dump had grown considerably after the fire had put an end to things they were still dependent on. Felix had connections everywhere and could acquire almost anything. Nothing was too insignificant or too much trouble for him to deal in.

Felix and Run-Run no longer lived in their ramshackle labyrinth of crates. They had found a more or less intact old van and with some help, they had humped it down the path to a spot quite close to the camping van. So now they all lived nearer to each other, with the camper a kind of central point. This also meant they became a little closer to each other's lives and had found out more about each other's daily activities. Felix seldom showed himself and no one really knew what he was up to. Allan reckoned he spent some of his time keeping his clothes in order. Even in the wet spell he was impeccably dressed, somewhat frayed here and there, but always clean and well-pressed. The dirt seemed to have second thoughts before adhering to his well-worn but always highly polished shoes, the only remnant of the drama that had brought these two strange brothers to the Dump and thus thrown them all together. Those shoes – and Police Constable Joseph Bean's identity papers Allan had hidden carefully just in case. . . .

Felix liked taking orders for things he could get through his own special channels, and in exchange he accepted what they had or found on the Dump, workable tools, household equipment, suit-cases, trunks and the occasional ornament that could be refur-bished and regarded as an 'antique'. He had recently had requests for bicycle parts and even whole bicycles, now much favoured on the black market in the back streets of Sweetwater. He accepted any wearable clothing and leather (provided it was not mouldy or rotting), footwear, panes of glass, and also gramophone records and books. Nothing was too ordinary or difficult for him to handle if there was a chance of a profit. In exchange he took bread-flour mix, soup concentrate and fats, tins of vegetable bacon, coffee substitute, detergents – much of it from military emergency camps, or so it seemed from the packaging. Very occasionally, Felix managed to get hold of some fresh meat, not the best, of course, usually fat and fibrous belly meat, pieces of backbone and bones for soup, but it was all received with enthusiasm because it could be made into stews which lasted for days.

Felix and Run-Run went into the city every evening at dusk, Felix first with a suitcase or bag full of barter goods and Run-Run at a suitable distance behind with an even heavier load. They left far too late to catch a bus, so no one knew how they covered the twenty kilometres into the city centre where most of the trading was said to go on.

One day Boy came back with a large bird he had caught, its wings almost touching the ground as he silently and proudly held it straight out, a victorious grin on his face. A drop of dark red blood dripped from the bird's beak. Allan couldn't make out what kind of bird it was, nor could he recall having seen one like it before. But on the whole they didn't see many birds at all.

Run-Run appeared just as Allan and Boy were wondering what to do with it. One glance was enough and he at once set about preparing the bird. He made a good fire and let it burn down to a

175

glow. Then he took the bird and buried it in the embers, making sure it was completely covered. He waited, Allan and Boy looking on, wrinkling their noses at the unpleasant smell of burnt feathers. Run-Run at last decided it was enough and dug the carbonized bird out of the embers, blew on it to cool it, then with practised fingers stripped off the outer layer of scorched feathers and burnt skin. Inside, the flesh was roasted through and juicy and tender. He carefully divided the bird and gave them a piece each. He himself ate the entrails.

After that they caught more and more birds; although they were mostly crows and the meat was bitter, they soon got used to that taste, too, and the birds became a valuable addition to their monotonous diet.

26

A busy trade had also developed along the Motorway at the lay-bys and exit roads. Standing at such places was prohibited, but as usual the prohibition, like motorway prostitution, proved to be one of many almost impossible to enforce. So people who needed anything, or had things to sell or barter, turned to the Motorway. For those from the eastern zones of the city and their large residential areas, the route was shorter than to the established market places in Dock Road.

Some went to the Motorway for other purposes – truck drivers, for instance, with loads they had managed to misappropriate during the day, perhaps shoes and clothes, but most of all food, tinned food in particular. Despite increased controls over rationing, it was relatively easy for drivers to appropriate considerable quantities, even if they didn't go as far as bribing the controllers with a share of the loot. Black market trade in provisions was a profitable business for some and the fact that this was effectively theft and receiving did not seem to worry anyone. No one regarded it as such. Nor did people who came up on to the Motorway for necessities regard the illegal trade as anything but adjustment of the uneven distribution. Some chain stores were favoured at the expense of others although in name they were all state owned. Everyone knew it. Corruption at the top was one of the most serious problems the administration had, and embezzlement, bartering and illegal black market money deals evened things out, with people taking the law into their own hands.

Not everything sold on the roadside was exactly first class. Damaged fruit and vegetables destined for the Dump often found their way up on to the Motorway, where traders had become so bold, they had set up regular stalls with roofs to protect them from the weather – though most of the deals were carried out between cars, man to man, and quickly and discreetly after a mumbled agreement. A good proportion of stolen goods also made their way there and the police still occasionally raided these illegal 'markets' – or as many as they could get to before the jungle telegraph had spread the word, leaving the parking lots and lay-bys deserted, strewn with rubbish, the flower beds trampled and the toilets stinking.

From the Dump it was easiest to get up to the Motorway by taking the old service road through the open ground behind the villa gardens, parallel to the foundations of the Motorway where it cut through the side of Abbott Hill. That track was used by Dos Manos on his twice-monthly visits to Doc Fischer, and from there they could climb up the bushy slope to the double row of barbed wire fencing protecting the highway. An extension had once been begun up there, intended for those wishing to park and admire the monastery ruins the hill was named after, outlined up on the top and surrounded by coniferous trees. There had been plans for souvenir shops and drive-in food-and-drink places of various kinds, but when the tourist trade declined and various economies were made, the project had been abandoned and all that was left was a row of empty concrete cubes where there were to have been kiosks and service stations. These were now occupied by traders and other wayfarers. But the line of rotating plinths intended for telescopes for those who did not wish to climb the steep path up to the actual monastery were still there, bare and useless.

It took half an hour to get there from the Dump, but Allan did the trip about three times a week with a bundle of things he had collected and hoped to exchange for food. If trade was bad and he was unable to find a market for his goods, he paid with money from his leather pouch, but that was a last resort. He preferred to beg. He gradually became a familiar figure, recognized by the regular traders who went there as often as he did. They often gave him odds and ends, and there was also always something to be found after they had all left in the evening.

Allan seldom spoke or mixed with other people, and he was much like the motorway bums hiking from place to place, swarming round the lay-bys, trading, begging or stealing, and offering all kinds of services for some food. He was even indistinguishable from the more established hucksters or the casual buyers and sellers. On the Motorway, most people looked roughly alike and that pleased Allan. He also liked the cheerful atmosphere among the traders. Friendliness between strangers was new to him. Although contacts were usually swift – people drove up, stopped, looked around, perhaps made a deal before leaving again, often several crowded into cars to save petrol – there was often time for a joke, a little cheerfulness, a shout, a handshake. Naturally there were disagreements, but rarely quarrels. Nor did many speculators and profiteers appear to make their way out there, so there was little usury.

People mostly drove out with articles they could do without to exchange them for things they needed, and the bartering was carried out congenially. Finding necessities in this way seemed to have released an initiative in many of them, going much further than just thinking out what could be acquired in exchange – and for what. This opened up opportunities for many other activities and initiatives, creating co-operation and flexibility because there were no rules or regulations, only understanding and common sense to go by, and that merged with social convention, making it freer, more distinctive. A *creativity* that had not been there before appeared to have been let loose, and people grasped at it, used it and slowly learnt to make good use of it. That was the atmosphere on a good day on the Motorway, when crowds of people came in old cars with their offers, desires and will to let the situation guide them, to improvise, make the best of it. They were people who had begun to see the seriousness of the situation but were not yet suffering any direct need. These were people who had the vitality to get out of their prescribed patterns when necessity demanded it. Such vitality still existed, and so did helpfulness – to some extent unbridled in a situation in which necessity and fierce bargaining prevailed – it worked still, in a way, but for how long?

All this was new to Allan. His experience of mixing with people had largely been in Sweetwater's barren entertainment areas, on crowded pavements, in the crush of supermarkets, in a past now apparently more distant and unreal than ever.

One morning when he was up there early – it must have been a Saturday from the amount of traffic – he was hanging around one of the stalls where some people were crouched round a Primus and a saucepan of some delicious-smelling soup, and he saw Mary Diamond getting down from a long-distance trailer which then roared straight on. She looked exhausted and he felt an unusual warmth as he took in the picture of her standing there by the roadside, awkwardly uncertain for a moment, automatically brushing back her hair and straightening her skirt. A cold north wind was blowing and she shivered in a short open jacket over a skimpy blouse. He did not move. She saw him and came over. They rarely met in the presence of strangers.

'You look cold,' he said. He had a rug slung round him and looked like a farm worker from the hills.

'It doesn't matter. It'll pass.'

She rummaged in her plastic bag for a cigarette.

'Haven't you any warmer clothes? It'll soon be winter.'

She shrugged.

'These are my working clothes, in a way.'

'Here, have this.'

Allan had two rugs he was hoping to barter for tins of food. They were precious now winter was coming and all fuels were in short supply – even oil and electricity were now rationed.

'Don't you need it?'

There was no force behind her words. She was very cold and gratefully accepted the rug he handed to her.

'I must get back,' she said. 'I must get some sleep.'

'Wait,' he said. 'I'll come with you.'

As they were talking, Allan had seen another vehicle just stopping. A van. The driver was sitting expectantly behind the wheel. A man went over to him. Then another. . . .

'Wait here,' said Allan. 'I'll just go and see what he's got.'

A moment later he was back, without the rug but with something heavy in a bundle.

'Come on,' he said.

He went first down the steep track towards the service road. As they walked past the huge motorway pillars, he stopped and turned to her as she stumbled and slid behind him. They were more out of the wind there, cars roaring above their heads and dust mixing with the rain into a sticky layer over everything. She was easing her way down sideways, one hand on the slope, one leg stretched out so that he could see her olive skin far up her thighs. Every movement she made excited him. They had not been together for over a week. Since the fire they had not found it easy to find suitable places, and the end of their regular meetings was torment to him.

She had expected it. It had been so long and she understood him, but she was tired. She hadn't slept all night and hardly at all the night before, yet had earned very little, a few packs of cigarettes, a little money, two free meals. Things had changed. She pleaded with him when he tried to press her up against the cold concrete.

'Tomorrow,' she whispered. 'Can't we meet tomorrow? It's so cold and I'm so tired. Please.'

But he wasn't listening. He could hear nothing but the roar of the cars above and the urgency of the blood in his veins. He had hold of her and nothing was going to stop him now. Her name was on his lips, but largely as a grunt of pleasure. She put her hands against his chest and tried to push him away, but she was so weary, she gave up and fell in with him because she just wanted it over and done with as quickly as possible. She was not even sure she really liked Allan. She sometimes thought him egoistic, crude and unimaginative. He was unlike many men she had come across and he lacked humour, but there was one thing that distinguished him from all the others. He wanted her. To have *her*. He made that clear in his taciturn, clumsy way and the strength behind his desire for her overcame her, drew her to him, even now when her back ached and her eyes were smarting with tears of exhaustion.

After that they met fairly regularly on Abbott Hill, largely because he wanted it, demanded it. She laughed at him and called him a romantic fool wanting dates in the green as her dark eyes flickered and blazed. She came as often as she could, and they lay together in the shelter of those huge concrete pillars, often directly on the damp ground when he forgot something to lie on.

'Just like the old days in the Palisade,' she said, but he paid no attention, not even taking in her sarcasm. Anyhow, her past meant nothing to him. To him it did not exist.

They both missed the quiet hours at the petrol station, when she looked at motoring magazines or made coffee for them until closing time, while he saw to the pumps and waited until it was time to turn out the lights, pull down the dirty blind and turn the key in the door.

Stilling his hunger for her and exercising force on her was no longer enough for Allan, not even the most important thing.

One evening Lisa lost a front tooth. They were in the camper gnawing at the hard bread and she suddenly lowered her head and spat the tooth out into her hand. With a giggle she held it up for him to see.

'Look at that. I'll soon be as pretty as Mary.'

She was lisping through the gap and she looked like an eight-year-old.

Lisa knew Allan and Mary met on Abbott Hill. It was no longer possible to hide, but she had accepted it. As long as he didn't leave her on her own, she was satisfied, as long as Mary looked in occasionally and told her stories and gave her advice. Mary also helped her domestically. She was practical, quick and efficient compared with Lisa, and she was kind and friendly. Lisa admired her and looked forward to her visits.

Lisa was now at the stage when a pleasing peace had descended on her. Everything she did, she did even more slowly, more lazily than before, and she saw everything that happened round her through a screening veil that subdued contrasts and conflicts, even the physical discomforts of pregnancy. During her first pregnancy she had swallowed 'pinkies' to calm her nerves, stumbling around in a bemused state. Her present state was much the same, but this time it was real, brought on by her own constitution as a natural defence against excitement.

She stretched out on the mattress, lisping and running her hand over her belly. For the first time for months, she felt a need for Allan to be near. She smiled at him. The fire crackled under the stove, for they kept it on nearly all the time now it was so much colder. The roof had been improved and it had walls on three sides now, so made a kind of extension and gave them shelter from the wind.

Two buckets of water were heating on the stove. Doc had insisted Lisa was more particular over hygiene. He had also advised her against sex, but she didn't have to worry about that, not that evening anyhow, now she had got him to feel with his tongue the gap where her front tooth had been.

27

Doc's practised old hands ran gently over Lisa's belly, feeling for the position of the foetus. She was lying with her knees up and peering at those hands, looking up into the lined old face as if trying to assure herself he was pleased and all was well. He looked over his glasses and gave her a friendly pat.

'Everything seems to be in order,' he said. 'It's not big, but it's in fine form.'

She smiled proudly, as if he were an authority and she had passed a difficult test.

In the course of their consultations, they played their childish games, he being the father and she the daughter – or grandfather and grand-daughter. He often gave her small presents or something good to eat, and they spoke in intimate baby-language. Even when he was advising and instructing her, he spoke as if to a child, stroking her head, tickling her under the chin to get her to smile if she seemed sad about something. She looked forward to their meetings, the feeling of security and of being protected they gave her. He was even considerate when examining her internally, making it almost seem like a game, a game that aroused a faint, almost pleasurable feeling of guilt in her, just as when she used play with herself when a child.

Now and again she dreamt of living with Doc in his ruin of a house, enjoying his friendliness and care, just playing and being looked after, but she knew that was impossible. Nor did she really know whether she wanted to when it came down to it, although she was often lonely, particularly since Allan was obviously distancing himself from her. She could also hear Marta's groans through the thin wall when she and Doc were laughing about something.

Marta's jealousy prevented Doc going to the camper to see Lisa. He would have preferred to do that over these last few weeks when it was not good for her to walk that long and difficult way. But the sick woman's accusations had become so wild, he was frightened she might do harm to herself if he went away, perhaps in a fit of rage and despair. She had decided that his connection with Lisa was damaging to both the girl and the child, that unborn child she had fastened her last hopes on with such intensity. She seemed to be frightened that Doc would do harm to the two of them, Lisa and the child. She kept throwing his past in his face, telling him that this was a life he must not destroy as she thought he had 'destroyed' so many young girls in the past. On the other hand she was obsessed with an idea that that Doc's help would turn out to be for the best, as if that would be evidence that he had *always* only wanted the best for his patients, in the past, too, when he was involved in his detestable illegal practice – then her long life of bitterness and reproaches would turn out to lack any true reality. She was unable to resolve this conflict and that filled her with hatred and confusion.

So Lisa had to go to Doc. Once a week, she wearily made her way along the muddy paths. Her time was approaching and Doc had to make sure everything was all right, the foetus where it should be, and she herself healthy, lacking nothing, getting enough sleep and not overstraining herself. He had become completely wrapped up in his patient and she made no protest. It all created a tie between them that was difficult to imagine breaking after the child was born.

On her way back, Lisa had stopped to rest several times. She obediently chewed on the sprig of parsley Doc had given her. It was late autumn now and vegetables were scarcer than ever. Doc had noticed the missing front tooth and scolded her for not taking the calcium he had given her to make sure she had enough in her meagre diet. The calcium had tasted so horrible, she had thrown it away, but she had not told him. She thought the parsley was unpleasant, too. She liked tinned food best and anything that didn't come out of a tin seemed unattractive to her, almost inedible, as if not *prepared* enough to be eaten. Even months on the Dump and her almost constant hunger during pregnancy had not cured her.

A dizzy feeling of exhaustion made her stop for a moment. She could sense something else beneath her rather dulled indifference. She wondered vaguely how much longer she could continue like this, blown up into an unrecognizable shape, weak and useless, a burden to them all. The instinct to be rid of her burden was now so strong, she no longer even dreaded the coming birth, as if an emotional cycle in her was developing in time with the physical changes. She was now *longing* to give birth, her body was longing for birth, to get it over and done with and bring the long wait to an end. Then she would at last be able to hold this child she felt moving inside her. When she had had Boy, the terror of what was going to happen had been so strong she had taken pills until she was mindless. More than once, she and Allan had talked about having the child adopted so that she would not have to have anything to do with it, so much had the thought of bringing a child into the world and then looking after it frightened her.

She went on, slowly waddling along the shore, every step a conquest. It was raining slightly again, milder now than it had been for a long time. She was gazing vacantly ahead at her feet in the oversize boots, one foot in front of the other, mustn't stumble, mustn't get lost. Her back ached.

She suddenly noticed the shore had changed – why hadn't she seen it before? It was no longer lifelessly brown and yellow as it had been all summer. The ground was now covered with growth – grass and green leaves, a few flowers here and there. Low bushy plants had shot up and now their narrow, leathery leaves were wet with rain. She was enchanted by the change. She had been so entirely absorbed in herself and what was going on inside her, everything else had been ignored. The sight of the green shore exploded before her, tumbling over her like a wave, the impression of colour, movement and change overwhelming. After all these months, did this mean a change, now that she was suddenly *seeing*? Did this mean her waiting was over?

She stopped to rest again and sank to her knees. She was quite calm, simply faint from the sight of the greenery, the small, almost colourless flowers, long runners over the hard sandy ground, rooting themselves on the way, winding round each other. She could see insects crawling over the flowers. Perhaps insects fed off the flowers, or perhaps the other way round? Perhaps they weren't even flowers, perhaps just dead ones that withered in the winter but did not fall. She didn't know. All she felt at that moment was a profound unity with everything living, growing, creeping and crawling. She ran her hands over the green plants the rain had brought out of the dead soil. She felt completely at one with this moment, as if no past or future would ever be able to take it away. She wondered vaguely whether she had the strength to get back. No, she couldn't. That didn't matter as long as she could stay there feeling the cool dampness of the leaves on her fingers. She feared nothing, a crystal calm descending over her, and she enjoyed every second as she sat there, every breath drawn like a gulp of fresh water, and she knew her time had come.

Nor did the sight of a man coming along the shore affect her. She stayed where she was. As he came nearer, she saw it was Run-Run and he was carrying something. When he was quite close, she saw it was a sack and something was moving inside it. He stopped a little way away, nodded, then concentrated on what he was doing. He put the sack down, loosened the strings and rummaged around inside with one hand. A sound came from the sack, loud and strange, a cry. Run-Run smiled broadly and pulled out a peculiar kicking creature, an animal about the size of a dog which kept letting out complaining little screams. As he held the animal firmly with one hand, he made a noose on a piece of rope he had had over his shoulder, threaded the noose over one foreleg and let the animal go while holding on to the rope. The animal made a few clumsy leaps on its long legs, trying to shake off the rope, but then gave up and stood looking at Run-Run and Lisa with large, colourless eyes. Its grey coat was rough and shaggy, its body angular and shapeless, although it could clearly move very quickly, and occasionally skipped about as it kept letting out its odd short screams. Run-Run was staring intently at it. He clapped his hands with satisfaction, took out an iron bolt and fastened the other end of the rope to it before hammering the peg into the ground. Then the animal walked round in a circle nibbling at the grass, now and again raising its complaining voice and showing them its stiff little pink tongue.

Lisa had got to her feet. Run-Run, the animal, the way he was treating it, had disturbed her peace. She couldn't take her eyes off the creature dragging its foreleg and shrieking. She had never seen anything like it and it made a deep impression on her. In her state, she couldn't bear anyone or anything that was hurt. The tethered creature was an ominous sign, its feeble bleating a bad omen. It looked more like a deformed dog with hardly any tail, a rough dull coat, long neck, pointed little head, thin fragile legs and hoofs. She shuddered with horror. She had had so many dreams recently, dreams in which she had gone through one birth after another, each creature more deformed than the last bursting out of her exhausted body. This animal, limping around, nothing like anything she had ever seen before, brought her dreams to life. She clutched her stomach. She must not get worried, not be frightened, not now, she *knew* that at once. She was afraid. She must get back home and creep under cover.

Then she heard a voice, Allan's, coming from nowhere. She couldn't make out how he could have got there without her seeing him, not realizing that she had been standing with her eyes tightly closed and her arms clasped protectively round her stomach, while Run-Run had occasionally glanced at her, unworried, as he crouched down trying to get the kid to eat some tempting green grass he had pulled up and held out to it.

Allan had been coming from the service road, the bleating

attracting him to the shore. When he saw the two figures, he at once recognized them and took a short cut across the maize field through the villa gardens. As he got nearer he saw Lisa swaying, her face white. He ran up and caught her just as she seemed about to fall.

'What's the matter? Are you feeling bad?'

She started violently when he touched her.

'*Allan*!'

'Are you all right?'

He held on to her arm, resisting the temptation to shake her. She stared wildly at him, as if just woken from a dream.

'Do you want to go to Doc? Shall I take you to Doc?'

He spoke to her as if to someone unpredictable, slowly, painstakingly. Then she came round and shook her head.

'No . . . no, thanks. It's nothing. I was afraid. That . . . that thing there.'

She nodded at the kid. Run-Run was still crouched down trying to feed it, unmoved by their presence. Allan looked at the animal with interest. He had heard that live animals could be bought in Sweetwater. The shortage of meat was beginning to be precarious, and he understood the wisdom of what Run-Run was doing. Animals could be kept out there, especially now when the grass was growing so well after the rains.

'What *is* it, Allan? It looks like . . . like I don't know what!'

'It's a goat,' he said, relieved nothing worse had happened and already much more interested in the goat than her.

'It won't hurt you.'

'Why has he got it?'

'To keep it here to eat grass and fatten, I think. When it's bigger he can slaughter and eat it.'

'Don't say that!'

As if it were not enough to have to envisage anything so horrible, he was now adding other kinds of horrors. In her mind she saw Run-Run with his knife leaping on the poor creature, stabbing it to death and the blood spurting. Moaning, her knees sagged and the weight of her heavy body pulled her downwards, gravity helping to relieve her of her burden. But she managed to stay upright and nothing happened, except Allan clearly thought she was all right and had gone over to Run-Run and the goat. The sight of another human being approaching frightened the goat again and it bleated loudly. Lisa stared at it dancing at the end of the rope. Run-Run and Allan were amused, holding their arms out as if trying to catch it and frightening it even more. Lisa could only see the knife and blood spurting out over the grey coat, and nor was she calmed by Allan's laughter or Run-Run's antics – there was something frightening in their behaviour, threatening, wicked – an ill omen.

She cried out, but heard her own voice whimpering almost like a child's.

'Don't cry, Lisa. Don't cry, Lisa.'

Then she saw a third man, this time someone she was sure she did not know. The way he was walking told her he was a stranger, striding purposefully across the sand, occasionally making a false step and almost stumbling, but going on as if nothing had happened, as if it were important to subdue the uneven ground beneath his feet. There was something menacing about him, far too decisive, clumsy and unnatural out there, and the way he held his head up as if his chin was just above water. He came towards them very rapidly and she saw he was in blue-grey uniform with a cape of the same colour flung over his shoulder, similar to social workers' uniforms. In one hand he had a square object, a plastic briefcase with metal fittings, an official briefcase. He was wearing a peaked cap.

She finally collected her wits sufficiently to cry out a warning.

'Look! Over there!'

Allan and Run-Run spun round in alarm and saw the man. He was so near now, flight was out of the question, and anyhow considering Lisa, that would have been impossible. They stood still, all three of them waiting for the man to cover the last stretch.

Once close to them, Lisa saw that he was not threatening at all, in fact not at all impressive in his crumpled uniform, a small, corpulent, middle-aged man with steel-rimmed glasses and an ill-fitting cap, his shoes and trousers muddy from the long walk across the Dump. The briefcase was the only clean object, like a foreign body. Some of Lisa's fear left her – a man like *that* couldn't be a danger to them, could he? But then a gust lifted his cape and she saw those buttons – once again cold steel seemed to go through her. Those buttons, tunic buttons with the official insignia on them. She recognized them at once – the buttons Boy had found and taken off . . . that corpse.

The man cleared his throat and looked first down at the ground, then up at the three people in front of him. He cleared his throat again and spoke, this time with his eyes fixed somewhere far behind them.

187

'I'm from the Social Services, East Division. I'm investigating the housing situation of those most deprived – if you'll excuse me.' He cleared his throat again. 'I'm to investigate you here.' His tone of voice was conversational, impersonal, with an undertone of apology smoothing the edges, as if regretting his very presence on the Dump as much as they must do.

'Is it true you live here?'

A moment went by before Allan realized the stranger was talking to them, his presence incomprehensible as well as the way he spoke. But when the man started staring at them one by one, then cleared his throat once again, it was at last obvious and he nodded.

'Yes.'

'Oh. How many all told?'

Allan hesitated, unwilling to give information to strangers, anyhow, particularly anyone in uniform. He disliked anything to do with the authorities, who kept asking unanswerable questions which never had anything to do with what concerned him. He had found that when they had lived in Sweetwater. His reluctance to answer had often meant he was refused benefits he was entitled to, housing benefit and child benefit. He reckoned this man must be harmless, a housing survey and something for the statistics. He still shrank from giving information to an official and it worried him that the man had come all the way out here to collect his information.

'How many did you say?'

Impatience had crept into the man's voice.

'Oh . . . six or eight.'

'Did you say eight?'

'Yes, six or eight in all.'

'Aha.'

The man was suddenly very busy. He raised his right foot, propped it against his left leg, put the briefcase on his bent knee, opened it with a snap and took out a bundle of papers in various colours, then began leafing through them, mumbling to himself. It sounded more like singing than speech, a song with incomprehensible words, the rise and fall of the notes like birdsong.

'Uh – uh. Hmm-mm. . . . Let's see now. . . . Now here we are. . . .'

He extracted a couple of sheets, put the others back, snapped the briefcase shut and fished a pen out of his top pocket, all the time on one foot, balancing the case on his knee. He seemed to find a certain satisfaction in carrying out this little performance with them looking on.

'What is your name?'

His pen was ready, shining like a sharp weapon, the file his desk.

'What's that got to do with you?'

Allan was now very much on his guard. He was going to keep his name out of it at any price.

'I have to fill in this form,' the man said patiently.

'What form?'

'An application to the Housing Department for allocation of housing.'

'We don't want to apply for housing.'

'But, my dear man.' The man flung out the hand with the pen in it. 'You can't go on living here . . . on the Dump.' The birdsong rose and fell in disbelief.

'Why not?'

'Now listen.' A touch of sternness had crept in. 'First of all, you have no *permission* to live here. This is public property and no one is allowed to live here without permission. You could be in trouble if I reported you. You must see that. It's also an important part of social policy that everyone, and that means *everyone*, is given a decent place to live. That's not easy in the present situation but the department does its best. We think it's the only way to halt social decline, you know, criminality, social apathy, falling morale.'

His eyes fell on Lisa, and he stared in astonishment, as if looking at something he had never seen before.

'This is your . . . eh?'

'She's my wife.'

'And she lives with you out here?'

'Yes.'

'But . . . in her condition.' The birdsong leapt an octave. 'And as long as you live here. . . .' He looked around with disgust. 'As long as you live in unregistered housing you are not entitled to benefit. Have you considered that? And your wife ought to be under supervision. Have you arranged for the birth? Or fixed it with a peripatetic clinic?'

'No.'

'But. . . .' The man's voice died away for a moment before again regaining strength. 'But that's criminal neglect. Your wife doesn't look at all well. And. . . .'

'We're all right.'

The man was clearly upset and put his raised foot down again. His song raced down through the octaves.

'You must be aware of one thing,' he said, almost menacingly. 'And that's no one in our society can go around doing exactly as he pleases to the detriment of himself and other people, *and* to society. Do you understand? Do you also understand that I cannot disregard circumstances of this kind? It is my *duty* to send in a housing application for you. If you hinder me in any way, I will have to go to the authorities and have you evicted from here by force and taken elsewhere. So. . . .' He raised his pen again. 'Your name please.'

Allan glowered at him in silence. The worst that could have happened had happened. The authorities' interest in their existence on the Dump, the authorities' *presence* out there where uniform, gait, way of speaking were simply so out of place, so grotesque and unreal. To be allocated an apartment by the social services would mean two rooms in one of the half-empty skyscraper blocks of the satellite towns in the North West Zone, where the suicide rate was higher than anywhere else in Sweetwater, exactly what they had barely escaped by moving to April Avenue.

What could he do? Lisa was rigid behind him, as pale as death, her eyes revealing she was scarcely aware of what was going on. Run-Run was a few steps behind her, his expression forbidding. At last left alone, the goat was tripping round in a circle, grazing.

'Well?'

The man's voice was now threatening. Allan was contemptuous, but an ungovernable rage was rising in him. This was the *Enemy* here in front of him. What could he do? He could knock him down, but what would he have gained by that? Impotence began to make itself felt, a dangerous feeling. What chance had he now? If he refused to do what this idiot said, they would have the police on their backs. If he gave his name, they would be moved all the same. What if this ridiculous little man in his crumpled uniform never got the chance to make his report? He could feel rather than see Run-Run a few steps away, taking in every word, immobile, as watchful as an animal. No one knew how much he understood. And Lisa? She was as if turned to stone, staring fixedly at the stranger, as if his tunic needed all her attention.

Allan's dark glare must have shown the hatred stirring in him, for a more conciliatory tone came into the man's voice.

'Naturally, "force" and "eviction" are very unpleasant words. I realize that some people . . . how shall I put it, don't *like* conforming to that kind of regulation. I know that – I meet a great many in my job, believe you me. We could perhaps discuss details. Perhaps I could arrange for your case to be – shall we say, *postponed* for a while. You know, we have so many. It might take some time before your case comes up. A year, two perhaps. You might have changed your mind by then?'

Allan saw the man was now ill at ease and trying to do a deal with him. No doubt he wanted to get back to the office, willing now to interpret the regulations for his own sake. But there was a condition.

'However, I must have your name and some other information so that I can fill in this form. We have our routine, you know.'

He had again propped the briefcase on his knee. It had stopped raining for a while, but now it had started again, raindrops making circles on the yellow form.

'So, your name is. . . .'

Sharp and expectant, the pen hovered just above the paper.

'Allan Ung.'

He had to gain time, to think out what was best to do. He had to make a decision while the man was writing.

'Allan Ung.' The man wrote, then stopped with a frown and looked closely at Allan.

'Allan Ung,' he said. 'That sounds familiar to me. I never forget a name. I've not forgotten a name in my fifteen years of the service . . . yes, there is something familiar about that name.'

He opened the briefcase slightly, thrust two fingers inside and extracted two or three pinned-together, stencilled sheets with close columns of words (names?) on both sides. He ran his finger down the columns, one after another, his lips moving soundlessly. Then he found what he was looking for and his face lit up.

'Allan Ung. Here we are. I knew I'd seen that name somewhere.'

Allan was as tense as an animal about to pounce. His name on a list! What could that mean?

'A description of you has been sent out, Allan Ung.'

The man's voice had turned exaggeratedly calm and friendly.

'What?'

'Nothing to worry about. You're only wanted for questioning. An explanation. . . .' he added when he saw Allan's closed, blank expression. 'Concerning a fire at a petrol station in the East Zone.' He started reading out aloud, peering at the fine print. 'A certain Mr Sweetness has given your name as a witness to it, and our

Peacekeeping Force is naturally interested in as much information as they can find.'

Allan's expression must have frightened him, because he went on in the same semi-cheerful, semi-assuring voice, like a doctor to a patient.

'As you almost certainly know, the two forces work together to some extent. Particularly when when it comes to missing persons, we in the Social Services can be of some assistance to the Peacekeeping Force. That applies to simple routine matters such as this.'

Now there was an abrupt, almost feverish touch in the man's disarming friendliness.

Allan still could not speak. Sweetness! Sweetness had reported him! He could no longer think straight, he was so enraged. He was stamping one foot like an animal about to attack. The man in uniform also noticed. As he went on in the same tone of voice, emphasizing this was only a routine matter and it would take at most fifteen minutes of Allan's time, he rapidly shuffled his papers together, snapped shut the briefcase and prepared to leave.

'Well, then, there's no point in my wasting time standing here in the rain and filling in forms,' he bleated cheerfully. 'I'll tell you what you can do. When you report to the Peacekeeping Force – that must be within three days, remember – then you can pop into my office – we can arrange for you to be vaccinated then, too. Everyone has to be vaccinated against influenza, as I suppose you know? My office is in the same building – we run the two services together as much as possible – seventh floor, room 107. That's easy to remember, isn't it?' He was speaking carefully, as if to a child he had no wish to frighten. 'Well, then, East Social Centre, seventh floor, room 107. Within three days. That's the law. You have a duty as a witness to report and make a statement. I must be off, I suppose. Goodbye.'

He attempted a smile, turned away half-apologetically, then turned back again.

'Are you sure I shouldn't arrange for your wife's admission? She really does not look at all well.'

'No!'

The paunchy little police-spy left with his glossy briefcase, retreating with measured and relieved steps along the shore.

Lisa could feel rather than see Allan's rage. There had always been something terrible, something uncontrollable about his fury once kindled, and to see him there, his face chalk-white under the wild hair and beard, stamping his foot, really terrified her.

There was another thing – Run-Run was also standing slightly bowed, as if ready to pounce, tense and concentrated, and she at once sensed that between them lay a deeply intuitive understanding, a savage common determination to do something terrible – it confirmed everything that had been worrying her since she had left Doc. She couldn't let it happen, but what could she do?

She saw them seeking each other's eyes, their movements alert, supple as those of animals. She saw Allan nodding to his mute, agreeing ally, a slight, almost throw-away nod which in any other context would have been meaningless, anyhow not binding, but at this particular moment between them it meant an insane pact sealing their cold-blooded decision.

Without a moment's hesitation, Run-Run turned and left with great springy, gliding strides, half-way between walking and running, making a wide detour across the shore so that he could cut off the little official, whose back was now disappearing on a straight course beyond the low mounds.

In her mind, Lisa saw what was going to happen, and she at once remembered the considerate words he had spoken before leaving (no doubt simply an official reaction on seeing her condition). That made it even more impossible, inconceivable. But she saw the morbid thoughts that had bothered her all day materializing, slowly and elaborately, as if before her own eyes, unreal, but still horribly real – the grey goat, Run-Run creeping up, his knife raised, the spurting red blood, unimaginably red and fresh. She could see Run-Run far away, a shadow between the mounds, and still just see the plump back of the little man who had tried to help her, the man with the shiny buttons, those buttons that had told her clearly what was going to happen.

But she couldn't let it happen, whatever Allan thought, however enraged he was. She couldn't let it happen. She must do something, shout or warn him. She opened her mouth and cried out, but he was on her at once, raging, his hand over her mouth, tipping her over on to the sand, hissing in her ear words she couldn't make out, squeezing the breath out of her with his heavy body on top of hers, his big hand clamped over her mouth so that she couldn't breathe.

When he loosened his grip, she struggled free and got up. She knew there wasn't long to go now and the thought of the little man was ousted by a much stronger imperative to extremes far beyond what she thought she could cope with, telling her she must get back, get home, lie down, get ready — she suddenly ran as fast as she could, staggering and stumbling through the grass. She scarcely noticed when she fell, but just went on, scrambling along on her hands and knees, her stomach swaying beneath her body and weighing her down.

She crawled on with sand in her mouth and blood dripping from her nose on to her hands (blood on the goatskin), now and again strange gutteral sounds coming from her throat.

Then he was there again, a hand under her arm to help her to her feet, but she was so limp in his grasp, he had to use both hands to heave her up and prop her body against his, pulling one arm over his shoulders and holding on tight. They stumbled along the shore, he mumbling into her ear: 'He was a police spy, Lisa. Don't you see? He had my name on a list of people they're looking for. Sweetness grassed on me, and now they think I had something to do with the fire. Didn't you see how he wanted to get back and tell the cops? I haven't a chance if they get hold of me, Lisa. Do you see? He's the *Enemy*, Lisa. If we'd let him go, it'd have been the end of us. D'you understand what I'm saying?'

She couldn't answer, could hardly hear. She had enough to do putting one foot in front of the other, listening to the voices inside her. She had felt the very first pains, the fleeting touch of the first shadow of pain, a trembling and faintly unpleasant feeling in her kidneys and lower back. Was she sure? Yes. She was not wrong this time.

She plodded on, slowly, methodically. It had started. It might take hours, all day, all night, but it had started. She was walking, still able to find the strength. She had to get back before the waters broke. She suddenly remembered the huge volume of fluid wetting the coarse sheets of the hospital bed. And the shame. She didn't want Allan to be there when it happened. She would ask him to fetch Mary. And Doc.

28

Mary made sure there was plenty of hot water. She sent Boy and Allan out to fetch more wood for the fire, although it was pouring with rain and there was not much hope of finding anything dry in the dark. When she wasn't giving them orders, she sat in the camper holding Lisa's head in her arms, humming and wiping the sweat off her cheeks, trying to comfort her between pains.

Doc was sitting in a corner with a watch in his hand, checking the frequency of the contractions. His torch shone with a sharp glaring light over the mattress where Lisa lay moaning. Doc had made no objections to Mary's presence, although he thought this dark-skinned woman was reducing his authority with her relaxed, instinctive competence. But he was comforted by her presence. The responsibility of bringing Lisa's child into the world under these conditions was weighing heavily on his failing memory and medical knowledge.

'They're beginning to be a little more regular,' he said. 'Shouldn't be long now.'

Lisa was lying on her side in the middle of the floor on a clean white piece of linen. A bundle of clean boiled cloths lay within reach alongside the bowl of water and soap. Doc had equipment in a small satchel, stethoscope, scissors, rubber tubing, needles, clamps, some packs of compresses, some medicine he had managed to acquire. Between contractions, it was quite quiet, as if they were all gathering their strength for the last lap, the only sound the ceaseless rattle of rain on the roof. Lisa gasped and made grateful little grunts when Mary put a hand on her back and massaged her, then cried out when she felt another pain on the way.

Doc cautiously pulled on a rubber glove and gently put his hand on Lisa's hip. She started – she had been dozing between pains.

'Let's just see how things are going,' he said gently.

He folded back the rug and fumbled a little before finding his way, sweating, his eyes narrowed behind the thick lenses.

'It feels as if the opening is beginning to be good,' he said, relieved the girl's pelvis was not too narrow.

'Two or three more, then we can begin to press a little.'

'We'll press the little scamp out,' said Mary, now stroking and massaging, calming them all with her monotonous humming as she rocked in a slow rhythm, as if her own heartbeats inside that warm body were emerging from the rocking which seemed to be filling the whole camper.

Allan and Boy were outside tending the fire in the dark, the rain hammering on the tin roof above them. They didn't talk. Allan sat still, shaken by what was going on, though not really scared. Birth was natural. Births occurred every day, every minute. But, he started every time he heard Lisa moaning – then pulled himself together and told himself that this was 'nature's way' and births were always like this, pain part of it, nothing alarming in itself. That was difficult to get used to. He had grown up in a society which had done everything to camouflage outward signs of human suffering and the culmination of suffering, the natural culmination of life – death.

He spat angrily into the fire. Saucepans of boiling water were on the metal plate and because the chimney pipe was leaking again, the fumes made his eyes smart. Boy was crouched beside him, cutting up a piece of leather into narrow strips which he then plaited together into a tough supple thong. He also shivered every time he heard the moans from inside, his thin face pale under the dirty fringe Allan cut with a knife whenever it hung over his eyes. His reserve since he had teamed up with Run-Run had gone, and he was now helplessly childish, clearly oppressed by the drama he understood so little about.

'What's the matter with her?'

He had suddenly turned to Allan with the question, the first time he had even mentioned what he had seen going on.

'She's going to have a baby.'

'What does having a baby mean?' the boy said. 'Does it hurt that much?'

'She has had the baby inside her for a long time,' said Allan, pleased to be able to break the silence. 'It wants to get out now, and that's when it hurts.'

Boy's face showed a glimpse of understanding.

'Like rats!' he said eagerly. 'Babies come out of the stomach like in the rats. I saw a rat once under a box, down in a kind of hole full of wool and bits of paper, like a bed, and then suddenly some little ones came out, pink all over, and they couldn't even walk. Run-Run showed them to me.'

Boy was as familiar with rats as he was with all other life on the Dump, while to Allan the increasing number was a constant source of annoyance. He killed them whenever he got the chance, but at this moment he had no wish to break this rare contact with his son.

'Yes, something like it. Only it's a human baby coming, a brother or a sister for you.'

'I don't know what a brother or sister is,' said Boy. He went on

196

working on his strips of leather – none of them knew what he was going use them for.

'Is it that small?' he said after a while, holding his hands slightly apart.

'A little bigger, about that big,' said Allan.

'No wonder it hurts,' said Boy, and he went back to work.

Inside, Doc and Mary were helping Lisa over on to her back, telling her she must now try to help by pressing down every time another pain came. She didn't seem to take in much of what they were saying to her, absorbed as she was with the waves of pain running through her body, occasionally giving her a moment to breathe out before again tearing her apart and throwing her helplessly into the arms of the two people beside her. Thrashing about as if drowning, grabbing their clothing, clawing at them, as if dragging them down with her into the chasm of pain she kept being hurled into. Doc held her under her knees and lifted, while Mary pushed her body forwards, pressing her chin down towards her breast.

'Press now, Lisa. Press now. That's right. Clever girl.'

'I can see the head,' said Doc. 'I can see the head, Lisa.'

He was wheezing, breathing heavily. A segment of firm new tissue became visible in the swollen opening, white in the torchlight. But Lisa was utterly exhausted, unreceptive in Mary's arms, panting and waiting for the next wave. When it came and lifted her away again, she screamed, beseeching other powers, everything outside her anguished body to come to the rescue. Doc seized her legs and lifted them up and back while Mary pressed her head up and down.

'Hold your breath now, Lisa. That's right. Just hold your breath and press down.'

It took a long time. The skull and its sticky wet hairs on the soft cranium, like parchment through which the baby's brain could clearly be seen, slid forward, then sank back again, forward, back, in and out in time with the waves, pressing on the torn opening. But it could not get free and sank back with a sigh. Everything was going too slowly. Doc held her knees, groaning, sweat pouring down his face and misting his glasses. Mary went on comforting Lisa and wiping her face with a damp cloth.

One more heave.

Then it came, tearing the skin, red blood flowing and mixing with the waters and excrement on to the linen cloth. The squashed little head, glistening with moisture, the face compressed under the slime and scum, was suddenly an object between Lisa's thighs. Doc seized it with both hands and pulled cautiously, while Mary whispered into Lisa's ear.

'It's here, Baby. It's over.'

The next contraction sent the slippery little body out on to the sheet, where Doc took hold of it and held it up.

'A girl!'

His cry was hoarse and triumphant, smothered by his relief when he saw and felt that the little creature he was holding was perfectly formed.

'A girl!' Mary repeated. 'You've got a girl, Baby. It's all over.'

Lisa was lying quite still, almost unconscious, and then a few moments later she managed a slight smile to show them that she understood and was grateful for their help.

Meanwhile Doc reached for the scissors he had sterilized and the blunt blades cut slowly through the cord, leaving a drop of blood on the baby's stomach – then a compress and a bandage made of strips of a pillow-case – he was sweating profusely – in the old days two or three swift actions would have been enough. But now he seemed to take ages fumbling with the unfamiliar niggling task – the baby still hadn't cried. He must do something to get her to cry, to start the delicate process of life . . . he put a teaspoon handle into her mouth to find the tongue, but that didn't help. He pushed the thermometer up into the tiny blocked nose, but not a sound came from the baby, its little arms and legs wriggling helplessly.

'Let me have her.'

Mary held out her hands. Doc reacted obediently, trembling and sweating, anxious that nothing should happen *now* it was over and everything had gone so well. He could hear his own breathing rasping in his throat and the light from the torch drew sharp shadows in the deeply lined face.

'Careful,' he stuttered. 'Careful. . . .'

But Mary took hold of the wet, wax-coloured infant, laid her on her back on the broad palms of her hands, lifted her up to her face and blew briefly and hard on to the narrow chest. The response was immediate – a long whistling hiccup, followed by a pitiful shriek, so faint it could hardly be heard above the rain rattling on the tin roof. The babe was alive! All was well. Everything had gone as it should. Doc busied himself with the afterbirth while Mary cleaned and washed the baby, its colour now beginning to return to normal.

'A girl!'

Mary's face was radiant as she stood in the camper doorway. She could just see Allan and Boy over by the fire, and someone else now, Smiley. Smiley had come stumbling and cursing through the rain, on a 'confinement visit' as he called it. He was in a good mood, having cheered himself up beforehand, and he willingly shared the bottle he had brought with him. Since his arrival, he had been holding forth to Allan on how selfish and irresponsible he was to bring a child into the world at all when the world was as it was.

'We're the last castaways on a rotten sinking craft,' he had proclaimed. 'Life-jackets thrown overboard long ago. Human beings have known that for fifty years, but they've continued in the same way. At first they had the idea of solidarity to fall back on, the dream of a just society created by free and equal men. They hadn't reckoned with the society that actually existed – a coercive society of human beings dehumanized, their opportunities for change in a positive direction slowly undermined – pulling the foundations of solidarity from beneath them and turning people into natural enemies. I tried to write that in a poem once. Huh! Did I tell you I once wanted to be a poet? But that was before paper rationing made the printed word so damned exclusive. Ha, ha, ha.'

Smiley was in great form, but every time a sound came out to them, he was also still, as if what he was lavishing his irony on was nothing to do with the real drama going on inside.

He greeted the news with enthusiasm.

'A girl! Did you hear, Allan? A little courtesan – given a little time. What do you say? Well, drink to it then, man!'

Allan drank and went over to Mary standing in the doorway.

'How is she?' he said in a low, embarrassed voice. 'Did it go well? Is everything all right?'

'Oh, yes. She's just flat out, but otherwise she's OK. She's asleep at the moment.'

Mary's face had an unfamiliar gentle look about it.

'I looked out for you up there today,' he said.

'Oh, did you? I didn't go today,' she said.

'Can I see you tomorrow?'

Allan didn't mind that Smiley could hear him, *must* be able to hear him if he wanted to.

'Maybe,' said Mary with a vague nod, apparently not interested.

'I'll be there tomorrow,' he insisted. 'Are you going, too?'

'I might. I told you.'

Her dismissive attitude annoyed him. He reckoned the birth of the baby had something to do with it, but that couldn't distract him from the elation he felt in her presence. He seized her arm and pulled her towards him.

'Mary. . . .'

'Let go!'

Her voice was sharp, but the movement she made to free herself was gentle, almost reluctant. Without another word, she went back into the camper.

Then Doc appeared.

'Well, well, now,' Smiley cried out, as if he had been waiting for a chance to drown the whispering in the doorway. 'Here's the quack himself. Glad to see you. Come on over and have a drink.'

Doc was smiling broadly, pleased and relieved everything had gone so well. The baby was small but perfectly healthy as far as he could see. He took a drink from Smiley's bottle. It warmed him. The fire warmed him. The atmosphere was almost friendly, the rain splashing down still, but they were reasonably dry under the tin roof. He sat down on the crate Allan pulled up for him. Boy was lying curled up in a blanket by the wall on the other side of the fire, coughing occasionally in his sleep.

'You ought to get him inside,' said Doc. 'He can go in now. He oughtn't to lie on the ground.'

'Hey, you haven't given the girl a name yet, have you?' Smiley said to Allan. 'What's it going to be?'

Allan looked down. He hadn't thought about it, a name for the child not a matter of importance as far as he was concerned. When Boy was born, they had tried out several names before settling on one, one that didn't annoy him. But now it seemed suddenly important to make a choice, as if a name meant something, as if giving his child a name meant giving her an amulet for health, strength and good fortune once it was pronounced. So the choice had to be good. A name was suddenly something more than a sound, a distinguishing mark; it was important. It had to be a name that meant something to them all, marking a point in time, an event, the birth of the child and a testimony of identity – symbol and exorcism.

Allan looked over at the other two men, one on a car seat, the other on a box, sitting round a reeking fire. Then Mary came into the doorway again, filling it as if to guarantee that mother and child would be allowed to sleep undisturbed.

'Let me have a look at her,' he said to Mary, and she disappeared back into the camper. A moment later she was back and handed him the little bundle. He looked at what he could see of his child, a tiny head of downy hair, eyes hidden behind wrinkled eyelids, flat nose, a beautifully formed little mouth pursed into an offended expression. She weighed nothing. He concentrated but was unable to fathom anything from the small sleeping features.

Then another downpour struck the ramshackle shed with wild force, thundering on the tin roof, and a fierce gust of wind rattled the loose walls. The noise woke the baby. She opened her eyes wide and for a moment peered at the fire and the night beyond, then fell asleep again.

Allan stared intently at the child.

'Rain. . . .' he said. 'I think I'll call her Rain. Yes, Rain,' he said again, affirming that the child had been given a name.

29

The record rainfall caused Sweetwater's water and drainage systems to collapse, and although the damage was reparable, the weather did not improve enough for repairs to begin, so the destruction simply grew greater. Drains already almost blocked from lack of maintenance simply could not take away the floods of water flowing through the streets. A high tide whipped up by the onshore wind made the situation totally chaotic in the low-lying parts of the city, flooding cellars and basements and making some stretches of streets impassable. Water seeped in everywhere, undermining streets and filling building sites. The mains burst in several places and then floodwater got into the drinking water, causing a health risk for those still fortunate enough to have any water in their taps.

The influenza epidemic grew worse and the appeal to every person to be vaccinated had not been taken up by many. Loudspeaker vans drove round, followed by mobile vaccination clinics, but a great many people were still dying of this new and pernicious virus, against which they still had no effective vaccine. The vaccine available was based on a related virus infection and was insufficient for more than a small minority. Health-authority decrees had gradually become so numerous and extensive as the situation deteriorated generally, new decrees were seldom met with anything but cynical indifference.

Nor was the medical picture of this new infection entirely clear. Its course seemed to vary considerably. Some people had it lightly, while others were severely affected. Some went into a coma after a day or two of sore throat or something like a minor cold, while for others it could last for weeks, with high temperatures and pains in all their joints.

A hundred people died during the first week of the epidemic in Sweetwater, eight hundred in the next. These figures were unusually high, although people were used to 'flu-type viral infections causing many deaths every year. What was critical about this situation was that the epidemics never seemed to be quite the same, so the previous year's vaccine was only useful to a limited extent and no help at all to those with the least resistance, particularly children and the old.

Boy was the first to fall ill. His cough got worse and worse and in the end he was so weak from fever, he couldn't even get out of bed. Then Rain fell ill. Lisa noticed her coughing when she was five days old, and sent for Doc. He came at once and examined the baby, who was already feverishly hot.

'She must have caught it from Boy,' he said.

Boy's eyes were feverish, his cheeks blotchy and his cough persistent.

'Have you milk for her?' said Doc.

Lisa did have milk this time, but the baby was weak and underdeveloped and not very good at sucking.

'You must try to give her what you can,' Doc said seriously. 'Press out a few drops on to a spoon. You mustn't give up. There are antibodies in mother's milk which might save her.'

But the next day, Rain's temperature was up again and she was struggling for breath, neither opening her eyes nor even trying to take in nourishment.

'We must try penicillin,' Doc said to Allan. 'Talk to Felix. Maybe he can get some.'

Felix could. The next morning, in exchange for two cakes of scented soap, part of the contents of a box of finer (and now priceless) toilet articles Allan had found, he brought four penicillin ampoules, a hypodermic syringe and a packet of milk-powder. He put the things down neatly in a row on the table in front of Doc and Allan and snapped shut his black artificial leather briefcase with metal fittings (he had driven the unfortunate official's car into the city and left it in a multi-storey car park after removing everything that could be sold).

'Difficult to get,' he told them. 'Everyone wants penicillin now. A lot of people ill.'

Doc filled the syringe and gave the baby an injection. Then they forced a little milk into her mouth.

'All we can do now is to hope,' Doc said.

It didn't seem to make any difference. On the fourth day, Rain went into a coma. Lisa was exhausted from lack of sleep and worry. She tried desperately to squeeze some milk out of her aching breasts, and she managed to get some down Rain, but very little.

'All we can do is wait,' said Doc. 'She's had all the penicillin she can take.'

The air in the camper was heavy and damp, clothing and cloths hanging up to dry everywhere, and it was still raining. Doc gave the last dose of penicillin to Boy. He was coughing as before, his face flushed with fever and he was showing no signs of getting better – or worse.

Allan had just come back from Abbott Hill. He had tried to barter for cough sweets, aspirin or anything that might help, at least for Boy, but there was nothing to be had. It was possible to get a quota of ordinary medicaments at the numerous mobile health centres, but that meant producing a vaccination certificate. Vaccination could be carried out by producing 'evidence of residence', in practice the same as an identity card. Medicines could only be got at chemists on prescription and they had to be paid for with money.

As soon as he saw Doc's gloomy expression and Lisa's pale face, Allan knew there had been no improvement. Rain lay in her basket, still struggling for breath, her face red and sore, her eyes closed and fists clenched, an almost inaudible wail rising and falling with each breath as she fought against the disease.

'I couldn't get hold of anything,' he said grimly.

'Nothing'd help, either,' said Doc. 'Not now. Not at this stage. All we can do is wait.'

They heard steps outside, then Run-Run opened the door and peered in, a bunch of leafy twigs in his hand. As so often, he made a sign that he wanted to make tea, and Allan nodded. Previously, miseries of this kind would have made them retreat completely from the outside world, as if anxiety and despair in themselves demanded so much strength and concentration, mixing with other people would have been impossible. But it was different now. The children's illness concerned them all, leaving none indifferent, no longer the sole concern of the parents. Life had to go on. They had to work, find food, struggle to keep alive, as before, and none of them could change that.

Lisa was lying back against a pile of bedclothes, still unable to get about much. Mary came to help her with the baby, her dark face radiant each time she picked the child up and held her in her arms. Over the last few days she had also helped with housework, washing clothes and cooking for them all. Like the others, she was worried, but each time she passed the infant's basket she couldn't keep back a cheerful cry.

'Look at her! She hasn't given up. They can't finish off my little one that easily.' She seemed to refuse to believe influenza could crush this life she had helped bring into the world. Lisa sat, hollow-cheeked, with dark rings under her eyes, staring vacantly in front of her, her face drained of colour. Her tears had dried up as hope had gradually faded and her thoughts circled round a wish that she had never brought the child into the world just to be taken away again. She was also hoping it would happen soon, quickly, so that she could begin to forget and at least escape this pain.

To Allan, Mary's visits meant a new phase in their relationship. He had soon seen she would reject any approaches as long as Lisa was nearby. At first that had annoyed him, but when she had been willing to continue meeting him wherever they could be alone together, he had reluctantly accepted it. Her very presence, her great heavy body in the camper with them aroused him almost unendurably.

He also became aware that she was quick and skilful at getting the work done. With Smiley, she mostly lay about on the car seat, smoking, painting her nails or sleeping. But in the camper she revealed a resolute efficiency. He looked on with wonder as she did the washing, cleaning and cooking. He helped as best he could, but she took over the moment she stepped through the door, and it never occurred to him to protest. He found he could *rely* on her. She would turn out to be strong and resourceful in a fix, just the qualities needed on the Dump, and much more so if conditions should grow worse. Her strength and skill made him admire and respect her in a different way from before, and when she didn't come one day, he felt the loss more deeply than purely sexually.

But that was still there and drew him to her every moment he was near her plump, earthy body.

Run-Run was busy at the fire outside, Doc dozing with his chin on his chest and Allan squatting on his heels inspecting the store of canned food he had hidden in a crate. Boy's cough kept coming from his corner. He was showing no signs of improving.

Run-Run opened the door, a cup of steaming liquid in his hand. He went over to Lisa and held it out, but she didn't move, almost as if she wasn't aware of him standing in front of her. He grasped her gently but firmly by the shoulder and shook her. He held the cup out again and, like a sleep-walker, she took it. Then Allan and Doc were given a cup each – it tasted rather sickly, but not unpleasant. Run-Run went over to Boy and tried to get him to drink some.

With three adults plus Run-Run and two sick children, the camper was overcrowded and hot.

'I must get on home,' said Doc. 'It's getting dark. I must go and see to Marta. I can't do any more here, but if there's any change, come and fetch me at once.'

He was about to get up, but Run-Run stopped him and pointed appealingly over at the corner where Boy was.

'I can't do anything more for him, either,' said Doc wearily. 'He's had penicillin, and I think he's got a chance, but he's under-nourished, so has little resistance. But you never know with these infections. He's got a chance. He's stronger than I thought. That's all I can say.'

Run-Run appeared to be listening to what Doc said. Then he pointed at Lisa, who was sipping her tea and occasionally running her hand over her breast. There were two dark patches on her colourless dress where her milk had seeped out. Then he pointed at Boy again and put his forefinger into his mouth.

They stared at him without understanding, and he repeated the gesture. When they still did not understand, he went over to Lisa, now aware something was going on, and put his hand lightly on her breast, pointed at Boy, then folded his arm under his chest as he rocked sideways as if rocking a baby.

'He means she should breast-feed him.' exclaimed Doc.

Lisa stared blankly from one to the other, too exhausted to make out what the conversation was about.

'It's an idea,' said Doc, nodding to Allan, his voice quite excited.

'It couldn't do any harm, anyhow. Can you get her to do it?'

Allan nodded. He went over to Lisa. Run-Run had retreated.

'Doc wants you to try to give Boy some milk. . . .' he began, but she didn't understand, just looked vacantly at him. He tried again.

'Give him the breast . . . your milk. Do you understand? It might make him a little better.'

'*Boy*,' she whispered. 'Am I to give *Boy* . . .? I can't do that.'

The disgust she felt at the thought of breast-feeding her big son was violent. She had distanced herself from him recently and he was almost a stranger to her. And now Allan was asking her to *breast-feed* him!

'No, I can't. I *can't*,' she cried, appealing to Doc.

'Lisa, please,' said Allan.

'No, let me go.'

He had grabbed her arm, his eyes ominously angry.

'He's ill,' she whimpered. 'They're both ill. Nothing is any use. It won't do any good. It'll soon be all over.'

He hit her with the back of his hand, hauled her to her feet and shoved her over towards Boy. Doc seemed about to intervene, but then sank back again with a sigh and put his hands over his eyes. What was happening doubly pained him. Both children were dangerously ill, little hope now for the babe, and then to see Lisa suffering like this. He was not sure he could stand any more.

'Try!' said Allan, standing over her like an executioner.

Sobbing, she put her arm under the boy's neck and pulled his head into her arms, then unbuttoned her blouse and lowered her aching breast to his face. At first there was no reaction when the nipple went into his half-open mouth, but then a few drops of milk moistened his dry lips, his tongue moved and he seemed to swallow.

'You must suck, Boy,' she whispered, pressing his head against her breast. 'Suck now.'

She was more awake now, the sight of her son's thin flushed face apparently putting an end to her reluctance.

'Suck now!'

Boy swallowed as his mouth filled with the pale sweet milk and gradually he began to suck, hesitantly at first, with long pauses in between, but then more strongly and purposefully, dozing off in between. Lisa sat with his head in her arms, watching him and feeding him each time he wanted more.

Allan woke early next morning and listened, woken by the quiet after the rain. The days of persistent drumming on the roof and corrugated iron outside were over and the silence was deafening. He could hear Lisa breathing beside him and Boy occasionally coughing. Not a sound came from the baby's basket.

He got up and fumbled for the matches. He was supposed to have been keeping watch on Rain, and had agreed to sit up while the others slept. He had done so for a few hours, then had nodded off. He had to watch out for the slightest change in her condition. Doc had not held out much hope, but Allan couldn't believe it – as long as she was breathing. In the end he had lain down, promising himself a short rest, a brief shut-eye. . . .

He at last managed to strike a match and light a candle. He looked into the basket.

At first glance he thought she was dead, her colour had changed so much, now pale and greyish, her eyes sunk in the dark sockets, the eyelids so transparent he could see the network of tiny blood vessels. Her mouth was closed, but the cupid's bow threw a shadow in the hollow below her lower lip and made it look as if her mouth were half-open. He had been prepared for this. He had already come to terms with her loss and had consoled himself with the thought that it was good it was happening now, so soon, before they became really attached to her, before she became a person. But the sight of her in that brief moment when he thought she was dead caused a knot of inexplicable pain in his chest. He had been prepared for it, hadn't he? He would have to carry her across the tip in a plastic bag, hide her somewhere where she would soon be covered over and buried under tons of garbage. He might have gone to the trouble of putting her body in a box to protect her from the rats. He had thought of everything, made plans, his way of protecting himself against all misfortunes. But. . . .

The covers moved and the baby drew a deep, sleepy sigh. She was asleep, resting peacefully! She had thrown it off! He put the back of his hand against her smooth, cool cheek. The fever had gone. There was hope.

He groaned and hid his face in his hands, his relief producing emotions against which he had no defence. He stared at the tiny hand momentarily waving about. Five small fingers, five fingernails, perfect, as if made of wax. He stared at the hand until he could no longer see it, until he could see nothing at all, until he found himself kneeling by the basket, found himself weeping,

weeping as he had not done since he was a child. In those days he could weep as easily from joy as from grief, long, long ago, in an earlier life, another distant world of dreams he could perhaps capture a few memories of at this moment, but which he found it hard to believe had ever been his.

30

When it was obvious Rain was over the crisis and getting better and stronger every day, life seemed to begin ebbing out of old Marta.

She had followed the child's birth and illness in a state of great tension, with hope – and no hope. She had showered Doc with questions and reproaches, calling him a wretched quack who couldn't even keep an infant alive after having brought it into the world. And at the same time she sent him over with ointment, fine linen sheets and two soft woollen blankets for Rain, beseeching him to get the child into hospital. He told her wearily that no hospital or doctor could have done better, as there was no cure and the waiting lists in all the epidemic departments were long. But his reply only upset the sick old woman even more. She started keeping Doc awake at nights. The long night when Rain's crisis came to a head, he didn't get a wink of sleep for her scorn and harsh reproaches. He was literally driven out of the house at the crack of dawn, when he set off over to the camper. On the way he met Allan, who told him of the babe's improvement, and he could see for himself that she was miraculously free of fever. He turned back to tell Marta the good news, and she broke down completely, weeping and raging for hours until she fell into a daze of exhaustion from which she never really emerged.

'She's lost the will to live,' Doc growled, shaking his head. 'She seemed to lose hold of her own life the moment I told her the babe was out of danger. Can you understand that? It won't be long now, if things go on like this.'

Doc and Allan hurried along the shore. It was chilly, the wind biting, the heavy clouds gone and an icy cold sunlight trickling down through the mist, now higher and apparently more distant than any of them could remember seeing it for a long time. The rainy season was over and winter had come, the factory buildings over at Saragossa sharply outlined, as if they had suddenly been brought closer. But the water between was colourless and dead where no wind rippled the surface.

208

Doc had asked him to help bring in the last of the vegetables. Allan was to have half of them. Doc couldn't use all of them himself, he said. In his mind, he reckoned he would soon be alone.

'But you must make sure the young ones eat vegetables,' said Doc for the umpteenth time. 'Particularly little Rain, when she starts taking solids.'

He had been on a quick visit to the camper and found all was well with the infant. She was slightly listless and underweight, but with no after-effects as far as he could see. Then she began to take in a little nourishment and started to suck. Boy recovered more slowly. He was still coughing and his temperature came and went, but he also seemed to be improving. Doc advised Lisa to go on breast-feeding him, but to be sure there was enough left for Rain. Lisa was also recovering, largely resting, with Mary helping her, apparently enjoying the extra work and treating the baby as if she were her own.

Run-Run came towards them leading his goat. As he passed them, he grinned broadly and drew his finger from ear to ear, pointed at the goat and patted his stomach.

'What's he up to now?' said Doc once they were well past him.

'Slaughtering the goat,' said Allan.

'He makes me uneasy,' said Doc. 'For no particular reason. He's helpful, and he seems to be able to do lots of things. But he doesn't really belong. He belongs in another era, another world. He's like some kind of primitive creature who acts on an impulse, without thinking, without conscience. He's like an animal . . . do you know what I mean?'

'Yes, I do.'

Allan had never told Doc about the official from the Social Services. The thought of that episode occasionally made him feel faint, the knowledge of his own part in it was so impossible. But then he recalled the man's bleating voice and the lists of names with such startling clarity, he knew that nothing else could have been done. But he had not told Doc, nor did he think he ever would.

Run-Run was busy. None of them ever knew what was going on in his head. They never knew how much he took in, of words, expressions and gestures, or how much he understood of what was going on around him. He reacted according to his own interpretation of events, sometimes incomprehensibly, at other times with his own strange logic, as if he were suddenly able to interpret the signs around him more completely than they did, so was able to take precautions for immediate as well as future needs. Thus this handicapped, unpredictable man was at an advantage because he had nothing but his intuition and senses to go by, unconditionally, and he never doubted their validity.

Just as he now carried out what he was doing with precision and sureness, with no careful plan, but with none of his elaborate operations apparently having any connection with what was going on around him. He first collected as much of the driest firewood as he could find and stacked it up on top of a heap of medium-sized flat stones in a low-lying place in the shelter of some large mounds. Then he lit the fire. It took a while for the damp wood to burn, but he persisted, knowing exactly what he had to do. Run-Run could light a fire under the most difficult conditions. When the fire caught, it soon flared up and then Run-Run added more wood.

Not far away from the fire, he set about digging a trench with a dustpan to which he had fixed a handle. When it was about a foot or so deep, he straightened up, the job done. He threw more wood on the fire and set off along the shore towards the villa gardens, trampling through the tall bracken and searching round until he finally found what he was looking for by the remains of a wall – a low, thick-stemmed, subtropical ornamental palm tree with large, succulent and glossy leaves. He cut down as many as he could carry and hurried back.

The bonfire had burnt half-way down, so he put on more wood before concentrating on the dead goat, now hanging up by its hind legs on a log jammed into the rusty skeleton of a crane some way away. Blood was dripping blood from it, fresh red blood falling into a pool on the ground. With a practised hand, Run-Run skinned the animal, rolled up the pelt and put it to one side. Then he washed the carcass in a bowl of water and hung it back up to dry for a while, the entrails he wanted to use stuffed back in the cavity. After cutting the carcass down, he took the armful of leaves over to it and packed it into layer upon layer of fresh green palm leaves. When that was done and the carcass was completely covered, he carried the whole over to the trench.

The fire was now nothing but embers, and equipped with the dustpan and a stick, he began to rake hot stones out of the embers and take them across to drop them into the trench. He rolled stones too large to carry down the slope with the help of his stick and boots. The bottom and sides of the trench were soon covered with hot hissing stones. Then he carefully laid the carcass on top, the outer leaves sizzling as they curled up from the heat. He quickly stacked more stones on top, then heaped earth on top of them. When he had finished, there was nothing to be seen except the burnt-out fire and a heap of earth as large as a dog's grave. He stared at it with satisfaction. It had all taken him several hours.

Two days later, early in the morning before the first sounds could be heard from the factories across the water, Marta sighed for the last time and died without being reconciled to her husband or her own destiny. Doc washed her, dressed her in her best dress, combed the stiff grey hair and laid her out on the bedspread, then hurried along the shore towards the Dump to get help from Allan.

Outside the camper, he tried to explain to the sleepy Allan what he had to do.

'She wanted to be buried on Abbott Hill. She said she wanted to be in "Christian soil". You must help me get her up there.'

Allan stared at him. Buried? On Abbott Hill? It was beyond him that anyone should have special wishes about where he or she should be buried. There had been little talk about burying the dead in the old way for years. Everyone was cremated by law these days.

'I promised to see she was buried there. I think I owe her that. Yes, I *must* keep that promise.'

As he stood there, grey and exhausted, he appeared to have shrunk, the wind tossing his white hair about. Allan still did not understand. Why should Doc think he owed Marta anything? She had plagued his life and now she was dead. But he raised no objections. Doc was asking a favour of him and he neither wanted to nor was able to refuse.

It took them some time to get away and in the meantime their voices seemed to have carried the news of Marta's death to the rest of them. Gradually, one by one, they appeared. Felix and Run-Run came by and joined them. Felix shook Doc by the hand and bowed.

'It pains me,' he said.

Mary came down the path to give Lisa a helping hand. Lisa must have heard what they were talking about, for she appeared in the doorway, dressed, apparently ready to leave. Even Smiley came

211

stumbling sleepily down the path and although little had actually been said, he asked what all the chatter was about.

They all seemed to take this gathering together because of Marta's death as a matter of course, and Doc hardly had to explain that he had promised to bury his wife on Abbott Hill. They understood at once and nodded, even Smiley abandoning his usual cynicism for a moment and agreeing with the arrangement.

So they all went to Doc's house, Lisa with Rain in a shawl tied over her shoulder. Her strength was coming back now and she was looking much better. Boy was still weak, so was allowed to ride on Run-Run's shoulders. They made a motley caravan as they trekked along the strip of shore in the chilly winter sunlight.

Allan and Smiley carried Marta. They took the service road for a while, then turned left, continued under the Motorway and started climbing up the ridge on the other side to get to the path leading to the monastery. It was heavy going up the steep scrub-covered ridge. The body was wrapped in a rug and Smiley and Allan each had one end over their shoulders. No one seemed to mind this form of transporting a dead person. In fact they seemed to be united in their joint effort to get to the place decided on.

The tourist path they followed for the last stretch was of stone-laid steps, so it was easier going. At intervals there were small open spaces for visitors to stop and admire the view. Below them, Paradise Bay spread out towards the broad bay. The Dump looked like a wilderness, a strip of hilly, barren desert along the shore. The steely twin ribbons of the Motorway sliced through the landscape, from up there like open countryside, then the Motorway vanished into the great curve of the bridge across the bay.

The little burial procession did not stop to admire the view. They struggled on, out of breath, sweating and determined to reach the monastery.

Inside the ruined monastery walls, the old churchyard was bordered by thick hedges that to some extent had resisted the climbing plants and weeds. Gravestones were leaning or had fallen, ravaged by age and erosion, some flat on the ground, others completely overgrown, visible only as hillocks beneath thick mossy grass. The most important graves were by the east wall, some small baroque mausoleums built in the old Catholic style, their ornamentation long since removed by souvenir hunters and vandals, but the columns and massive stone coffins still remained and they could see two great slabs of cold glossy marble.

'Here,' said Doc, pointing. He had led them up to a simple sarcophagus with neither roof nor edifice, but with one plain stone at the end, so worn by wind and rain it was impossible to read the inscription carved into the granite.

'This is where she wanted to be,' he said. 'She chose the place herself. We used to come up here sometimes before she was taken ill.'

He and Felix started heaving the heavy lid off the stone coffin. Carefully, Smiley and Allan put the body down. It had been hard work and Allan was exhausted, Smiley sweating and breathing heavily, but he looked at Allan with his usual, faintly demonic smile.

'Old Marta is not the only one to want to rest her weary limbs up here,' he muttered quietly so the others shouldn't hear him. The bundle on the ground between them was almost hidden in the long grass.

'Look at our dear Mary over there. Has she told you this is her favourite place for "excursions" – with clients who don't like messing up their car seats. It's nice and cool lying on marble when it's hot.'

'Shut up, Smiley,' said Allan. He was strangely affected by the realities, what he saw behind the talk, perhaps because on the last stretch he had walked behind her, admiring those broad hips and strong thighs tensing to lift that heavy body up the slope.

'All right, all right, I know you're touchy on that score, but I thought I ought to put this little ceremony into some perspective.'

Allan turned his back and went over to Mary and Lisa, who were sitting on another stone busy with Rain.

There were no ceremonies.

Once Doc and Felix had the slab off, they all stood round the stone coffin. It was quite empty apart from a layer of earth at the bottom. The contents of the grave had presumably been removed for reasons of hygiene. But the actual coffin had been left for its 'cultural value' – the city's income from tourists visiting the monastery on Abbott Hill had been considerable.

When Doc gave a sign, Allan and Smiley lowered the body inside and thus Marta was laid to rest in the only spot of 'Christian soil' left. The authorities had long since taken over the allocation of places of burial and the rituals had been performed by a representative of the health authorities.

They all helped to put back the heavy stone lid. No one said anything. Everything was now just as it had been when they had come, even the derelict souvenir kiosk leaning heavily against the wall. Run-Run took Boy on his shoulders again and they started getting ready to go back.

All traces of their presence vanished the moment a wind blew, playing in the undergrowth, the plants again creeping over the ground, as if no one had been there for years, perhaps even for centuries.

Run-Run skilfully removed the top from his earth-oven, whipped away the stones, knocked off the leaves, and there was the goat, roasted through and reeking. He took out his knife and hacked off generous pieces for them all, fresh, delicious meat, so tender that they could literally lick it off the bones. At first they had just stared, but then they ate, devouring this rare delicacy. Smiley went back to the station wagon and brought a bottle of liquor. Doc had maize bread and salt. They sat round the crackling fire keeping out the cold of the wind, which even in this sheltered spot got through to them.

'It's a cultured civilization that buries its dead with a party,' cried Smiley. 'There's hope for us after all, you'll see.'

He passed the bottle round and they all took a swig except Run-Run. He was crouching by the fire, gnawing at a thighbone he had cut off for himself, slowly, methodically, not gorging, but also without leaving a shred of meat on the bone. Lisa was tired. She was sitting by Doc, her head on his shoulder, Rain asleep in her arms.

Allan could feel a glow of well-being spreading through him. The rich food, plentiful for once, and the strong drink were both flowing in his veins. He stared at Mary talking to Felix on the other side of the fire. She should have been sitting by him. . . .

Late afternoon and the sun had sunk into the mist behind Saragossa. A jet plane drew lines of condensation in the sky, the body of the plane glinting high overhead. Smiley was at once on his feet waving his arms about.

'Look!' he shouted.

He meant the plane and the tracks floating behind it making magical patterns in the sky.

'I can't see one of those damned things without wanting to shoot it down,' he said, his fingers machine-gunning it down as he leapt round in a mixture of pantomime and war-dance. His mood was infectious and soon they were all on their feet, shouting and yelling, pointing at the plane and dancing round with their hands above their heads – it was intoxicating, liberating after so much food and strong drink. They danced round each other, releasing tensions, as if they had rid themselves of a great burden. Wildness seized them and left them as the intensity of their dancing and yelling increased and faded.

In the middle of all this, Allan and Mary were standing together, so close he had to hold her and whisper:

'You must stay with me tonight.'

It was not a casual suggestion or a drunken proposal. It was serious, a prayer. His stomach full of heavy nourishing food and his blood thick with liquor, he knew what he wanted, what he needed – he *needed* her. He needed this woman close to him, her body, her practical skills – they had become necessities of life to him. He had no doubts.

'Listen, you're to stay with me!'

She smiled at him, smiled, but kept her distance, measuring strength, her arm in his grip, smiled, but let him wait, let him beg for it.

'Oh, am I?'

Aroused, breathless, almost to the point of irritation, he said, 'Yes. Yes, Mary. Tonight you're to stay with me.'

'Am I, indeed?'

Danced round him, inviting, unapproachable, accommodating, unavailable, baring her teeth and stroking her arm. She had reined in many a man who had not known how to control himself. But he had won, he was the stronger, and she knew it, was subdued and brushed softly past him, whispering, 'Cut it out now. . . .'

A promise or a warning as the others leapt round in their wild war-dance and Run-Run's smile spread from ear to ear as he threw more wood on to the fire. Even Felix was seized with madness and jumped up and down on the spot, letting out shrill, bird-like cries.

She was with him when it grew dark and the others had gone back. Doc had long since gone back with Lisa to the camper to make sure Boy was all right – he had been put to bed as soon as they had got back from Abbott Hill, for he was still far from well, and Lisa was exhausted after the trip and the festivities.

215

Smiley was the last one left at the feast, snoring, lying on his side with his legs drawn up to his chest and his back to the remains of the fire, chewed bones and other remains of the meal scattered all round.

Inside the camper, they undressed as quietly as possible. Allan pushed Lisa carefully over towards the edge of the mattress so that all three of them had room, and when he and Mary sought each other out, they did so quietly, so as not to disturb the others' sleep.

Afterwards he felt less lonely as he lay in the darkness, the bottomless darkness which every night nullified Time on the Dump. He pulled her to him and whispered that she must stay with him now, be with him — anything else was inconceivable. Through the enveloping darkness, he sensed her reply as compliance, an avalanche of earth as she laid an arm across his face, a century of scents . . . although he could hear her teasing laughter and knew she was smiling.

Lisa, undisturbed by these sounds and movements, half woke, turned in her sleep and crept closer to the warm body between her and Allan, close to it, seeking safety in the arms of this earth-mother, as she slept the sleep of the exhausted, her thumb in her mouth, a shadow of stubborn, inviolable childishness on her young forehead, over which life would pass, then glide aside, leaving no trace behind it.